alien places

Atul Kumar

A hypothetical scenario that might happen. One day an alien species might contact us. Not in the movies, but in real life. Following technological advances that are perhaps currently beyond our imagination, they might send a representative to visit Earth. They might already be on the way. They might genuinely want to understand some key issues affecting humanity and how we interact with our environment. They might not want all the detail; just an overview. And to do so, they might ask their representative to be shown a limited number of places that encapsulate what we as humans think they should know.

In *Alien Places* Atul Kumar embarks on an imagined voyage with this hypothetical alien. He meets the alien at the International Space Station, before commencing a world tour of ten places to show his alien visitor: Cairo, Los Angeles, Ho Chi Minh City, Beijing, Queensland, Geneva, Amazon Rainforest, Easter Island, Challenger Deep and Antarctica. Atul explores how these places, in combination, give a sense of some key issues facing humanity and our interaction with the environment.

Whizzing the alien through a broad range of concepts, *Alien Places* explores what such a world tour might reveal to ourselves about humanity, our ability to survive and thrive in the long term, and what we might learn from our alien visitor.

Alien Places
An Imagined World Tour with an Alien Visitor

Atul Kumar

ATUL'S EARTH

Alien Places

An Imagined World Tour
with an Alien Visitor

Atul Kumar

alien places

Atul Kumar

An Imagined World Tour with an Alien Visitor

Alien Places: An Imagined World Tour with an Alien Visitor

Published by Atul's Earth in 2019

ISBN: 978 1695458 475

Cover design, interior design and *Alien Places* logo designed by Creative Byte.

Atul's Earth logo designed by Pete Nicholson.

Photo of the author by Dave Dodge Photography, with clothing provided by Head Fudge.

About the Authors

Atul Kumar was born in Cardiff in 1979, and graduated in Geography at the University of Nottingham in 2000. After gaining an MSc in Environmental Management at the University of Nottingham in 2001, he travelled the world for two years before returning to work for environmental organisations and charities. He is now a fundraising consultant for environmental charities, presenter, writer, actor and voiceover artist based in Bournemouth.

Alien is a being from another galaxy. Gender neutral and called simply Alien, it is friendly, peaceful and inquisitive. At first it appears to want nothing more than to report back to its own species a balanced and insightful understanding of humanity and its interaction with its environment, through the medium of visiting ten places. What can this encounter say about us, and our relationship with Earth? As the journey progresses, we learn more and more about the real reasons for the mysterious alien's visit.

CONTENTS

Arrival

'Earth'. Funny name for a planet. It's a bit like calling a planet 'Mud'. Or at least, that's what an alien might think. *Alien Places* is all about thinking from that kind of different perspective. It's about taking a step back – a really big step back. And viewed from a distance, a list of more objective names for this particular planet might include 'Ocean', 'Sea', 'Water' or even 'Cloud'. And that's just the surface, as visible from a distance. Perhaps an alien would be more interested in the substances beneath the surface, and find it more appropriate to name our planet 'Magma', 'Mantle', 'Iron', 'Silicon', 'Aluminium', 'Potassium' or 'Magnesium'.

Or perhaps an alien would find it more appropriate to name our planet after the most abundant life form, and so we would be living not on 'Earth', but on 'Pelagibacter Ubique', naming our home after the single-celled virus organism found throughout the oceans.

> *How inappropriate to call this planet Earth, when it is quite*
> *clearly Ocean.*
> Sir Arthur C. Clarke, author of 2001: *A Space Odyssey*

'Earth' is the original misnomer. A sign of things to come, perhaps. A metaphor for our self-important anthropocentrism, possibly. A red flag to an alien, conceivably. A symbol of our complex relationship with objective reality, maybe. What does this planet-naming error say about humans, and our relationship with Earth?

For the rest of this book I refer to our planet as Ocean. You'll get used to it. How disappointed Arthur C. Clarke would have been to have openly communicated such an excellent insight, and yet no one ever acted upon it. Someone has to. Taking responsibility is inherent in the psyche of environmentalists. And so I raise my literary glass to Sir Arthur across time and space, and take up his challenge to question what could be described as our most stubbornly persistent example of linguistic anthropocentrism.

This book is all about big thinking in ways that, for me, are only really possible by cognitively stepping away from our planet. The tool of the alien helps us to question everything we assume to be fundamentally unquestionable. The alien viewpoint is to see

1

our planet with fresh eyes, bringing practical rather than purely philosophical benefits, with implications for policy making.

Alien Places is an exercise in empathy – to imagine yourself as an alien. You can learn a lot from looking at yourself from someone else's perspective, and there are real advantages to doing this. Chess players rotate the chessboard in their mind, to understand how their positioning looks from their opponent's point of view. In the First World War one of the British military strategists had a life-sized painting of their German opponent hung on the wall behind their desk. It was probably quite a shock for colleagues entering the room for the first time. Why did they do that? To help get into character, as if they were the German military leader. They rotated model battlefields to see the arrangements of British troops from the German perspective.

Humanity is now at war again. This time we are at war with ourselves on a species level, locked in battle between the sustainable and the unsustainable, the helpful and the harmful, survival and extinction, to be or not to be.

Alien Places aims to keep the lessons learned from interaction with the hypothetical alien grounded, practical and solution focussed. This is the appropriate stance for a writer communicating in the midst of a climate emergency, at a time when public discourse and policy making is in a state of denial about this reality, preferring instead to concentrate on the stasis of Brexit, Trump, and other situations that could be described as minor admin details in comparison to the extinction of humanity via environmental Armageddon.

So this book is far more ambitious than a philosophical or metaphorical meditation on the insights we might receive from such an encounter. Humans are currently at war, for example, with climate change. It is worth taking a moment to clearly think about who exactly is the enemy of humanity as a whole at this point in the twenty-first century fight against climate change. Yes, within humanity there are opposing views, but if we take humanity as a collective, and if we step outside of our anthropocentrism, perhaps an alien would observe that humanity is essentially battling the elements, with the atmospheric and oceanic system itself. That system is based on physics.

What have humans picked a fight with? Physics. I'm not here to mess about with unclear answers. The alien and I are here, literally, to save the world.

'Choose your battles' is a phrase of wisdom that humans have not heeded. We have, most unwisely, picked a battle with physics itself. Needless to say, we can only lose. And yet when growing up I thought, perhaps naively, that humans like winning. The alien and I have a little fun with the concept of winning as our world tour progresses. To help humanity to win its battle for survival, I offer all the solutions I can in this book, as many nuggets as I can, gained over my professional career and education before that.

But I can't solve humanity's tendency towards suicide without help. And I don't just mean help from my fellow environmentalists. Or even politicians. We need all professions to step up. For example, I urge psychologists and sociologists to explain the human mass psychology of suicide immediately, and more publically than they have felt able to do within their professional constraints so far. How does this book help them to do so? Well, from an alien's perspective, I think an earnest description of professional constraints would not be good enough. If such professionals are held back, for example, in diagnosing the psychological condition of Donald Trump that led him to withdrawing the United States from the Paris Agreement to address climate change, then those professional constraints very obviously need to change.

Need. An over-used word. From the perspective of an alien, the word 'need' in this context would perhaps not be used as an expression of subjective preference, 'wouldn't that be nice', opinion and so on. Need for an alien might be more visceral, more grounded in the reality of not drowning humans by filling their lungs, evolved to use gases rather than liquids, with the floodwaters of a melting continent. Need, when human survival is the only yardstick, the only objective criterion on which we can all agree.

Taking our lead from the British military strategist in the First World War, perhaps we can win only by thinking from the perspective of our planet's atmospheric and oceanic system. A far more chilling prospect than any human threat. Our enemy has no mind. It has no personality to plead or reason with. No option of a good nature. No sentimentality to appeal to. If we emit gases that heat up the system, then the system heats up. There is only the mindlessness of physics itself. Film-makers have often played on the terror of such a robotic and unfeeling enemy, such as in the first instalment of *The Terminator*.

This isn't the movies. This is real life. And whilst the 'good guys' won at the end of *The Terminator*, humans will not and cannot win a battle against physics. Perhaps we need to rethink what it means to win. Sometimes winning means not getting into the fight in the first place. Or if that's too late, then withdrawing as fast as possible. It is too late for humanity to avoid entering a battle with our atmospheric and oceanic system, but we can, and need to, withdraw immediately. In practical terms, withdrawal means stopping the emission of more greenhouse gases, and then literally withdrawing some of the gases already emitted. Carbon sequestration, if you want the fancy technical term.

Our planet, now called 'Ocean' remember, has an atmosphere, not a brain. To an alien, it would probably be very clear that our planet is not somehow special, not excused from physics, and not different from all the other planets that work according to cause and effect. In the case of observations about climate change, the levels of particular gases in the atmosphere are the cause, and average global temperature is the effect. The cause and effect relationship is based on physics. An alien would probably not think that our average global temperatures depend on human opinions. If there is more carbon dioxide in our atmosphere, our atmosphere will simply warm up. All fairly obvious to an alien, I would expect, because they would have somehow made use of their knowledge of physics to get to our planet in the first place.

Perhaps the phrase 'Mother Earth' is partially responsible for leading humans into a false sense of security that 'Earth' will somehow look after humans, regardless of their actions. It will not. It cannot. It has no brain. It has grey matter, but that's the iron core of molten metal. 'Mother Earth' has no interest in human political opinion. It is not a mother. It is a ball of various materials. We don't think a dung beetle's ball has a brain, a personality and an ability to care proactively for the insects that live around it, so why should our planet?

To an alien, it's probably very evident that the planet Ocean cannot have thoughts about Brexit, Trump, or desperately urgent human health and social issues that humans might consider more important than the environment. The cause and effect relationship between carbon dioxide and global warming continues according to the laws of physics, regardless of where humans focus their minds, and regardless of what humans prioritise and deprioritise.

My repetition of that concept in different ways within this Arrival chapter is not accidental, but strategically intended. The importance of this idea to continue can't be emphasised enough, as the future of humanity depends on accepting it. So I have used the nomenclature shift from Earth to Ocean as a practical method to constantly, permanently remind all humans of this brainless, harsh reality.

What response would we give to our alien if, on arrival, it reports that its own planet is burning up because there are a few people in power who act as if objective laws of physics can be put on hold while they debate something else? 'Welcome to somewhere more rational?' I could not say that with honesty.

Yet human vested interests are getting in the way of responding in accordance with the same laws of physics that humans accept in all other circumstances. Indeed, such 'disagreements' are often communicated on social media via smartphone devices, implicitly accepting that the laws of physics still apply to their smartphones. We do not have a choice. The laws of physics apply. There is no negotiation with gravity when you are falling: neither at the individual level, nor metaphorically at the species level.

Human thinking is responsible for getting us into various environmental problems. Human attempts at getting us out of this mess have not worked. I think the solution is simple. We need to think as if we are not human. We need an alien perspective. Need, in this book, means survival of humanity. *Alien Places* is therefore nothing less than an attempt to change the reality of impending human extinction.

> **We cannot solve our problems with the same thinking that we used when we created them.**
> Albert Einstein, Theoretical Physicist

In case you're wondering, or in case this book is being read many years after the year 2019 when contact with real aliens might have been made, it is perhaps worth clarifying that an alien hasn't really visited our planet as of 2019, as far as I'm aware. For now, the alien is imagined. Hypothetical. In other words, I wasn't really selected by the United Nations to show around an alien. I didn't really show it ten places. What you are about to read is an imagined world tour, but the lessons, concepts and solutions are very real. And for the rest of the book, I'll be talking as if the world tour were real. This is where the imagination begins.

So my imagined alien visitor chose to visit our planet for reasons that were progressively revealed as the journey unfolded. The alien was a lot more benign than our former adversaries in the First World War. It was not our enemy, but our neutral observer. To learn the most from this process, it was important that we didn't fear the alien, or be scared of sharing information that it could use against us. We wanted the alien to understand humanity as deeply as possible, and so we assumed the intentions of its visit were peaceful, and either neutral or positive. Trusting our alien was integral to learning from it.

After a short lesson from my guest in how to tune into its brainwaves, we communicated one-to-one using telepathy. Then I acted as translator when interacting with other humans during our globetrotting. Our planet doesn't have a mind or a personality, but my alien sure did. In the forthcoming chapters you will meet an alien with quite a multifaceted personality, appropriately blended with mystery and blankness where required to help humanity with a particular insight. The alien's periods of blankness were important: they allowed us to transfer or project our own thoughts onto it, so we could see and hear them more clearly for what they really were.

Telepathy was the alien's preferred method of communication. But that telepathy was not an equal, two-way affair. It was on the alien's terms, not mine. It shut down and came back according to the alien's preferences. Such was the dominance of its highly evolved communication method that, as our imagined journey progressed, I learned that its mouth was not really functional at all, and was purely decorative. Nevertheless, it was generally a very polite alien, and its first telepathic message to the human species was an apology: that our telepathic connection was imperfect.

The alien's periods of blank silence could be thought of as holding up a mirror to humanity. When we explain something to an alien, how do we feel when we say it out loud? Do we feel embarrassed or ashamed, or proud and convinced we are on the right path? If we don't feel happy about our actions, can we swallow our pride and change? When we look into a perfect, neutral mirror, do we like what we see? If we are really honest, maybe there are a few things we would like to change.

But humans are not good at change. Perhaps an alien would even diagnose our species as neophobic: having an extreme or irrational dislike of anything new or unfamiliar. Perhaps the human mind has evolved to associate previous ways of doing things that did not lead to death, with safety. But at a global level regarding environmental issues, for example, we are not on a safe path. We need a new relationship with change. We need to think about change as if we are not human.

I hope the telepathic communications, silence and blank expressions of the alien can help humanity towards new, perhaps radical self-awareness, insights and changes that might otherwise not have arisen. Radical not for the sake of being radical, but in the case of climate change, simply because the physics requires changes in atmospheric carbon dioxide levels to be radical.

In this book I usually avoid the word 'science', because in our current culture, some humans have started to use that word when they want to debate its findings, such as when its implications go against their vested interests. Its brevity as a single word facilitates its dismissal. And to clarify, I am referring specifically and only to the word 'science', not to science itself. Nomenclature is a recurring theme of this book. I prefer the phrase 'cause and effect'. This phrase clarifies and reflects back to us our philosophical attitude towards the notion of objective reality, and forces us to think about whether reality is related to human interpretation or not. Human survival depends on our ability to move on from playing games with objective reality.

Is my use of an alien to communicate environmental solutions a gimmick? Well, I think an alien is a practical, multi-purpose, Swiss army knife of a gimmick.

I think they're fun, but I understand that aliens aren't for everyone. You might prefer the analogy of running. I have chosen the alien because it can also connect with other analogies: humanity needs to walk to the starting line in the race for real, practical and perhaps radical solutions. At this starting line, an alien can help us to get into the starting blocks by helping us to accept the objective reality and known laws of physics. Without that help so far, our start in the race has been awful. An alien can then pull the trigger for us, by clarifying we need to get going immediately, not after Brexit is sorted and Trump leaves office, and whichever distractions replace those distractions, but immediately launch into full sprint to resolve the climate and other environmental crises faster than those crises can make us extinct. This is the real human race.

The human race against atmospheric warming is not metaphorical or philosophical. We are literally racing against atmospheric warming. Lagging at the back of a race and asserting the words 'I'm not racing' does not mean you won't lose the race and be classified last.

To use another analogy: one can disagree that one is falling from a tall building, but those are just words. Simply asserting 'I disagree' during descent does not stop the splat. We need to move on from disagreeing with each other, and unite on the most basic level imaginable: accepting the physical, natural laws that we all are operating within. In our current culture we seem to value debate over action. Anyone closing down a debate is deemed outrageous. Well, that needs to change: it's not ok to debate whether the laws of physics apply to us or not. It's not ok to debate whether or not to pull the cord of a parachute whilst falling. You need to pull it, then have a debate about it later, if you must.

One of the challenges of the environmental sector has always been that success is when something doesn't happen. For example, humanity has not been wiped out by the expansion of the hole in the ozone layer. That is because we implemented solutions that worked because they were based on simple physics. There will always be people who say the avoided scenario was never going to happen. Those people need to be ignored. I think an alien would also ignore those people.

We must pull the cord, then accept that some people will say we were never going to splat, despite that being physically impossible. To paraphrase the biologist Richard Dawkins: one of the benefits of being human, rather than another animal, is that humans can look over distant time horizons and think about the future before it happens, and change our course accordingly. If we can't pull the cord when humanity is falling, we are failing to use our unique abilities as humans, and acting as if we don't have that ability.

There is probably some sort of pleasingly curvaceous, normal distribution or buttock-shaped line graph one could draw, whereby the questioning of objective reality is useful to a point, reaches a peak of usefulness around the centre of the graph, and then drops back down to being deeply unhelpful. Let's start this book at that peak; we've considered the notion that we could get lost debating the concept of objective reality, and we could listen to the people that deny objective reality. I have of course been referring to climate deniers, and I am ending their presence in this book right here in the Arrival chapter, symbolic of their limited role in the future not just within this book, but within humanity overall.

Cause and effect is simply about how and why things change, regardless of whether humans agree. Cause and effect happens regardless of how humans observe or interpret changes. Cause and effect is where a productive search for solutions begins. Cause and effect is what the alien used to traverse the multiverse to visit us.

There is hope for humanity, because there is cause and effect. There is a cause and effect sequence of actions that continues to heat up our atmospheric and oceanic system. And there is a cause and effect sequence of changes that slow down temperature increases, and their associated problems for humanity.

Now more than ever does society need help with thinking from different perspectives, and the alien perspective can provide us with a fun framework for doing so. For some people events in 2016, such as the public votes for Brexit and the election of Donald Trump, were surprise results that highlighted a new, social-media-driven phenomenon. Many of us are now living in our own echo chambers, following on social media the people that tend to agree with our own perspectives. We need to break out of our echo chambers in order to plan more effectively for the long-term survival of our species.

One way of interpreting this book is as an exercise in science communication. That exercise has started already by explaining my caution about the term science itself. Having spent most of my life studying and working on environmental science and management, I can't help but notice a recurring, fundamental problem of anthropocentric thinking: the idea that it's ok for humans to think from their own perspective. Is that really ok? I think the evidence is against that now, given that we are not taking the actions that will prevent our own extinction. A solution is perhaps instead to think from the perspective of other beings such as an alien, or even entities that don't think at all, such as the atmosphere and the planet itself.

We humans are all, in a sense, in one human echo chamber. Well, who better to help us out of the human echo chamber than an alien visitor?

It would be an understatement to say there are a lot of problems with how humanity interacts with Ocean. That makes it a challenge to find a way to communicate these issues in a representative, yet positive, fun way. That's why I have chosen an imaginary alien to help with that challenge of communication.

This thought experiment could be carried out using any places on Ocean, to raise any issue. Whilst part of the challenge is to give a balanced overview of humanity to an alien, it is also impossible to do this as a human. Recognising my own limitations, therefore, I must confess to, and build on, the particular interests that I have, which are primarily environmental. Any human answers to the question of where one would show an alien would be inevitably somewhat biographical. One way of interpreting this book is as a blend of environment, travel and biography of the author.

With an emphasis on environmental and geographical issues, I have kept references to other issues as broad as I can. Other issues raised include philosophical, scientific, cultural, historical, political, religious, and artistic aspects of humanity. With such a wide range of possible issues, I have emphasised those where I hope that alien engagement would help public understanding.

I wouldn't wish to claim that this book constitutes a comprehensive list of the most important issues facing humanity. Rather, I have emphasised some key topics where I hope the alien perspective will help humans with the challenge of change.

Although clearly a hypothetical scenario, the reality of the situation is that an alien might actually visit Ocean. It might happen. And it might happen in your lifetime. Occasionally things happen within our own solar system that take us by surprise, and on timescales so fast that we don't see them coming.

On 19 October 2017 Robert Weryk in Hawaii observed the first known interstellar object to pass through the Solar System. It was named Oumuamua, the Hawaiian word for scout, or 'first distant messenger', but only after it was concluded to be probably not an alien spacecraft. Until then, the possibility of it being an alien spacecraft was considered so plausible at the time amongst scientists around the world that the name was provisionally suggested as Rama, the name of the alien spacecraft in Arthur C. Clarke's 1973 novel, *Rendezvous with Rama*. Oumuamua left the Solar System within two months, such is the speed that interstellar events can take place. Maybe the next object flying into our Solar System does turn out to be an alien spacecraft, with a peaceful, inquisitive alien wanting a world tour of Ocean.

In that sense this book is not hypothetical at all. Half the fun of writing it has been to take seriously the possibility of an alien visitor wanting a world tour. If this really does happen, and for whatever reason I have been summoned to the United Nations in Geneva, plonked in some sort of comfortable, large chair surrounded by anonymous people in dark suits and sunglasses, given a tablet and told neutrally that I'm now in charge of the alien's itinerary, where would I really take the alien?

In this book I describe the imagined world tour that I undertook with my alien visitor. It was a tour of all seven continents. We visited ten places of various scales – city, regional, continental. In some places we spent more time and raised several themes, whereas other places we visited so the alien could learn a more focussed set of insights.

Each place was introduced to the alien with a song, and so over the course of all ten places an *Alien Playlist* was built up, with re-interpretations of their meanings that intentionally showed a different perspective on them. Similarly, part way through our exploration of each place, I set up a makeshift cinema in our surroundings, and played a film for the alien, usually on my tablet. This built up a series of *Alien Film Nights*. The songs and films aimed to entertain and enrich the experience and understanding for the alien, with each revealing something about humanity, or representing the concepts raised at each place.

My imagined alien adventure started at the International Space Station, where I

A L I E N P L A Y L I S T

Anything Could Happen
by Ellie Goulding

My meeting point with the alien was the International Space Station, where I played this song for the alien. The lyrics introduced the idea that humans typically go about their daily lives thinking within a relatively narrow range of options of things that might happen. Humans need to remind themselves to stay open-minded, which does not necessarily happen naturally. At least, not to the extent of expecting an alien visitor. In other words, I was warning the alien that humans are going to be surprised to see it. This is despite being intellectually aware that at some point in a vaguely anticipated future, some form of human–alien interaction most probably could happen.

This book is in some senses a way of helping humanity to psychologically prepare itself for a benign alien visitor. The human mind does not easily accept major, sudden events such as the arrival of an alien species. Repeated psychological preparation would help. We need to remind ourselves in advance that the events in this book, currently imagined, really could happen.

arranged to meet the alien to establish the basics. Here we worked out how to overcome all the practical barriers and details that in reality would probably prevent this whole hypothetical scenario from working. We found solutions such as how to protect the alien from forces natural to humans, such as our planet's gravitational and magnetic fields. We considered issues such as preventing making each other ill by accidentally spreading harmful bacteria. After learning that aliens also sneeze, I armed it with the noble, flappy, human technical device of the tissue.

A L I E N   F I L M   N I G H T

Arrival
(2016)

Before we completed our preparations for arriving on Ocean at the International Space Station, I showed the alien this film. The story captures some of the initial challenges that humans might face, if or when a life form arrives from another world. The lead character, Louise Banks, is a linguist. The overarching message of the film is that basic communication will be the first challenge, including the mystery of the arrivals' intentions for coming at all.

One of the dramatic pinnacles of the film is the potentially disastrous miscommunication between the arrivals and the humans. A sentence from the alien species is translated differently by different nations on Ocean, with a particular symbol being translated as either 'weapon' or 'tool'. The alien needed to know that during our world tour, similar misunderstandings may arise.

The film also highlights an even more fundamental potential difference between humans and alien arrivals: understandings of time itself. For the arrivals in the film, time was not linear. Banks is assisted by them to see premonitions of the future, present events and past memories as almost indistinguishable. The alien needed to know that it also may have a very different understanding of time and space from current human thinking.

As we floated and bobbed about in the International Space Station, I explained to the alien the itinerary that we had ahead of us. I wondered if the alien was here somewhat against its will, flung from its family home for bad behaviour and sentenced to two weeks on a less evolved planet to think about what it has done. Or perhaps it had been planning this visit for years with great optimism. Or maybe it had been absent-mindedly scratching a lottery ticket whilst double-screening with a television and smartphone, and learned it had won not cash, but an interplanetary holiday. My curiosities were answered during the course of our world tour.

This book may appear on the surface to be fiction, but its concepts and practical aims are non-fiction. Some would describe it as an example of creative non-fiction. By creating and using a fictional alien, it aims to help to change things in the real world for the better. It aims to be a practical toolkit for policy makers, helping them in the present and future to make better decisions regarding environmental policy. There are many other books and articles on the market that directly advise environmental policy makers what to do, and what to change. Chris Packham et al.'s *People's Manifesto For Wildlife* in 2018 springs to mind as an example: it's not exactly an unclear document. Beautifully illustrated, cogently argued, relentlessly helpful, ahead of its time. Each section ends with concise policy recommendations ready for implementation by Government.

So what does the alien perspective add to the environmental policy debate? Well, the answer is not to replace the recommendations of publications such as Packham's. Rather, the alien perspective helps environmental policy makers to understand the absurdity of not acting on such recommendations.

It's one thing to talk amongst ourselves as humans: it feels like quite another to talk to an alien. Try telling an alien that we are fully aware our children are increasingly likely to have their lungs filled with the floodwaters of a melting continent as a result of ignoring our climate crisis, but we're busy talking about something else called a backstop relating to Northern Ireland and the Irish Republic. Would the alien say: yes, keep talking about the backstop, not the massive, melting continent of Antarctica?

The alien perspective is therefore a way of correcting our priorities. I'm not the first to write about this. The simple model of 'Important' and 'Urgent' applies here: human instinct is to stay focussed on things that are both Important and Urgent, like the backstop. But actually, it is more strategic to deal with those things quickly, and spend more time on the strategically more important things that are usually 'Important' but 'Not Urgent', such as climate change, which was arguably not as urgent in the 1970s and 1980s as it is today. If ignored, Important and Not Urgent issues move into the category of becoming Important and Urgent, hence the Extinction Rebellion protests of 2019, where the argument was effectively that, having been ignored as an Important but Not Urgent issue for decades, climate change has now shifted to the Important and Urgent category. But UK Government bandwidth since 2016 has been catastrophically dominated by Brexit, something else that was Important and Urgent. Hence the preventative principle inherent in the environmental sector: to prevent ourselves from becoming overloaded with multiple issues that are all Important and Urgent.

As we are overloading ourselves with Important and Urgent issues, and so choosing to focus on the less Important, Urgent issues, then I think the alien perspective helps those in power to make hard choices about which to deprioritise. And I believe an alien would deprioritise issues that are ultimately minor, such as the UK's relationship with Europe, or the US' relationship with Mexico, so that humans can instead prioritise action on existential environmental policies such as resolving the climate crisis. Indeed, perhaps an alien would understand the importance of nomenclature, and along with renaming our planet, also rename environmental policy as existential policy.

So this book is not an imagined world tour for environmental policy makers to read, chuckle a bit about, forget and move on. It is written far more ambitiously than that: philosophically to empower voters, and the environmental policy makers they elect, for ever. This of course can only be achieved via a considerable dousing of humour. A little jumping ahead, a little taster of what's to come, is necessary to help understand this.

Alien Places aims to help environmental policy makers to stand, shoulder to shoulder, with an imagined alien at the base of the two ancient, metaphorical columns in Cairo whenever they are faced with a difficult, subjective debate. It aims to help environmental policy makers to understand when to make big changes, and when to make small changes, as they peer in their minds over the edge of the skyscraper in Los Angeles with an imagined alien, watching the survival tactics of a BASE (Building, Antenna, Span, Earth) jumper with a large, rather than small, parachute. It aims to help us all to join the alien at the bench on Easter Island during a total eclipse of the Sun, and remember that it is usually difficult, unwise or impossible to generalise in totality. And perhaps most importantly of all, environmental policy makers must forever stand in their minds at the Ceremonial South Pole, showing their aliens the literal and metaphorical blank canvas of Antarctica, as they contemplate humanity's unwritten future, where international co-operation and change can happen for the better.

I have enjoyed delving into the question of which places to show an alien, firstly as a simple essay question as a Geography undergraduate in 1998, and then in a podcast series, and now in this book. I find the concept essentially limitless: there was too much to say to fit into this one book. I hope to continue the discussions in podcast or radio interviews for many years to come. The concept clearly stands the test of time for me, and I hope it does for you as well.

In 2013 NASA's Voyager 1 space probe became the first man-made object to leave the Solar System and enter interstellar space. I learned from the alien that the co-ordinates provided by Voyager gave the alien its map to get here. For the next probe to leave Ocean containing information aimed at aliens, I hope, of course, that it includes an e-version of this book.

You would almost certainly choose different places to show your alien. I am interested to hear where you would take your alien and why, and I invite readers to tell me about your places by email, social media, or join me for a podcast interview as part of the *Alien Places* series. You can contact me via my website: www.atulsearth.co.uk

PART 1:

need
to
know

CHAPTER 1
Cairo, Egypt

 A L I E N   P L A Y L I S T

Tilted
by Christine and the Queens

As we made our way from the International Space Station to the surface of Ocean, I played this track for the alien before our arrival in Cairo.

Humans have a wide range of interests, values and concerns. We are a species searching for a balance between different elements of our existence. Some aspects of our lives are directly in competition, even conflict, with each other. As a visual metaphor for this, the music video is performed with the singer and dancers constantly trying to keep their balance.

The lyrics were also intended by the song writer to highlight that humans sometimes portray and present themselves as different from how they really are. The very existence of make-up is a simple example of this, hence the reference to the magic marker.

Each individual human usually believes they are actually good, if perhaps a little tilted or out of balance. Even the most evil or sociopathic humans usually believe they are actually good. The alien needed to know this. For its own safety, it needed to know that not everything on Ocean can be taken at face value.

On arrival at Cairo's airport the alien and I waited patiently for our bags to emerge from the carousel. I nodded politely to passengers waiting at the same and neighbouring carousels, trying my best to normalise the situation of having a companion of such other worldly appearance.

It was a short alien. Green. Leaf-shaped, jet-black eyes that drew you in, as if they were squashed black holes. Its eyes gave nothing away, no minor muscles surrounding it for expression. I wondered if the alien had made use of interstellar black holes to reach our planet, with an intergalactic version of the slingshot method used by Apollo 13, harnessing the moon's gravity to return the craft to Ocean. Perhaps the alien's space vessel had cavalierly slung shot to get here, using the gravity of whole galaxies – one hand at the wheel, the other downing a whisky. The alien had two arms and two legs, by the way. That much was familiar.

As we waited for our bags, I gave our human observers increasingly purposeful, stroppy looks back, as if to suggest that their staring was unwelcome, if not downright rude. My visual arrows turned into vocal daggers, but very British ones – subtle, unclear, unappreciative 'tssk' noises. Not quite to the extent of an antagonistic 'what are you looking at?' but certainly trying to communicate that it's impolite to stare, even at an alien. It occurred to me that maybe the alien didn't mind, and that perhaps I was getting lost in my own, anthropocentric reaction to the open-mouthed gawping of my fellow humans.

Our bags appeared and we hoisted them onto our trollies. Like a child learning unquestioningly from a parent, the alien copied me, with a telepathic 'tssk' sound effect included. Which seemed rather pointless, as the alien then confirmed that only I could receive its telepathic noises.

An Egyptian gentleman approached the alien and offered to carry its bag. I intervened quickly, giving the gentleman a coin and courteously waving him on his way, before he could realise that he was only the second person in human history to interact with alien life. I explained telepathically to the alien the nature of its first proper interaction with a human other than myself.

'The human's motives were more self-interested than was initially apparent. He needed money to trade for essential products such as food and housing. He might not have had the skills to make his own. He may not have been receiving sufficient income from other sources,' I added, feeling listened to by a motionless alien. 'Maybe there aren't many other people who require his skills in return for money.'

The alien's void eyes were mesmerising. I wondered what it was thinking, and having recently established our telepathic connection, I expected to find out soon.

'So the unemployed gent did what he could,' began the conclusion of my first intergalactic explanation, 'by offering to carry your bag, hoping for a coin or two in return.' My employer for this tourist guide gig on steroids was the United Nations. Temporary contract. They had prepared me with the latest, highest specification tablet from a leading global tech company. I was to use this tablet at various points during the world tour with the alien. The tablet had excellent Internet connection, and had also been preloaded with various useful facts and figures, charts, quotes and other information that my employers thought might come in handy for an alien.

A wise person should have money in their head, but not in their heart.

Jonathan Swift, Satirist

From our practising at the International Space Station, I knew that a quiet, cranial whirring noise tended to precede an incoming telepathic message from the alien. So with my first telepathic missive complete, the whirring began, and the alien was quick to indicate that it understood the situation thus far.

'We have a similar system at home,' started a voice in my head concisely. It added: 'We also divide the jobs that need doing between individual organisms, then receive and trade indirectly with tokens: what you call money. The system allows flexibility in the products and services received in return.' Despite expecting the incoming voice, I needed a moment to accept it was not an airport employee speaking over the tannoy, but rather, my first receipt of casual telepathic chitchat with an alien in Cairo.

We reached the line of taxis at the airport. An Egyptian driver lifted my bag, and then the alien's bag, from our trollies into the boot of the taxi. He alternated an increasingly panicky look between his human and non-human customers. I had avoided the option of public transport on this occasion in order to reduce the alien's interactions with humans as much as possible until we were to reach Beijing, the fourth stop on our world tour, where we had planned a welcoming ceremony and formal announcement to the world. The plan was that until then, we would find the alien some sort of disguise or clothing that would hide its unusual origins. I had been hoping at least to get to some shops to find the alien something to wear, but as the taxi driver seemed suspicious already, I needed to act more quickly. I offered the professional driver a few Egyptian pounds in exchange for his baseball cap, which, appropriately, sported a small stitching in the shape of Tutankhamun's burial mask. Deal done in an instant, I wondered whether I had offered an appropriate price, or whether the anxious taxi driver simply wanted to skip the haggling custom, and return his day to serving purely human customers as quickly as possible. I placed the cap on the alien, stood back, squinted, then felt reassured that the alien could now pass as a short human at first glance.

Wisdom begins in wonder.

Socrates, Greek Philosopher

The alien looked out of the taxi window in wonder. It was captivated, lost in its own, intense curiosity as we travelled from the airport. Our taxi passed through a high-quality residential sector, and then by contrast, through an area of Cairo known as the City of the Dead. The alien seemed almost hypnotised by the blurring buildings rushing past. Knowing that any words spoken out loud might confirm to the taxi driver that fifty per cent of his passengers were not human, I gave a brief explanation for the alien telepathically. Unnecessarily, I later learned, I pointed my frontal lobe towards the alien when emitting my thoughts.

'Some people have more money, more possessions and higher quality houses than other people. Some people in Cairo have little choice but to live amongst ancient tombs in the City of the Dead, rather than the purpose-built dwellings you saw along the road a moment ago.'

'I understand,' said the alien neutrally. I felt it wanted to be left alone for a few moments to absorb its first views of Ocean from ground level.

I returned my inner thoughts to devising further tactics for explaining the appearance of the alien to people it would encounter. The cap would help, but we needed more of a plan, some sort of ruse. I was momentarily distracted by the thoughts that my United Nations sponsors had perhaps either overlooked this detail during our planning, or alternatively, found it amusing to see the alien and I struggle with the challenge of anonymity. Finally, I wondered if it was an intentional experiment in how humans react when they are met with an unplanned and unexpected alien encounter: an experiment that would have been nullified had we announced the alien's arrival to the world in Cairo rather than Beijing.

'Please tell other humans that we're on a stag do, and I'm in a costume,' said the alien telepathically, whilst still looking out of the taxi window.

Brilliant. The alien had clearly done some research into the human stag do cultural practice of dressing up a male groom-to-be in some sort of silly costume and parading him around for ridicule on a Saturday night. There was no time like the present to test out the hypothesis. It might work for the alien, at least until we got to Beijing. I instructed the taxi driver to stop, using the universal method of flapping some currency at him. He needed no further encouragement, and halted the vehicle with considerable enthusiasm.

The alien and I lifted our rucksacks onto our backs, and began a saunter. We were still in the City of the Dead area, and gravitated towards its centre. I noticed that wearing our bags on our backs made it easier to appear that we were drunk, lost, confused and staggering on our fictional stag do.

We encountered some locals, who pointed at us and laughed.

'Your friend an alien? Your friend an alien?' They had no idea.

'Yes,' I began, and surprising myself with an indignant feeling of wanting to defend my companion, added: 'and don't laugh at dwarves, please. Where are we?'

'Our home. Please have a seat, human, and human in alien costume.'

The plan had worked. I was impressed with the alien's foresight that this simple tactic would work so easily.

'We're on a stag do,' I lied, nose metaphorically growing. 'He's the stag. He's had about eight pints, so not saying much right now. We got separated from the rest of the lads at the airport. I think the best man deliberately gave us tickets to Cairo. We thought we were going to Prague.' I rolled my eyes at our imaginary prankster friends.

We were believed with guilt-inducing sympathy, and sat on some dusty steps. We were offered a warm, red drink each. We chatted and asked residents of the City of the Dead about their living situations, and asked why they didn't have the jobs or money to live in purpose-built houses, as did the people living in the higher-quality residential sector we saw in the taxi. Pretending to be drunk, it turned out, was a great excuse to ask humans basic and personal questions in order to teach the alien.

Their answers included a recurring theme that they lacked the skills to get a good job because they previously lived in the rural areas farther south in Egypt, where fewer people had access to education. They explained that this led to exclusion from the places, dwellings, activities and technologies that required an abundance of money.

After asking City of the Dead residents why they moved to Cairo in the first place, the alien then appreciated one of the basic issues driving human distribution in the world: the growth of large cities, partly because of population growth, and partly because of recent decades of rural to urban migration. This migration had been caused by a range of push and pull factors, mostly with their roots in the acquisition of money. The human population of the world, I extrapolated, is now mostly urban.

The alien needed to know that most humans are now found in cities, and whilst the reasons are varied and complex; it needed to know that the basic need for money is a recurring theme that drives human geographical distribution, movement and behaviour.

Overconsumption and overpopulation underlie every environmental problem we face today.

Jacques Yves Cousteau, Conservationist and Film Maker

The alien quickly grasped the basic reality that the human population grows when more humans are born than die. I received no telepathic reply when I asked its view on how the population of a species can and should be managed. It's a burning question for humanity: it underpins all other environmental problems, including climate change. I resigned myself to the reality that the alien was not going to be giving me many answers on this world tour, at least not explicitly, or not yet anyway.

Using the tablet I presented the alien with a chart, prepared by an anonymous executive at the United Nations, that showed the recent falling of the death rate in Egypt, largely as a result of improved medical knowledge in recent decades, compared with the continuing high birth rate. There are many reasons for the birth rate not dropping in immediate response to the death rate dropping. These include gender and cultural issues relating to contraception, and a time lag before people can be confident that their children are more likely to survive now than in previous decades.

We boarded an overcrowded bus, and the alien experienced first-hand a simple example of one of the many problems of overpopulation in Cairo. The alien's body was partially compressed and crushed as more and more people got on board. We escaped at the next stop and walked the streets, frequently passing homeless people asking the alien for specifically one American dollar or, occasionally, exactly one English pound. The alien suggested we both do so.

'Not necessarily for the homeless person's benefit, but for mine and yours. To make us feel happy, through the act of helping another person. That's as good as most species get,' said the alien concisely. I realised I was in wise company. I made a note of this on the tablet, to report back to the United Nations.

In stark contrast to its moment of wisdom, the alien then looked excitedly at boring examples of refuse left in the streets. Each time, it looked expectantly at me, as if I should be explaining every object it saw, however mundane. Its expectations of me as an interplanetary tour guide, now that we were settling into our first walking tour of the city, had become clear. I had wondered what level of detail the alien would be interested in, and had prepared myself psychologically for this sort of scenario. So I politely talked for ten minutes about the arguably tedious yet not entirely futile human practice of gum chewing, and all imaginable issues around gum disposal, both of the product and its wrapping, and the intended methods of disposal versus actual. My monologuing would not have filled a full ten minutes, had it not been for the regular alien encouragement to continue, like a dog panting at its owner to throw yet another ball for it to fetch.

Talking of dogs, I spotted dog excrement a few steps ahead of us on the pavement, and wondered nervously if I would shortly receive a telepathic request to explain that as well. The alien spotted the poo. Luckily for me, the alien then got distracted with a bodily function that seemed similar to partial choking.

'Your air is polluted,' said the alien accusingly.

'Sorry about that. On behalf of my species, I mean.'

The alien stumbled off balance. I found it a couple of steps in a doorway to have a sit down. Immediately an Egyptian teenager ran up behind the alien, opened its rucksack, stole a bundle of Egyptian pounds, then swiftly disappeared into the bustling streets. The alien stood defiantly, albeit at a considerably lower height than the sprinting adolescent.

'May I vaporise it?' asked the alien with restraint that revealed its impatience.

'The teenage thief?'

'Yes,' said the alien, lurching forward as if to start a pursuit.

'No. Sorry. We have a heavily flawed legal system to deal with criminals.'

I had to hold the alien back from chasing the thief, and in that moment felt like I really was on a stag do that had turned into a fracas on a Saturday night. I managed to talk it down telepathically. I felt pleased with my ability to influence the impulsive behaviour of a species from another galaxy. Telepathically, I emitted a thought about the human custom of dealing with such situations with an admittedly vague concept of proportionate response. The alien accepted this with a blend of speed and reluctance.

The alien had already personally experienced a number of problems associated with overpopulation and crowded cities in less developed countries. To demonstrate a short-term solution to these issues, I took the alien on an excursion to the site of the new capital city being built 40 kilometres away on the outskirts of Cairo, in an attempt to reduce the population pressure and problems in Cairo.

Whilst walking around this undeveloped area, I noted that it was predominantly a collection of individual building sites, brimming with impending connection to each other. Overall I felt a sense of optimism in the area, but wondered why the alien was telepathically silent. I changed tack, and asked the alien to keep in mind the concept of population growth throughout our world tour. At this point I got an agreement from the alien, with an addendum that it was looking forward to hearing more throughout our journey about how humans are dealing with global population growth as the key issue underlying all environmental problems.

Back in Cairo I took the alien to Giza, the area with some of the most well-known ancient monuments on our world, including the Great Sphinx, the Great Pyramid of Giza, and a number of other large pyramids and temples. The atmosphere at the site was electric: tourists swarming and jostling to get better views, guides reciting their explanations, locals circling with various tactics to make a few Egyptian pounds. It felt like we had arrived at the first truly important place on Ocean for the alien to visit.

Like a parent in a supermarket, I regretted turning my back for two minutes. I was inspecting a generous offer of two traditional-style necklaces for the price of one from a local, smiling lady wearing a shop. Instead, I bought a small toy camel as a souvenir for the alien. When I looked around, the alien had been coaxed onto the back of what had become in my visual absence a fully upright, real camel. A thin rope from the mouth of said camel led to the rough hand of a local Egyptian man, keen to earn money from tourists.

The alien insisted to me telepathically that it had been allowed onto the camel for free, without mention of payment. The alien's money supply had been depleted by the Egyptian version of Usain Bolt, and it was wisely reluctant to overspend at such an early stage of our world tour. I waited and observed with amusement to see how the alien intended to deal with the issue of being allowed off the camel. On, you see, was free. Off, now that's where the money came in.

Perhaps cruelly, I watched with morbid fascination as the alien and the Egyptian struggled to communicate. The alien, I noticed, seemed unable to use its mouth to speak out loud, but telepathically, I was picking up a torrent of angry phrases and disbelief at the trickery of humans. The Egyptian, I observed, seemed frustrated at needing to shout at yet another blank-faced drunken man on a stag do. I marvelled at the interaction, wondering if the Egyptian had any idea he was interacting with a being from another world, or was in fact firmly assuming his camel detainee was in his early twenties, wearing an alien costume as punishment by his friends for being the first in their group to be getting married.

I slipped a note to the Egyptian, and at a grunt from the human, the camel dutifully bent both front legs first, then rear, and the alien's ordeal was over. The alien had learned the pervasive nature of monetary transactions with humans, and the idea that almost nothing comes for free in human society. It relayed to me telepathically that it was making a mental note to proceed with caution when dealing with apparently altruistic humans: a theme it had remembered from the song we listened to in transit from the International Space Station to Cairo.

Alien mental notes, I learned, were permanent. It told me that its memory, and brain generally, functioned less like the spongy material within my skull, and more like the hardware within the tablet in my bag. The alien had requested a human tour guide, rather than tablet tour guide, as a compromise, on account of humans having limbs. Charming. Alien memory is apparently not perfect, it concluded, but also had no resemblance to the fleeting nature of human retention it had detected in my brain thus far on our world tour.

Tempting as it was to retaliate by rubbing in the alien's camel naivety, I remembered that I was technically a United Nations employee for the next few weeks, and so probably should hold back the worst aspects of human nature whenever possible. I was also genuinely impressed with the responsibility the alien was taking for maximising its own learning, by deriving general principles from its camel episode. I gave the alien the benefit of the doubt that it would also understand there are always exceptions to any general principles it was deriving.

I guided the alien's attention to the Sphinx, and explained that it is one of the world's oldest and most treasured monuments. I explained that urban air pollution is causing damage and putting the head of the structure at particular risk, with some researchers predicting that, without structural intervention, it will fall off by the year 2200.

Looking at the view of the Sphinx with the three largest pyramids in the background, I asked the alien to rotate its gaze one hundred and eighty degrees in order to see the contrasting view of tourist developments and a Pizza Hut outlet, about three hundred metres away. With onlookers present, I pretended it was no big deal that the alien rotated just its head, not its body, to do so. A quick pat on the back of the alien signalled for it to rotate its head slowly back to normal, and generally not to draw attention to itself. Rather than telepathically, I explained out loud with slightly too much volume, trying to distract our audience from the non-human head rotation, that Pizza Hut is a multinational company. With my best air of distractive authority I listed loudly the pros and cons of such companies: often criticised for being culturally and aesthetically insensitive and bringing limited new jobs for locals, but also intrinsically linked to the global capitalist system, as we would expand upon when we arrived in Los Angeles. That vocal distraction, combined with the alien's baseball cap, seemed to deceive the impromptu audience that I was educating a human.

The Sphinx–Pizza Hut juxtaposition exemplified the contemporary sense of place in Cairo, whereby one half celebrates the heritage of the city, and the other acknowledges Egypt's dependence on tourism for income. After the alien completed its gradual head rotation back to its usual position, we surveyed the opinions of the locals in the Sphinx area. We asked their thoughts about Pizza Hut's location, and Western influence more generally. From their answers we found that many resented tourists because of their non-Islamic behaviour, such as drinking alcohol and not covering up the majority of their bodies. Thus the alien better understood the views of Muslims who felt their country was under cultural siege. It was a simple way to introduce to the alien the concept of cultural difference.

We spent an hour squeezing through ancient corridors in the dark interior of the Great Pyramid. The immaculately constructed passageways and hidden chambers were of particular interest to the alien. Cryptic hieroglyphics covered the walls, with occasional explanations from our guide. The alien seemed well ahead of the guide, however, and to be reading the hieroglyphics with greater ease than a parent reading *The Very Hungry Caterpillar* for the eleventh time that evening to a toddler. At the end I explained that we would discuss the Great Pyramid again before we left Cairo, but our next stop was to be a market.

Walking through the densely crowded market was more like playing rugby against your will than taking a pleasant amble. The bustling market was a cacophony of mixed sounds and accents. The running theme was haggling.

'You break my business,' claimed a stall owner with earnestly gesturing hands. He was pretending to weep melodramatically in response to a tourist refusing to pay the first suggested price for a largely unnecessary item of memorabilia. A fridge magnet, maybe. An ornament in the shape of the Great Pyramid, perchance. The tourist pretended to walk away, and the stall owner chased. A few seconds later, and a deal was done.

Most of the local stall owners spoke enough English to sell items to tourists. However, later in our tour of the rural areas south of Cairo, which received fewer tourists, we found fewer locals able to speak English. Linguistic adaptation, I concluded, was again on the basis of money.

I instructed the alien to perform an observational survey of gender presence in public spaces around the city, and then later in more rural areas farther south. The alien counted more women on the streets in Cairo than in the rural areas, where they were not allowed to be seen unaccompanied in public according to some humans within Islamic culture, demonstrating the differences in gender issues in different areas of the same country.

That evening I sat with the alien on the banks of the Nile. With the sounds of the ancient river lapping calmly around us, I explained that humanity has within it different and opposing views of its own history here on Ocean. These tend to fit broadly into one of the following four categories: natural selection and evolution over billions of years, intentional creation by a supernatural being, the influence of extra-terrestrial beings such as the alien's own species, or that humanity is operating within a computer simulation run by more advanced beings.

> *A people without knowledge of their past history, origin and*
> *culture is like a tree without roots.*
> Marcus Garvey, Jamaican Political Leader

I clarified for the alien that these broad categories have a variety of differences within them, and that new theories and insights are constantly being developed, adding nuances and important differences to our understanding of the universe and our place within it. Indeed, the very presence of the alien was shedding new light on all four categories.

By the river we were joined by various locals going for a walk. We invited them to join us for a conversation before they continued on their way. We met both Muslims and Coptic Christians, and asked them all about the reasons and evidence for their beliefs. At the next place on our world tour we compared their answers with the evidence for evolution as shown at the George C. Page Museum of La Brea Discoveries in Los Angeles. The opposing views professed in each place, and by each group, helped the alien to understand the tension not only between religious believers and non-believers, but also between Western and Islamic communities, often referred to as the main global tension following the end of the Cold War. These tensions have been manifested in what has been described as a New World Order since the events of 11 September 2001, and many subsequent terrorist atrocities, some of which have taken place in Egypt itself.

Some events in Cairo in the past hundred years could be interpreted initially as suggesting supernatural or extra-terrestrial activity. However, as time, knowledge and science have progressed, apparently inexplicable events or superstitions have tended to become fully explained. Cairo could therefore act as a microcosm for the alien to understand the progression of human knowledge.

With this in mind I took the alien to the entrance of Tutankhamun's tomb, and explained that following its opening in 1922 there were debates around the reasons for subsequent deaths amongst the team or people connected to the team that discovered it. Such ideas developed from a mysterious 'Curse of the Pharaohs' hypothesis, to the analysis that the 11 deaths were actually spread out over 10 years following the tomb opening. The supposedly linked deaths took place across a wide range of people, including those only distantly connected to people involved with opening or visiting the tomb. Over time this led to an acceptance that, as opposed to there being a proactive 'curse', the deaths were more likely to be explained as being within the normal range of the expected death rate of the population.

'What would be the physical mechanism of the curse?' asked the alien, both wisely and telepathically.

'Exactly. Well, potentially there might have been a release of airborne bacteria on opening the tomb,' I replied.

'Hmmm,' said the alien, a noise that I decided, perhaps erroneously, to interpret as the alien being unconvinced.

Shortly after visiting Tutankhamun's tomb, the alien became ill with what on Ocean we would call the common cold. The alien reassured me it would not be fatal, and would pass in a day or two. With that reassurance, I then found all aspects of the alien's sneezes both visually and audibly amusing. It quickly made full use of the tissue I had given it at the International Space Station; promptly filling it with intergalactic snot, then handing it to me and in return receiving another fresh vessel in which to collect further nasal gunk. The exchange continued into the evening. I speculated that the alien had, over the course of several hours, handed me its own body weight in mucus. The nasal discharge factory remained productive overnight.

We had checked into a large tourist cruise boat, which was more like a floating hotel, moored on the banks of the Nile. Fellow passengers slept with their cabin room lights off. If someone was observing the boat from the outside, they would have noticed one cabin room still had its light on, with an alien and a human in symbiotic harmony: a steady rhythm, a dance of sneeze, blow, hand the tissue to the human, and repeat. Boat staff were brought into the dance, handing me new supplies of tissue and toilet rolls, and disposing of the used ones. I marvelled at the convergent evolution that had been going on in different parts of the multiverse, which had independently led to dealing with a cold virus using the solution of startlingly similar slime, albeit in significantly different quantities.

Between sneezes we conversed telepathically with a depth and reflective insight quite at odds with the stringy mucus we were physically dealing with. We found it tempting, yet concluded it unwise, to abandon rational analysis based purely on our own personal experience. We resisted reverting to a superstitious interpretation that the alien must also have fallen victim to the curse of Tutankhamun's tomb. The larger data set of evidence and logic was the more enlightened thought to focus on. Between sneezes we reassured ourselves that many thousands of other beings had visited the tomb's entrance without falling ill, and the alien had probably simply picked up a cold from that overcrowded bus, the market, or any one of the other crowded places we had visited so far in Cairo.

The next morning the alien was not feeling quite up to walking around again. We sat on the banks of the Nile during the daytime and started to get bored. I taught the alien a few human travel games that didn't require any special equipment: eye spy, hand clapping routines, that back-writing game where you have to guess which word you're writing on your partner's back, and so on. The alien hadn't heard of any celebrities on

Ocean, so we couldn't play that 20 questions game where you can receive only Yes or No answers in order to guess the name of the celebrity the other person has in mind. So after a while, we ran out of games.

I felt it was an appropriate moment to teach the alien about the human tendency towards pareidolia, the term for attributing meaning to random or coincidental features or events. Expecting it to join in the fun, I invited the alien to look at the sky and observe the clouds, where I saw what was blindingly obvious to me, a cloud pattern that resembled a human smiley face. The alien looked back at me blankly, unimpressed. It saw no facial patterns.

'This is an example of human anthropocentric tendencies that, if you're not careful, will lead directly to the downfall of your fragile civilisation,' said the alien matter-of-factly. Being rebuked is unsettling at the best of times, but especially so when done telepathically.

'It's insulting to the millions of other species you share your planet with,' continued the alien. 'Why are humans not interpreting other cloud formations as body parts of a woodlouse, a carnivorous pitcher plant, or now that you have a bit a technology, a DNA strand of bacteria?' asked the alien sarcastically.

I was for a moment pleased to learn that the alien had the personality tool of sarcasm within its range. A sarcastic alien: brilliant. We're going to get on great. But then I started to feel, perhaps quite rightly, jolly insulted as it feigned pride with a continued series of examples of non-anthropocentric interpretations of cloud formations in the Egyptian sky.

'That cloud looks like my waste recycling unit at home. That cloud looks like the left shoulder of a middle food chain animal that lives in puddles on a post-apocalypse planet in multiverse quadrant 7.2, universe minus 3,333,516, galaxy 902,131,885, as we call it. That cloud looks like a pebble that I've seen on countless planets. Perhaps you would like to choose which planet … oh, I remember, you're a human, you haven't exactly been to many planets now, have you? In conclusion, please tell your fellow humans, for your own good, that there is no mechanism for, or meaning behind, any cloud formation that relates to any species observing it.'

Crikey! With such a narky tearing down of anthropocentrism, I thought it positive that the alien at least seemed to have recovered from its cold. I reassured the alien that although most humans are aware that pareidiolic interpretations of cloud formations are meaningless, what is perhaps even more problematic is the attachment of meaning to coincidences more generally. For some humans this relates to their world view of how we have come into being. Such beliefs are inherently linked with hopeful feelings that their God or Creator sends them coded messages in the form of coincidences, rather than just saying the message rather more directly.

The alien had none of that either. A somewhat emotionally exhausted alien voice in my head recited, almost robotically this time, an explanation that confirmed my early suspicion about who was going to be the real teacher on this world tour.

'The most surprising situation of all regarding coincidences would be if there were never any coincidences, of any kind, on any planet. With an infinite number of events happening every nanosecond within humanity and every other species, you must expect coincidences to arise from this continuous flow of simultaneous events, without requiring supernatural causes to explain them.'

'OK. Thank you.' I swallowed the humble pie of utterly destroyed anthropocentrism. There were more examples of this to come during our world tour. I worried about how the alien was going to react to them.

We linked our discussion of coincidences to the broader idea that the alien had very much worked out by now: that humans don't know everything there is to know. Where there are gaps in knowledge, some humans will jump to assumptions, including invocation of mysterious or supernatural reasons, rather than sit with the rather more honest acceptance that we simply don't know. This concept, I relayed to the alien, is what the human poet John Keats in 1817 called 'negative capability': a proactive ability to not know, to settle on uncertainty, to conclude there is no logical conclusion given the information available. Many other humans, including philosophers such as Socrates agreed with this kind of idea. I was heartened to hear the alien's response.

'You don't know what you don't know. You have much to know about the multiverse before you can start to know what you don't know. Even my species doesn't know what it doesn't know, and we know a lot, you know,' said the telepathic voice. For the first time I detected the alien's sense of humour. It seemed to know that it sounded slightly silly.

Wisest is she who knows she does not know.
Jostein Gaarder: front cover of the book *Sophie's World*

To demonstrate our lack of knowledge, I took the alien, once recovered from its cold, to a site where modern scientists and architects had abandoned an attempt to reconstruct the Great Pyramid on a scale several orders of magnitude smaller, using the same equipment they believe humans had in 2589–2504 BC. Unable to complete the reconstruction, and hence unable to explain fully how ancient Egyptians built the Great Pyramid, some humans interpreted this as evidence of divine or alien intervention. However, as more and more documents have been discovered that describe the construction process of the Great Pyramid, such gaps in human knowledge are gradually being filled. The key to accept, of course, is that gaps in knowledge do not mean that those gaps must be filled immediately with any explanation, however irrational.

It was time to pull back from insights into the unimpressive antics of the human psyche, and teach the alien more about the physical basics of what humans are made of. It needed to know that the main component of the human body is water. This physical reality has far-reaching consequences for all aspects of human existence, including its geographical distribution.

Linked to this is the concept of the physical environment's limitations upon human activities. Only about four per cent of Egypt's land area is inhabited: the vast majority lies within 15 kilometres of the banks of the river Nile. Using a helicopter I took the alien just beyond the southern limit of Cairo, and asked my companion to perform a transect across the Nile, recording land use 32 kilometres either side.

Wearing earmuffs simply to satisfy our pilot that we were adhering to health and safety practice, the alien jotted down its observations about the pattern of human population distribution either side of the Nile. I explained that the surrounding Libyan and Arabian deserts were unsuitable for humans to build on, cultivate crops or conveniently obtain a water supply, and therefore few humans want to live there. This helped to explain the key issue of regional inequalities between different parts of our planet's surface; with landscapes tending to become more inhabited as the number of opportunities for people increased.

 A L I E N   F I L M   N I G H T

Quantum of Solace
(2008)

Each night in Cairo we stayed on the large cruise boat moored on the banks of the Nile. One evening the alien and I watched this film in the James Bond franchise.

Far from being marketed as a film with an explicit environmental message, the film made a crucial point about the relative importance of various natural resources. The dialogue in the first part of the film refers to the world's 'most precious resource', and leads the human audience to assume they are talking about oil. The twist in the film comes with the revelation that, spoiler alert – they are talking about water. The film highlights the potential for global conflict over water as a resource.

The uninhabitable Egyptian desert was an excellent backdrop for the alien to learn the fundamental importance of water to all aspects of humanity and life on Ocean.

Thousands have lived without love. Not one without water.

W.H. Auden: in the book *First Things First*

When performing the transect I also showed the alien on the tablet a series of photographs of certain parts of the desert from when they used to be arable land, but have since become desert as a result of humans overworking or clearing the land. This desertification introduced to the alien the key issue of human effects on the natural environment.

The next day I took the alien on an excursion to the Suez Canal, and explained that in 2012 seven per cent of all seaborne-traded oil worldwide transited through this canal. I asked the alien to count the different national flags on the ships, and deduced that the canal is widely used. To illustrate why, I helped the alien to place a piece of string on a globe, and linked Kuwait, a major oil exporter, with the US east coast, a major oil importer, firstly via the Suez Canal, and then via the Cape of Good Hope.

I explained that the longer journey would involve greater time and cost, and that a result of Ocean's continental physical geography was that the country which owns the canal can charge other people to use it, and thus earn money. The alien then understood the strategic importance of the canal, and appreciated that other countries would want to control the canal themselves, hence Egypt's conflicts with Israel, the UK and France in 1956–57.

From this example I extrapolated to the general principle that some countries want to own or control land that belongs to other countries. This helped the alien to understand why humans end up fighting each other at the international level. This theme was a recurring issue at subsequent places on our world tour.

Having understood water as one of the most basic physical needs of humans, the alien then requested I explain more about some aspects of the human mind. Good for the alien, I thought, to be more concerned with the deeper issues. It asked me to teach it about our relationship with objective reality. What an interesting question, I thought, and could think of no better place to take the alien than to a school, and to attend a maths class.

I explained to the Egyptian schoolteacher that this was a one off and that her class was not expanding by two on a permanent basis. The alien and I then headed straight for seats at the back of the class, like two new kids arriving at a school after their parents had relocated, and needing to set an immediate expectation that they were the epitome of the coolest of the cool kids.

The alien watched intently as the teacher proceeded with some basic sums. I had not seen the alien this transfixed by something since it saw that bit of chewing gum on the pavement. It gave me a telepathic running commentary on its thoughts.

'These small humans seem to count using their fingers. This means they use a system of base-ten, an act of switching their counting system around multiples of 10,

20, 30 and so on. It seems that all humans have ten digits across their two hands, so I can see the logic behind this system. I should point out, however, that this is entirely idiosyncratic to the particular quirks of human physiology. Other species in the multiverse use different base systems, obviously.'

The teacher explained to the students the method for successfully completing a few simple sums. The students were then given a test, with a maximum score of 20. The alien took part as well, and achieved the maximum 20 out of 20. However, on hearing the results of the small humans that took the test, the alien was shocked.

'Why did every pupil not receive 20 out of 20?' asked the alien telepathically, struggling to understand. 'They were taught just a few moments before the test precisely how to nail every sum bang on every time.'

I was pleased to hear the alien had picked up a few colloquialisms already.

'There are variations between humans in terms of quality of memory, processing ability and other cognitive functions,' I explained, knowing this was opening a potential can of worms. 'Although you, my alien pal, and indeed the tablet in my bag, have near perfect memories, at least to the point of a pre-advertised number of terabytes, this is not how the human brain works. Perfection is not an ability of any human brain in all circumstances.'

Only one student in the class of 30 received the full 20 marks, with the rest receiving scores ranging from 19 down to zero. Thus the alien learned a critical concept in understanding humanity: that when objective measures such as maths are used, the majority of humans do not achieve full accuracy. The vast majority of students in this test got at least one of their answers incorrect.

'In other words,' the alien rephrased sympathetically and with accidental patronisation, 'humans are usually at least partially wrong, and that being fully and comprehensively correct is numerically uncommon, unusual, or as you might even say, odd.'

The alien was then telepathically apologetic to its adult tour guide, insisting it was not intending to be condescending to us mere humans. What a considerate and polite alien. I believed it. It was an alien genuinely in shock. I had before me an alien sincerely desperate to understand why 20 out of 20 is the exception, not the norm.

'I was diagnosed with a cold after visiting Tutankhamun's tomb,' began the alien in an intriguing line of logic. 'In the same way, are humans that score 19 or below diagnosed with inaccuracy?'

'Umm...' Knowing the sincerity of its intention to understand rather than insult, I found it hard to disagree with the alien's perspective. It was a pure form of reaction to a situation to which we humans have become, perhaps dangerously, accustomed. One could indeed look at humanity as suffering from or displaying the symptoms of such a condition, using this numerical example, at least. The alien seemed genuine. I detected no antagonistic intention, but noted my own, fallible, human instinct to defend my species, whether it was right to do so or not.

'I am sorry this question distresses you,' said the alien. 'If humans are afflicted with an inaccuracy epidemic, I will report this back to the leaders of my planet, and we will discuss the ethics of making an intervention, if you so wish. We have solutions to help you with this, but I am bound by Interplanetary Legal and Ethical Agreements that prevent me from sharing them without going through the necessary authorisation first.'

This was the first suggestion, I later realised, that perhaps the alien was visiting Ocean for reasons a little more altruistic that the simple indulgence of a field trip. Perhaps it was ultimately here to help us, subject to a bit of interplanetary red tape.

'Thank you,' I began cautiously. 'I should also probably run it past my fellow humans before eliminating our innate ability to be inaccurate. Might be a few pros and cons to weigh up. Can I run that one past the United Nations, and get back to you?'

'Of course,' said the alien in a tone that seemed to lament the human condition as one diseased with inaccuracy, yet respecting our right to wallow in such a disease. I was reminded obliquely of a principle of caring for adults with autism: the alien was respecting our right to make poor choices, or to live within the framework of our own limitations, even if allowing those poor choices means allowing an element of self-harm.

I explained to the alien that there is a range of reasons for our inaccuracy epidemic. There is great diversity between humans in terms of our memory function, our likelihood of making mistakes, our reasoning and logical performance, and other intrinsic psychological factors that can affect answering numerical questions correctly. There are also perhaps more extrinsic or variable factors, such as nutrition, quality of sleep and personal circumstances that distract humans from full concentration. And then there are personality, attitude and motivational issues: humans might be capable of getting sums right, but can they be bothered? Are they right to focus on other things, and I didn't mean meaningless other things like some television programmes, but meaningful other things, like resolving climate change?

The alien decided it needed to hear from the students themselves. With its tour guide as interpreter, the alien discussed with the children their maths test results. The most interesting conversations were with the two pupils that got 19 and 18 in the test. The alien learned that they could have scored 20, but they intentionally made mistakes in their answers. When probed further by the alien as to the reasons why they did this, the pupils revealed that they did so in order to avoid being teased by the other students, which then may have resulted in forms of social exclusion. The cool kids, it seemed, do not score 20. To my surprise, this was not culturally specific to children in the UK or USA, and included these Egyptian children as well. Thus, the alien concluded, there were also fascinating group dynamics, social and cultural issues, and multiple assumptions combining to form a human vested interest in perpetuating our inaccuracy epidemic.

I was reminded of how some people glibly summarise the life story of Microsoft founder Bill Gates. To paraphrase, some say that if he had been one of the cool kids at school, then perhaps we wouldn't have Microsoft today. Founding an internationally successful, society changing technology company requires numerical accuracy, not being cool. Bill was probably capable of getting 20 out of 20, either literally or metaphorically.

This reassured the alien that our situation on Ocean is more complex than humans being simply incapable of getting things right. Sometimes we know the right answer, but externally communicate the wrong answer. I extrapolated for the alien to the more complex and current social debate around 'fake news', and the broader human struggle with accuracy, which often has its roots in some form of vested interest.

The maths test results showed the alien the diversity of human accuracy when objective measures are used. When subjective issues are raised that do not have clear, objective or numerical answers, the diversity of human responses is even greater.

In the evening on our last day in Cairo, I took the alien to an ancient site in the city, and selected two tall columns, engraved with hieroglyphics. In a metaphorical demonstration for the alien, I asked it to imagine that each column represented an opposing view of a subjective question, simplified as 'For' on the left and 'Against' on the right. Given the diversity of human responses to the maths test, the alien was not surprised to hear that when it comes to any subjective question, humans are collectively able to populate both columns with plenty of entries, certainly with at least one point in each column.

The alien was familiar with this method of thinking.

'On my home planet,' started the alien telepathically, its green head tilted back as it looked up at the 'For' column, 'we decide on a course of action by firstly populating both columns as thoroughly as possible, then assigning a weighting and numerical score to each entry, and then concluding on the basis of which column has the highest score.'

'Bingo. Do you do this consistently, in all circumstances?'

'Of course,' said the alien, seeming to wonder why I would question the method. It went on to describe how they use a software package to help. It sounded to me eerily similar to Microsoft Excel. The alien reported with some enthusiasm that they find this to be a wonderfully logical and consistently successful method of converting a subjective debate into an objective resolution, whilst recognising and respecting opposing views. On the alien's planet they have been using it for what humans would refer to as millennia, and they credit the method with nothing less than the method for preventing conflict and war, and for creating stable and lasting peace.

'No one is left feeling insulted or outraged,' explained the alien. 'All parties recognise that nobody's column is empty, and that there are genuine factors in both columns. One simply has to conclude on the basis of the scores, one way or the other, in order to progress.'

With a mixture of defensiveness and envy, I explained to the alien that, here on Ocean, this concept is not new, but it is also not always used. Human philosophers had given this method fancy names in the past, such as Dialectics, or Thesis, Antithesis and Synthesis, which dated back to the time of German philosopher Hegel in the late 1700s. Basic concepts of argument and counter-argument were around long before that, under varying terminologies.

'The problem for humans applying this method is one of consistency,' I clarified for the alien. 'We struggle with using this method regularly, whether that is in our minds, in writing, or using a computer. We struggle with identifying where an argument has been neutralised by a counter argument. We are lazy, and can't be bothered to assign points to both columns where valid points are expressed. We can't be bothered to assign weightings, and we can't be bothered to conclude according to scores. We are racked with a truckload of vested interests, but we are also aware that we really should use this method with objectivity,' I confessed, realising that teacher had turned pupil very quickly in my relationship with the alien.

'Are there examples within humanity where this method is used regularly?' asked the alien curiously.

'Hmm. Fields such as education and academia, perhaps, tend to be the sectors where this method is used more consistently, and the fields of politics and business are probably those where it is used less consistently.'

The alien emitted a sort of telepathic yelp.

'So those with the most influence use the method least?'

'Yes.' I replied, overwhelmed with an inexplicable, culturally British compulsion to add: 'Sorry'.

To the alien, this method of thinking was completely obvious, and not even in need of explanation.

Ashamed to be part of my species, I apologetically confessed to the alien that vested interests mean that humans often do not use this method. Human failure to do so is sometimes conscious, but sadly, usually subconscious. Humans can become so personally invested in one of the columns that they subconsciously draw a cognitive box around their own column, to the exclusion of the other column. In extreme cases, I confided, humans deny the existence of the other column. In some cases humans may assign weightings in a way that places an extreme emphasis on the value of intangible, unspecific feelings that are in reality, unarticulated vested interests. In other cases, humans are just lazy, and dismiss the objective conclusion because they have not bothered to assign numerical scores, weigh up and conclude based on those scores.

I explained to the alien that humans have computers that can help with this on a day to day, practical level, but we rarely use computers for this noble reason, instead preferring to use our top notch technology to watch videos of domestic cats jumping from sofas and narrowly missing their destinations. Debating by spreadsheet would mean setting up simple columns For and Against, making it easy to assign scores and calculate the numerical conclusion. But this is rarely done, except perhaps for the most diligent of university professors and debating societies.

I gave the alien the example of climate change: there are points in both the 'For' and the 'Against' columns regarding the hypothesis that humans are causing the observed changes. However, the overwhelming majority of evidence, logic and understanding of cause and effect means there are more points in the 'For' column than the 'Against' column.

With embarrassment at my species mounting, I admitted there was a human called Donald Trump. With my head held low, and kicking the Egyptian dust around a bit, I admitted that Donald Trump was the leader of the next country we were to visit. He was an example of what I described as a 'one column human'. I explained to the alien that Trump probably did this consciously, using an approach of first identifying his vested interest, and then allocating points only to the column that supported his vested interest. He might have been thinking he was doing what was in his own interests, but that is only theoretically true in the short term, not in the medium term. In the medium term, his actions were physically threatening the lungs of his own children and grandchildren to be flooded with the rising waters of the melting continent of Antarctica. That was not actually what he wanted, I believe. So individual humans work against themselves in the medium term, whilst thinking, due to the inaccuracy epidemic, that they are acting in their own short-term vested interests. Long-term thinking? Really long term? Well, that's not even discussed as a species.

This showed the alien both the source of and the solution to many of the problems faced by humanity: rather than one-column thinking that leads to problems, humans need more two-column thinking that leads to solutions.

Two-column thinking is a method used already by many humans, at least some of the time. Perhaps an example of a consistent two-column thinker, I suggested to the alien, was the previous leader of the United States, Barack Obama. Obama signed the global agreement in Paris to tackle climate change as a direct result of two-column thinking. However, his successor, Trump, seemed to be a one-column thinker, and as a direct result of that way of thinking, he withdrew from the same agreement.

So the alien learned that the two-column thinking method does not always come naturally, that humans need reminding to use it, and that humans will not necessarily elect to positions of power other humans with the ability for two-column thinking. On our way to the airport, my green travel buddy concluded our time in Cairo by suggesting placidly that using or not using the two-column method is simply a question of whether humanity will continue to struggle with conflict, or move beyond it.

CHAPTER 2

Los Angeles, United States of America

Can't Keep Living This Way
by Rootjoose

As we made our way from Cairo to Los Angeles, I played this track for the alien. The lyrics focussed on an individual, and I extrapolated them to represent the current way of living in the United States of America as a whole.

Human understanding of sustainability since the 1960s has led to a clear conclusion: the way of living in countries such as the USA is unsustainable.

I explained to the alien that the song lyrics could be reinterpreted to represent a dawning realisation of all humanity. Humans are increasingly looking at themselves and understanding that we need to change, but as a species we genuinely don't know how to change things on the scale that is required for true sustainability.

On arrival at Los Angeles airport the alien and I collected our bags from the carousel. I started pushing my trolley towards the exit, and noticed that the alien was not keeping up with me. I looked back and saw the alien motionless. It seemed to be staring into space and clutching a dollar bill expectantly, waiting for another human to offer to carry its bag. I realised from a distance, without telepathic assistance, that the alien was expecting to give a human that dollar bill in exchange for carrying its bag. It thought it had learnt from a similar situation at Cairo airport. The alien had extrapolated a little too much, assuming it had got the hang of the drill at all human airports on Ocean. Not quite. I reversed my trolley and explained to the alien that we were now in a more wealthy country, and despite there being many examples of poverty in Los Angeles, it was generally not at the level whereby locals offer to carry tourists' bags at airports, hoping for a dollar or two in return.

We jumped in a taxi and, whilst looking out of the taxi window, the alien took child-like joy in pointing out to me familiar features from its experience of Cairo. Pollutants from the exhausts of other cars, gum on the pavements, dog excrement, litter lining the roads, power stations, industry in the distance; all wonderfully familiar to the alien.

Perhaps it had been expecting something wildly different. I had promised ten different places after all. I explained that later in our world tour we would visit places unrecognisable from Cairo and Los Angeles. Easter Island and the Challenger Deep, for example, are very different places. For the moment, the alien rejoiced not only in the familiarity of the sights, but with the taxi window wound down, also with the sounds. It overheard humans speaking in American accents, as it had done when we were in the more tourist-dominated areas of Cairo, such as Giza and around the Sphinx.

As the alien seemed to be enjoying this familiarity, I decided our first stop in Los Angeles would be a Pizza Hut outlet, which the alien recognised from Cairo. Delight turned to disappointment as the alien realised there was no Sphinx visible from our window seats. I ordered our pizzas and moments after they arrived, the alien noticed I seemed keen to watch its method of eating. This turned into a game, with the alien enjoying the challenge of eating its food without me seeing how it did so. I was intrigued to see how it was eating, without appearing to have an operable mouth. With considerable brilliance the alien managed to devour its pizza only when my head was turned or, alternatively, during the microseconds of my blinks, leaving a progressively depleted plate.

I explained to the alien that humans often like to orientate themselves in a city new to them by going up one of the highest buildings, and getting a sense of the city with a bird's-eye view. I took the alien to the top of the tallest building in the central business district, where we had a panoramic view of the urban morphology.

'LA has sprawled to become one of the largest cities in the world by land area, as a result of being built around the use of the car. Most residents here are wealthier than in Cairo. They have been able to afford personal cars, and therefore to travel across the conurbation by car, for several decades.'

'I understand,' said the alien casually, walking with no fear right up to the very edge of the roof of the skyscraper.

'To get back down to street level, we will need to use the stairs or elevator, rather than jump,' I clarified for the alien. 'Humans have not evolved to fly, and so we require, rather unfortunately, a fully functioning parachute in order to break the fall and survive an impact with the ground resulting from a plunge of anything more than a few metres.'

Mid-exposition we were joined by a young adult human sporting a large backpack and a wild grin. He said no discernible words, but roared, ran, reached the edge, and essentially kept running. It was as if the edge of the roof wer<

The alien was alarmed. It had grasped easily the key
narrative: that human biology, gravity, impact managemen
were all connected and relevant to each other. Yet here wa:
to contradict all these connections. The alien and I jointly ,
the building, and were relieved to see the young adult hum,
parachute, then floated safely to ground level.

I took this as an opportunity to provide a metaphor for
a range of problems, some of them extremely urgent, as represented by a young adult
human plummeting to the ground at great speed. However, during our descent humans
are often in denial, over-congratulating ourselves with the very accurate statement that
we are still alive. On the tablet I selected for the alien a quote from the play *Macbeth*,
with only the briefest of digressions about who William Shakespeare was, and why we
like him.

> *'tis strange and oftentimes*
> *To win us to our harm*
> *The instruments of darkness tell us truths*
> *Win us with honest trifles*
> *To betray us in darkest consequence.*
>
> Banquo in *Macbeth* by William Shakespeare: Act 1, Scene 3

So the falling human is correct: 'tis true and honest that a falling human is still
alive during a fall. The impact with the ground is the problem. So it is also true that
they are also on a collision course. Without doing something tangible to change that
course, imminently they will become pavementally and thinly distributed. This in turn is
largely incompatible with the required co-functioning processes and three-dimensional
requirements of most if not all organs in the human body. In other words, soon they will
not be alive.

Humans are collectively, I explained to the alien, rather like this with climate
change. Many of us are still alive. Some have already died as a result of climate
change, but for decision-makers that are still breathing, by definition, their lungs have
not personally been filled with the floodwaters of melting continents: the sea levels are
rising, but they're personally still alive. Using this honest trifle to justify inaction on climate
change is to betray us in darkest consequence.

I continued the metaphor for the type and scale of environmental policy action
required to resolve climate change. Humans also often over-congratulate themselves for
making small steps towards resolving something. In this part of the metaphor, I reminded
the alien that the BASE jumper did not solve the problem of falling towards the ground
by making a series of small changes. The faller did not use a series of small cocktail

example, to break the fall. Rather, this particular human used one single, chute. And not only that, but the parachute was deployed not gradually, but nly.

Such is the nature of the environmental policy action required on climate change. Examples of humans over-congratulating themselves for making small steps to resolve the climate crisis include using energy-saving lightbulbs, or switching the engine off in their car while waiting to collect their kids at the school gates. Yet humans are not implementing the larger, sudden, game-changing solutions, such as suddenly changing their voting patterns towards political parties that are ideologically committed to implementing major solutions to the climate emergency.

'Our inevitable ban on using fossil fuels for energy production is…'

'…politically analogous to pulling the cord of the parachute attached to your species, currently falling at terminal velocity' completed the alien telepathically. How reassuring that we were now at the stage of completing each other's sentences for each other.

There are three levels of action required to resolve climate change. These three levels can be represented by a pyramid, which I asked the alien to visualise from its time in Cairo. At the top of the pyramid are governments, the middle level consists of businesses and organisations, and at the base of the pyramid are individuals. Government sets the legal frameworks and incentives, cascading them down to the middle and bottom levels to implement solutions, such as establishing and using renewable energy companies.

All levels are intrinsically linked, as individuals vote in governments, but it is important to be clear, amongst a current cultural fashion of individualism, that the primary power and influence is the top level. In itself the base of the pyramid has limited influence over its own strategic direction, with the key exception of voting in the government that decides that strategy at the top of the pyramid. For example, if governments continue to give subsidies to fossil fuel companies, rather than renewable energy companies, they are setting in motion a series of cause and effect factors that lead to individuals perpetuating their use of fossil fuels on the basis of needing to use the lowest cost option, regardless of which companies they would environmentally prefer to use.

Back to the BASE jumper metaphor: when we accept that individuals can make only small differences when placed as we are within a governmentally set framework, we see that individual actions are usually represented in scale by the small cocktail umbrellas. By contrast, only the government level is capable of changing the framework for individual daily actions. In other words, only the governments can pull the cord of the large parachute.

The emphasis on individuals is therefore misplaced if directed at individual daily actions such as energy-saving lightbulbs, and better placed when focussed on the action of voting in whichever governmental parties will pull the cord on climate change. Anything other than a sudden switch in mass voting patterns of individuals towards political parties that emphasise environmental policy in their manifestos is therefore like attempting to break the fall of humanity using a combination of small cocktail umbrellas.

I warned the alien that talking about politics can be very triggering for humans, and can invoke a descent not just into a pavement, but also a descent into relativism, whereby some humans insist every comment must be weighted equally. The solution, we concluded, was for humans to use the two-column thinking method advocated in Cairo for all subjective discussions, including how to resolve climate change.

'Why are politicians involved in decisions about energy production?' asked the alien.

I found this surprisingly hard to answer.

'On my home planet, decisions based on physics are made by physicists. This includes decisions on energy production methods. Politicians simply make the decisions about where to locate our energy production devices. They have no say in what those energy production devices are, or how they operate. The pros and cons of each type of unit, using the thinking columns, are assigned weightings by physicists, and concluded by physicists. Because those pros and cons are understood only by physicists, then only physicists weight and conclude. Sorry if that sounds a bit obvious.'

'No, no. You're fine, Alien my old chum. No need to apologise. Quite right. My bad. Or rather, our bad. Humans, I mean.'

I searched my brain for examples to share with the alien whereby, on Ocean, we have also put scientists in full and genuine control of environmental policy. I recalled the banning of Chlorofluorocarbons (CFCs) in 1989 in response to the crisis of the hole in the atmosphere's ozone layer. In this example, scientists effectively made the decision to pull the cord on CFC production. Politicians simply listened to the scientists, implemented that decision, and did the actual cord pulling.

After an ear-popping descent back to ground level using the elevator, the alien and I walked the streets of downtown LA for a while, until we found a place to hire a car. I selected a convertible, hybrid model, with options for both petrol and electric motoring. My alien companion had no valid licence to operate this vehicle. So I took the wheel and, top down to enjoy the sunny LA weather, drove the alien around LA, heading for the wide boulevards along the beach, lined with soaring palm trees. Somehow able to read the endorphin levels circulating in my system, the alien learned that humans tend to find this an enjoyable experience.

The alien noticed that humans in other convertible cars were completing the look with a dashing pair of sunglasses. We were waiting at a set of traffic lights when, before I knew it, the alien had snatched a pair of sunglasses from a passenger in a neighbouring vehicle. I apologised on the alien's behalf and offered to give them back, but the terrified victims sped away in what they believed to be a decision between their lives and their sunglasses.

'Bad alien,' I scolded. 'That's illegal.'

'I learned in Cairo that there are no consequences for theft on this planet,' said the alien neutrally.

Interesting behaviour, I thought to myself, which the alien overheard. I had until now assumed my alien sidekick was inherently law-abiding, and not just in fear of legal consequences. I had presupposed an inherent good nature in the alien. I still believed that to be true, despite witnessing the robbery. It was more like watching a two-year-old child steal a toy from a fellow toddler, rather than watching an innately evil being. Perhaps the alien was equally somewhat impressionable, especially given its reference to its own experience of being robbed in Cairo, and the lack of consequences on the perpetrator. I hoped its time on Ocean was not starting to be a bad influence on the alien, corrupting its otherwise innocent temperament.

It was generally a polite alien, and sometimes very considerate. At times, I felt its societal evolution was very obviously far in advance of ours. But I reminded myself it had come from an entirely different part of the multiverse, and so at some point in our world tour it was bound to demonstrate slightly different legal and ethical expectations from those encountered on Ocean. And besides, if that was the worst thing the alien did throughout our journey, I would be extremely lucky.

'We will need to talk more about law enforcement here on Ocean,' I said firmly. 'Just because you couldn't vaporise that teenager who stole your money, doesn't mean you can steal from others. Promise me you won't do that again?'

'I promise,' said the alien, sulkily.

'Good alien.'

After a minor struggle by the alien, followed by a brief, one-handed intervention from its chauffeur, the alien was able to wear the sunglasses the right way around on its face. They were slightly too large.

I had by now got the hang of not needing to point my head towards the alien whenever I thought at it. So, looking ahead whilst driving, but thinking sideways towards my passenger, I shared my thought that hybrid cars are the perfect encapsulation of where humans are in terms of their technological development. Within a single machine we have a literal transition from petrol to electricity, a metaphor for the societal transition from fossil fuels to renewables, from the unsustainable to the sustainable.

The braking system was able to harvest some of the heat generated from the brake discs, and convert that into energy to further power the car. This topped up the battery, in addition to plugging the car into a charging point. The electricity from the charging points came from the national power grid. Whilst the grid was not fed by entirely renewable energy sources, it was partially fed by such clean methods, and therefore involved fewer carbon dioxide emissions than running the car on fossil fuels alone.

From the coast we headed back towards downtown Los Angeles. The overall LA region is one that experiences natural phenomena such as earthquakes. Our hybrid vehicle joined the back of a long queue of traffic. At the front of the queue was a road bridge. Humans had stopped their vehicles before driving onto it. The ground, it appeared, had already been shaking from an earthquake for some time in this area before we arrived. The road bridge was empty of cars. It was wobbling rather like a jelly at a six-year-old's birthday party. Then it collapsed and disappeared into a cloud of its own dust.

'I'm pleased that no one is hurt. But this is rather inconvenient for us,' said a voice in my head.

We were stuck in gridlock. Car horns blared pointlessly. Drivers got out and stood, hands triangulated symmetrically onto hips, as if using the human body to make geometric shapes would somehow help clear up the confusion.

From people in the same predicament, we heard a rumour that it would take a full day to clear. We decided, like others around us, to abandon the hybrid car and walk. We headed, perhaps appropriately now that we were unable to drive, to the Peterson Automotive Museum.

The museum organised workshops designed specifically to teach children how automobiles had changed the way America operates. I left the alien in one such workshop, along with a group of six-year-olds, perhaps similar to those at the recently imagined birthday party with wobbly jelly. After an hour of walking around the museum, grateful for a little time to myself, I returned to collect the alien from the workshop. The workshop leader let the rest of the class empty. She took me to one side to inform me that my child, although non-verbal, showed surprisingly advanced Lego car-building skills for a six-year-old.

At the museum they had a DeLorean car from the film *Back to the Future*. Door wings up, the alien sat inside. I disappointed my new friend that this vehicle is not a real time machine. I then wondered why this would be disappointing rather than expected news for the alien. I probed fairly persistently, asking if time machines were routine devices on its home planet, but received no reply, telepathic or otherwise.

Back to the Future
(1985)

Back at our hotel I showed the alien this film, one of the classic blockbusters that epitomised the film industry driven by Los Angeles in the 1980s. The film combined genres of science fiction, action, adventure, drama, romance and comedy.

The film introduced to the alien some questions that occupy the human imagination. Scientists continue to battle with the conundrum of whether any form of time travel to the past is possible, and if so, how that would be possible without creating paradoxical situations.

Near the end of the film, I paused it during the final scene. Here a small, compact 'Mr Fusion' device was used to power the DeLorean car that had travelled back from the future. I explained to the alien that fusion power as an alternative and clean source of energy has been in slow development since the 1940s. One of the key technological solutions in the fight against climate change is to develop nuclear fusion devices that are small enough to be convenient, whilst also clean and safe enough to overcome the disadvantages of nuclear fission.

The alien quizzed me accusingly about why nuclear fusion had not already been developed on Ocean. Embarrassed at my part in the underdevelopment of my species, I confessed that vested interests of the fossil fuel industry had led to nuclear fusion receiving insufficient development funding. And to put a further damper on our otherwise excellent film night, I added that this is despite the potential of nuclear fusion as a pervasive, clean, game changing, 'parachute' solution to the fall of humanity via climate change

---

The next morning the alien was in another sulk, unimpressed by human lack of time machines. Perhaps it had been hoping for more from us. Over our muted breakfast I changed the subject, and explained to the alien the role of Los Angeles and Hollywood in the film industry, and that at least we humans are smart enough to imagine such technology and its benefits, even if not to invent it. This seemed to cheer the alien's spirits a little. We retrieved the hybrid car from its abandoned location by the collapsed road bridge, and drove to Universal Studios.

On arrival the alien tugged twice on my sleeve and pointed to a colourful visitor train packed with tourists: mothers holding their babies, fathers holding cameras, teenagers rolling their eyes, and an animated train guide standing at the front, explaining everything they saw. We jumped on board and through speakers positioned above our heads, heard about the changing trends in film over time. Unknowingly to the train guide, his train that day contained tourists from not one, but two different parts of the multiverse. This was thanks in part to the alien's cunning and now staple disguise of its baseball cap obtained in Cairo, and its oversized sunglasses, stolen here in LA.

On the visitor train the alien learned about why humans like to be entertained through film, and the importance of story-telling in human evolution as a means of passing on useful survival knowledge from one generation to another over a camp fire. Films play no less a functional role now, explained the visitor train guide, but more one of exercising the human imagination, escapism and a safe form of excitement in an existence otherwise dominated, if one is lucky, by a 9–5 job culminating in the dreary climax of the annual tax return. I sensed the train guide was speaking from experience.

'Many people on Ocean suffer a far more difficult existence than working in the same job day after day, after day, after day, after day, after day,' explained the train guide, now clearly revealing his thinly veiled biography. 'And yet many experience a far more profitable existence,' he vented with suppressed anger, giving the example of what he chose to describe as 'hideously and immorally overpaid actors in the Hollywood film industry'.

The inequality of incomes and fortunes is essential in capitalism.
Ludwig Von Mises, Economist

The alien was confused by the mixed emotions it detected from the visitor train guide. I had an idea to explain this important concept further for the alien. After a quick call to my United Nations employers to pull a few strings, I received an email with two e-tickets to attend the Oscars ceremony that evening.

Bow ties on, I explained to the alien that we were heading to a place that epitomised the contrasting fortunes of different people within the same industry. When we arrived the alien kept on its sunglasses, and the security staff seemed to assume the alien was a slightly pretentious method actor staying in character for the evening to show off. They erroneously ushered us directly onto the red carpet. The alien noticed a scattered selection of actors lining the flanks of the red carpet and talking with fans, signing autographs and smiling proudly for selfie photographs.

My otherworldly guest gravitated towards the sides of the red carpet, seemingly intent on copying the other actors. A lady wearing an X-Files t-shirt was beckoning the alien particularly fervently. I considered for a moment the option of allowing this impending sequence of events to play out, perhaps saying it was actually Tom Cruise in an alien costume, staying in character for his most immersive role yet that would blow everyone's mind in next summer's blockbuster. I could only envisage that scenario ending in disaster or, at best, spoiling the revelation in our forthcoming destination of

Beijing, where the alien's arrival on Ocean had a planned announcement with careful wording, rather than a screaming realisation by a fan flanking a red carpet. I thought better of it and steered the alien inside the building.

Immediately a glass of champagne was thrust into the alien's hand. The alien thought it had now learned what to do when a human makes an uninvited gesture of apparent kindness, and so reached inside its child-sized dinner jacket pocket to retrieve a dollar bill. I held the alien's arm in place and thanked the doorman with words, rather than money.

'It's ok, buddy,' I explained to the alien as we walked to our seats. 'We're now in a place of such lofty wealth that people might offer you champagne without expecting a dollar in return. The doorman is paid well through a monthly bank transfer, and although tipping is often appreciated in this particular culture when handed a drink in a bar, in this even more particular scenario, it is not expected.'

A telepathic voice in my head muttered something about excessively complex patterns of human interactions.

We sat at the back and, as the ceremony progressed and each nominee was named, I showed the alien on the tablet the fee that each lead actor received for their role in the various films. The figures were often in the range of $500,000 to $20,000,000 for a few months of work. I compared this with the average salary for Los Angeles of around $55,000 for a year's work. The alien understood that this probably accounted for the cynicism displayed earlier by the train guide at Universal Studios.

After the ceremony the alien and I walked across town to a catch the end of a fashion show. Again we witnessed wealth and opulence at the venue. We listened to a number of ingratiating speeches by immaculately dressed fashion designers. The alien was nodding off, and I marvelled at what seemed to be universal behaviour when falling asleep in an upright seated position: a lean forward, a jolt, a semi-conscious lean backwards, a drowsy attempt to re-gather composure, and a repeat of the cycle. I was transfixed at this otherworldly demonstration of intergalactic unity in the most unexpected of places and behaviours.

An eco-fashion designer began to talk, and I gave the alien a nudge. The designer explained the extensive environmental impact of the clothing and fashion industries, and current efforts to reduce the impact through solutions such as organic cotton, more durable clothing, and diversions of waste clothing from landfill. The designer explained their use of vertical supply chains: the sourcing of clothing materials from the same country, rather than incurring the 'fashion miles' needed to fly in materials from various parts of the globe to make each garment. Via our sixth sense of telepathy, the alien then asked me pertinent questions about the supply chain of its bow tie. I couldn't answer: the label on the bow tie was tiny, with minimal information. I concluded for the alien that the industry still has a long way to go in terms of both communicating and resolving its environmental impact.

We finished the evening by visiting a hospital in Los Angeles. We talked to staff on a night shift about their income. The alien learned that many of these workers, so critical to maintaining human life, were paid less than the average wage for Los Angeles. The over-recognition of high performers in the entertainment and fashion industries became clear to the alien, and again it was sympathetic to the visitor train guide's suppressed anger. I felt proud of my alien friend when it asked me to pass on the message to the hospital workers that, despite their relative under-recognition in terms of societal status and pay, they were no less high-performing super-stars than the highest paid, Oscar-winning actors it had seen earlier that night. It would have said as much directly to the hospital staff by itself, explained the alien telepathically, but it did not have a functional mouth: its mouth was purely decorative, having lost the need to use it for speech over the course of millions of years of evolutionary development relying on telepathy. I had guessed that. But I still didn't know how the alien ate.

The following morning I took the alien to Venice Beach, where we had a workout at an outdoor gym located on the sand, known as Muscle Beach. During our bicep curls I told the alien about the life story of Arnold Schwarzenegger, who used to body-build at this outdoor gym before becoming a successful actor and then politician.

I revealed to the alien that Arnold's story epitomised the 'American Dream' and the opportunities available to humans willing and able to commit to extraordinary levels of hard work. On the tablet I showed the alien a photograph of Arnold in his body-building prime. While Arnie's face was in shot, the frame was dominated by a single arm. I explained to the alien that this photograph demonstrates the physical results of consistent hard work. There were three parts to the arm: an initial triceps muscle that an average gym regular would have been proud of, had it formed the entire thickness of their arm. But on Arnie, it served merely as a sort of foundational layer of muscle. It was nothing more than an introductory prelude, a subservient platform for the headline act, the main part of the arm: the biceps muscle, which launched upwards, bulging to the stratosphere. Thirdly, like a star twinkling on top of a Christmas tree, the biceps signed off with a thick, throbbing vein that protruded upwards further, touching the top of the frame of the photograph.

The alien moved its gaze from the photograph to an average looking gentleman, mildly beer-bellied, walking his dog along the beach.

'Are they the same species?' asked the alien telepathically.

'Yes, there's just one species of human,' I clarified, and added with a mild understatement: 'lifestyle choices are largely responsible for the contrasting physiques.'

I elaborated for the alien that if it were let in to the dog walker's home, it might observe this human watching television, and possibly munching on crisps or other examples of the average to poor diet that typifies the vast majority of Los Angeles households. If let into Arnie's home in his prime, however, the alien would have seen a television that was switched off, but the room would have been filled with noise nevertheless: the grunts and heaves of bench presses, the clang of dumb-bells hitting the floor, the sizzle of fried eggs before their flappy journey into the protein-hungry jaws of a man-giant.

'Why don't all humans behave in the same way as Arnie?' asked the alien, understandably.

I explained that each human had different levels of motivation, and while Arnie could, should have been and was often celebrated for his achievements, his situation could also be interpreted as tragic: that for him it was impossible to feel fulfilled without such extreme achievements. In contrast, other humans may feel profoundly fulfilled, despite minimal achievements. And so the alien learned the complexity of humans on their journey towards the nebulous idea of happiness and fulfilment.

I added that the origins of such huge differences between individual humans were explored professionally by the vast field of human psychology. Different psychologies have their roots in a combination of genetics, circumstances in childhoods and other environmental and situational factors throughout a person's development. I clarified for the alien that Arnie was simply the metaphorical embodiment of high achievers in all aspects of human life, including business, politics, the arts, sports, and so on.

Much is said and written by humans on the topic of why some individuals succeed more than others, and I offered my view to the alien that a recurring characteristic of high achievers is one of clarity. Setting clear goals and working backwards from those goals systematically is a key factor that seems to distinguish and separate out the normal achievers from the highest achievers. I expressed this further for the alien using the form of a poem, which I called *Clarity Motivates*.

When Clarity was born it was clear from the start,
When she needed something she cried from the heart.

Fifteen months later her mum said to her,
Please draw a cat with beautiful fur.
Clarity knew what she needed to do,
And she drew a cat before she was two.

Fifteen years later she had an exam,
She'd done no revision and was trying to cram.
No genius is born with facts in her brain,
She left with E and it started to rain.
But Clarity knew what she needed to do,
She needed hard work for that exam, take two.
She remembered her reasons and there were a few,
A job and more money were good to aspire to.
She found out the deadline and worked back from there,

What revision to do, and when, and where.
She passed with an A, the first time in her life,
She succeeded in something and avoided strife.

Fifteen years later and Clarity was winning,
Not in exams but Olympic swimming.
Her deadline was 2020 and she'd worked back from there,
What training to do, and when, and where.

When Clarity stopped swimming she helped out a charity,
Transferring her focus to fixing calamity.
She's not a rare talent, not special in reality,
You'll succeed too, when you become Clarity.

The alien and I visited the Museum of Tolerance in Los Angeles. This museum used multimedia techniques to teach children about inequality and prejudice within our species. For example, ethnic minorities are often unable to get the jobs they are qualified for due to varying levels of racism. This means they are forced to take lower paid jobs, and in some cases resort to crime, such as the increasingly globalised drug trade. Higher crime rates in residential areas of lower cost housing then create a landscape of exclusion for those that fear for their safety.

> *We may have all come on different ships, but we're in the same boat now.*
> Martin Luther King Jr, Civil Rights Activist

From the museum I drove our hybrid car to Watts, an area of Los Angeles associated with lower cost housing and ethnic minorities. Sunglasses on, the alien joined me in spending a few hours doing a survey, asking individuals about their employment status. Answers showed that around seven per cent of people in Watts were unemployed. We repeated the survey in Beverly Hills, an area associated with higher cost housing and low percentages of ethnic minorities, and found an unemployment rate of just five per cent.

On the tablet I showed the alien average income data for residents of Beverley Hills, with 22 per cent earning over $200,000 per year, compared with the average for the USA of just five per cent earning more than this figure. I asked the alien to consider how much street lighting was functioning properly at night in Watts compared with Beverly Hills. After an evening of walking through both areas, the alien reported back to me that, using this metric, the authorities comparatively neglect Watts.

Speed Demon
by Michael Jackson

Continuing the theme of race, I summarised for the alien the life story of Michael Jackson. His appearance changed over the years as a result of a skin condition and burns suffered when filming a Pepsi commercial in the 1980s. He appeared to change from one race to another in a way that is almost unique in human history.

The lyrics of Speed Demon were inspired when the writer, Michael Jackson, received a ticket for speeding. In the extended music video there is a section at the end, showing Michael and a rabbit character enjoying a dance off at the side of the road, thinking they had escaped punishment for speeding. However, their speeding offence soon caught up with them. A law enforcement officer gives Michael a speeding ticket. Michael weakly attempts to justify himself, then reluctantly accepts the ticket.

For the alien the message was that breaking rules is often tempting for humans. This can even be a form of fun for children. Breaking rules continues into adulthood, where anti-authority sentiments can remain core aspects of human psychology, often subconsciously. The alien needed to know that this is a pervasive aspect of human psychology. Indeed many refer to this as a key driver for the British and American public voting for Brexit and Donald Trump respectively in 2016. Outrage and angry rebellion are in fashion in our current culture. Rebellious tendencies bring both helpful and unhelpful consequences for humanity.

We jumped back in the hybrid and drove to the secluded, far western end of the Santa Monica Boulevard, the heart of the Lesbian, Gay, Bisexual and Transgender, or LGBT, community in LA, to confirm a common pattern that certain types of minority are both geographically and socially marginalised. We then visited an ethnic enclave known as Little Saigon, with more than 189,000 Vietnamese Americans. I explained that many of these people were either refugees or relatives of some of the refugees that left Vietnam in preference for LA in the 1970s and 1980s, perhaps because they feared the political situation and war in Vietnam. We continued this theme later in our world tour, in Ho Chi Minh City.

Our next stop in LA was the Natural History Museum of Los Angeles County. Here the alien learned how oil was formed, and that it is a finite resource. I explained the global warming model to the alien, the problems of putting carbon that was once in the ground into the air, and the meta-solution of simply keeping that carbon substance in the ground. How exactly we achieve that is the challenge.

To really give the alien an idea of how quickly oil was being consumed, we sat at the side of a petrol station with clipboards and stopwatches to record the almost constant consumption. The relentless level of consumption was, of course, repeated at thousands of petrol stations across the globe.

I then took the alien to a wind farm and solar energy plant, so it could see for itself human efforts to find alternative energy sources. I explained that humanity has been aware of the challenge of finding alternative energy sources for many decades, but humans are proving to be slow to scale up these solutions. As long ago as 1980 humanity was well aware of the vested interests within it that were slowing the widespread deployment of clean energy.

> *The use of solar energy has not been opened up, because the oil industry does not own the sun.*
> Ralph Nader, Political Activist, in 1980

The alien was familiar with the concept that constant oil consumption cannot continue for ever.

'Even if the centre of your planet is nothing but oil,' speculated the alien, 'your oil would still run out if you continue to use oil faster than it's produced through sedimentation. Alternatives are needed for that reason alone, regardless of climate change.'

I confessed on behalf of my species that partly because the USA is organised as a free market economy, the vested interests of oil companies continue, and therefore the constant consumption of oil continues unchecked. I compared this to the organisation of Vietnam, which, under socialism, is in theory in a better position to limit oil consumption. This presented socialism in a positive light, but the very presence of Little Saigon in Los Angeles suggested a negative side to socialism, which I described to the alien as the lack of freedom of choice.

Before we left LA, there was one final stop for the alien – a gun shop. Relating to the concept of free markets and freedom more broadly is the issue of gun control. To demonstrate how easy it was to purchase guns in the USA, I gave the alien some cash, removed its baseball cap and oversized sunglasses, and let it walk into a gun store alone. The alien received excellent service, despite not being human or able to talk, write, or provide identification. It emerged from the store clutching an AK-47, and a bag of bullets.

Referring back to the two-column thinking introduced in Cairo, I listed for the alien the range of thoughts on both sides of the debate about gun ownership in the USA. In the column 'For' the freedom to own a gun was the ideological position, as stated in the Second Amendment of the US Constitution, of the right to bear arms. I clarified for the alien, like a dad making a bad joke, that this was not an encouragement to wear vests.

In the column 'Against' the freedom to own a gun was the equivalent counter-argument, in the ideological position of living in a safe society. Freedom is never total for all: the freedom to bear arms for one person takes away the freedom of another person to live without fear of being shot. The points calculation in the two columns was therefore 1–1 at this stage of the debate.

I presented the alien with statistics showing the lower numbers of gun-related deaths in most other countries on Ocean, compared with significantly higher numbers of gun-related deaths in the USA. The alien commented there was no equivalent counter-argument for this in the opposite column.

We conducted a thorough exploration of further points on both sides of the debate and assigned weightings. The alien noticed that the 'Against' column had accumulated more numerous and heavily weighted points. We recognised and respected the points in the 'For' column, whilst concluding that there were more numerous and more heavily weighted points in the 'Against' column. It was blindingly obvious to the alien, therefore, that policies in the USA must change to have greater gun control.

> *We do not have to accept this carnage as the price of freedom.*
> Barack Obama, speaking about gun control when President of the United
> States in 2016

On the tablet I found for the alien a news story, which summarised a shooting event in New Zealand in 2019. In that country, the Government responded by changing their gun control laws within a few days.

'So why haven't the laws been changed in the USA?' asked the alien.

'Barack Obama, when President, used the two-column method and comprehensively won this debate, but he still couldn't change the laws,' I lamented.

I heard a telepathic squeal of intellectual agony from the alien.

'Are you saying that comprehensively winning a debate does not necessarily mean humans on the losing side will agree they have lost?'

'Yes,' I admitted. Again I felt the urge to add: 'Sorry.'

'This,' howled the alien from its own brain to mine, 'is going to be a problem.'

Sensing I may be losing the species-level respect of my travel buddy, I tried to calm it down with honest elaboration, hoping that would help us to find a solution together. I revealed that human refusal to acknowledge defeat is due to vested interests so strong that the human mind can sometimes create a genuine delusion that its arguments have really not been outweighed at all. Other times, a human may recognise in their mind that their preferred column has lost, but factors such as pride or the challenge of change means they act as if they do not recognise their defeat, and continue with words and actions as if they have won.

'Not all humans are like that. Jacinda Ardern, the Prime Minister of New Zealand, understood when something needs to change. Barack Obama also understood,' I urged. 'So you might be a little hasty to write us all off. Obama understood which column had won the debate about gun laws, and he was not afraid of changing the laws. But he was limited in his ability to make those changes due to failings in the structure of the American political system.'

I was sensing a very unhappy alien. At least it had learned the complexities of humanity when it comes to implementing the obscenely obvious. But was that enough to prevent my frustrated pal from quitting the world tour after just two places?

I realised something serious was happening in the mind of the alien, and more importantly to me now, in the relationship between me and my new friend. A quiet whirring noise began in my head, overlain by a telepathic and strained yet diplomatic message from the alien.

'For your own good, it's probably best we end our two-way telepathic connection for now. You don't want to know what I'm thinking about humanity at this point in time. We'll reconnect later in our travels. Where's next?'

'Vietnam,' I said, miffed. My emotions were mixed. I felt shunned, yet relieved that the alien intended to continue our world tour.

There was an amusing plopping noise as we disconnected. Then silence.

CHAPTER 3
Ho Chi Minh City, Vietnam

 A L I E N   P L A Y L I S T

War
by Edwin Starr

Building on the concept of war that we introduced in Los Angeles, I played this song for the alien on our way to Ho Chi Minh City. The song expresses the reality that in war almost everyone loses. Indeed, perhaps the only ones that benefit are those in the funeral industry, assuming they were not personally involved.

The song, a clear protest song against the then Vietnam War, was released in 1970. There were many wars that I could have chosen to explore in depth with the alien. Perhaps more than any other, the Vietnam War was one that demonstrated most clearly the dilemma for humanity of how to organise the collective self.

The alien burped. Astonishing, I thought, for someone without a functional mouth. Then I remembered that as a boy, armed with a fizzy drinks can, a free afternoon and an encouraging pal, I had managed something similar. It was a sort of inward throat-burp. On this realisation that burps don't need operable mouths, all seemed well again, sitting next to the alien.

The burp occurred at approximately 35,000 feet above sea level. We were on our flight from Los Angeles to Ho Chi Minh City in Vietnam, the third of ten destinations on our world tour. We were not talking, but still together. I felt a bit like half of a married couple in that sense.

I couldn't hide my feeling of being shunned by the alien's decision to cut off our telepathy. In a very literal sense, it was impossible to hide this feeling; the alien could still access my thoughts, but it was no longer a two-way connection. How would it feel if I had the ability to cut off my thoughts, and chose to do so? The alien looked at me blankly whenever I addressed this issue in my mind, as if to remind me it could still hear everything, and it was not going to discuss its reasons, 'so back off'. The implied power differential was stark. 'Suck it up' was the message I wrote to myself on the blank canvas of the motionless alien face looking back at me.

I had been getting the hang of the telepathy thing, and if I was honest with myself, I had started to feel a bit smug about it. I had been entertaining initial thoughts about misusing this new ability to show off at parties, to gain insights into what particular ladies really thought of me, to teach it to the military, to make a few quid in poker games, to publish a 'How To Use Telepathy' book, or at least to get an article in a respectable newspaper. But on the flight I came to terms with the brutal realisation that I had no idea how to initiate a telepathic connection with a human. The alien had initiated the process. The alien had also then fine-tuned our connection. The alien had decided whether or not our connection would remain two way, or as it was at this point in time, one way. It was not something I could repeat. I tried of course, firstly by pointing my frontal lobe at a German gentleman across the aisle, only to receive a visual rather than telepathic castigation. Secondly, the brain of the air stewardess did not reveal her inner ranking of my appearance on a scale of one to ten; instead, I received a disappointingly normal vocal communication, asking me to take part in an informal, in flight quiz regarding which drink I would like next.

I became unsettled, desperate to re-establish the telepathic connection with the alien. I felt a heightened sense of loneliness. I had lost something that most people would never experience. I wondered if this was how first-time users of class A narcotics felt: up until that point in their life they were fine without the drugs, but after a single use they were hooked. I remembered the film *Trainspotting*, and speculated that soon I might also be curled up in a cognitive corner, shivering with withdrawal symptoms following the high of the out-of-body experience, convinced no one else could understand, wishing I had never experienced this addictive sensation in the first place, destined to find the rest of existence banal and so always hunting for the next telepathic hit. I then recalled the evocative title of Maya Angelou's autobiography, *I Know Why The Caged Bird Sings*. If a bird is born in a cage and has never known freedom that is one thing, but let it experience freedom and then cage it – well, that's something very different.

At this point the alien's head rotated a simple 90 degrees to face mine. The stillness and neutrality of its expression led me to guess its thoughts. I decided it might be suggesting I was exaggerating to call on such lofty literary references to express how I felt about losing our telepathic connection. Childishly, I pointed my frontal lobe at the alien and thought back a retort to 'connect us back up, then'. It didn't work.

So I was left really, really wondering what the alien was thinking. Why did it feel the need to prevent me hearing its thoughts? What was it thinking about our experiment at the gun store, and our subsequent discussion, that would be so damaging for me to hear? Did it mean that me personally, or humanity generally, should not hear its thoughts? Paradoxically, I was also comforted that it chose to disconnect: if it felt humanity had no hope, it might as well have let me hear the fate of our species, then left Ocean. Not doing so, I mused, implied we have a chance. The alien had rotated its head back to facing forwards, and was either pretending to read, or was genuinely able to read the magazine that it held upside down.

On arrival in Ho Chi Minh City, the alien noticed an airport sign referring to the city as SGN, meaning Saigon. In our time together so far I had experienced many character traits of the alien: patience, consideration, wisdom, sarcasm and anger to name a few, but its reaction to the SGN sign was different. Panic, perhaps. Somewhat out of character, I thought, and remembered that I was still getting to know this creature's personality. I postulated that the notion of even having a personality was potentially anthropocentric in itself.

My daydreaming was not appreciated. The alien gestured impatiently, pointing with a green quarter, rather than fifth, of the digits on one of its hands. The pointing was not static, but alternating between the 'SGN' sign, and the clearly listed 'Ho Chi Minh City' on its printout of our itinerary. We had arrived in the wrong city, so the alien seemed to be assuming.

I projected a silent elucidation to the alien, a quick telepathic history.

'Both are correct,' I began. 'The identity of the city had been in a state of flux. The official name change from Saigon to Ho Chi Minh City reflected settlement by different cultural and political groups, which in turn reflected the basis of ideological differences that led to a war that played out here.' I lamented the one way nature of the exposition, missing what might otherwise have been a telepathic noise emitted by the alien to continue into the depths of further detail, or to wrap it up. I decided on the latter.

'At the end of that war, the city was officially renamed Ho Chi Minh City, but diplomatically it was not felt necessary to replace every sign that said Saigon or SGN. Both are now culturally acceptable.'

The alien seemed satisfied with this and then, confident as anything, grabbed its bags from the carousel, looked around and paused, wondering if this time anyone would offer to carry its bag. On cue, a Vietnamese lady appeared and offered to carry its bag. The alien gave me a void look, and I perhaps erroneously projected onto the extra-terrestrial visage a meaning similar to a wink coming back at me, indicating that it had got the hang of the situation at airports on Ocean, and that it knew this meant we were again in an economically less developed or wealthy country.

I had by now spent around ten days with the alien, and so it was no surprise that at some point during our journey, the alien would need to visit a toilet. The aforementioned burp had alerted me to the existence of some form of internal bodily activity within the alien, and our various meals so far had confirmed the alien's need to eat and drink, even if I had been losing our cat and mouse game to observe exactly how the alien did so.

We approached the toilet area, and the alien was faced with a choice: left for male, right for female. I had not considered the alien's gender identity until this point, and had simply been thinking of it as gender neutral. It had suggested the stag do ruse, but perhaps that simply reflected my own gender: had I been female myself, perhaps it might have equally suggested a hen do ruse.

The alien stopped walking. Its Vietnamese bag handler dutifully stopped as well. The lady, perhaps also assuming the alien was on a stag do, gestured the alien to go left, towards the gent's. The alien shook its head. The lady then gestured right, towards the ladies. The alien shook its head. The Vietnamese lady was understandably confused, and looked at me in sincere confusion, mixed with fear. Helpfully, she noticed nearby was a toilet for disabled people, and gestured the alien towards it. The alien nodded. I gave our bag and toilet helper an appropriate number of Vietnamese dongs, and indicated I would take it from here.

Waiting outside the disabled toilets, I speculated as to what was happening behind the closed door. I had observed no obvious waste disposal orifices on the alien, although in order to be respectful, I hadn't exactly been looking closely for such features. When the alien emerged it looked exactly the same as when it had gone in. I realised that, without telepathy or a functional mouth, there was no point in me asking what had gone on in there.

Instead I decided to extrapolate a metaphorical lesson from the alien's first lavatorial experience.

'You have now experienced a clear example of a human thought concept known as the bifurcation fallacy,' I thought telepathically to the alien as we walked straight ahead, towards the exit of the airport. 'This is when humans present a false dilemma, or question that simultaneously imposes a pair of multiple choice answers, when there is at least one other option available. Male or female, for example, when in your case, it was neither.'

The alien nodded to indicate it understood. A tangent entered my mind about the alien becoming some sort of representative icon for the LGBT community on Ocean.

'If I may draw an immediate analogy with our current direction of walking,' I continued, 'consider if a human asks you now, not only where the exit is, but also then imposed on you the multiple choice answers of left or right as the only valid answers?' I asked the alien.

The alien looked at me as vacantly as the toilet it had just left.

'We would be forced to reject those options,' I suggested. 'Logically rather than evasively, we must introduce the third option as the only honest answer: the exit is straight on. That would be a physical reality rather than opinion, feeling or hunch.'

The alien nodded. It seemed familiar with the conclusion, but I wondered if, on its own planet, they struggled with the bifurcation fallacy in the first place.

I linked this back to the thinking method introduced in Cairo: for the purposes of a simple demonstration I had picked two columns, as humans are often faced with a valid decision between two and only two options. But in fact, just as there were thousands of columns in Cairo, so it was also important to remind the alien that there are often thousands of options for humans to weigh up. Sometimes the full range of options can only be summarised into three or four, rather than two, viable options. The principle and method behind the thinking process is identical, however: to add up the scores across several columns, rather than just two, and conclude according to those scores.

So the lavatorial dichotomy had taught the alien that nearly everything on Ocean is more complex than is possible to generalise or summarise. The need for brevity often comes, somewhat appropriately, as a BOGOF: Buy One Get One Free. Brevity almost always comes packaged with a free dollop of bias. There is usually no such thing as a summary that is not a biased summary, no simplifications that are not biased simplifications. Yet summaries and simplifications on Ocean are often pushed by humans with vested interests, using the bifurcation fallacy to the point of being impossible to be objectively correct, as evidenced by the metaphorical disabled toilet, and the emblematic direction of the airport exit being straight ahead.

In the heart of Ho Chi Minh City we found a side road harbouring a crowded café. Seats spewed onto the narrow pavement like the River Nile emptying into the Mediterranean Sea. The mainly outdoor seating arrangement dominated the business, with the minority of seats located inside a room the size of a suburban garage the alien may have noticed in Los Angeles. Money, I reminded the alien, drives a large proportion of human geographical distribution, whether on the macro scale such as the rural–urban migration discussed in Egypt, or on the micro scale, such as here on a side road of Ho Chi Minh City, where humans were distributed densely on small foldable chairs along a narrow pavement. This was perhaps driven, I explained to the alien, by the personal financial situation of the Vietnamese café owner, struggling to make ends meet, and seating new customers wherever possible in order to make a few more dongs. Having previously supported the multinational corporation of Pizza Hut with our culinary custom, it was time to support this local business owner.

'Welcome to Ho Chi Ming City' boomed the café owner, two arms raised. He looked to each side, inviting other customers to join him in giving welcoming, polite smiles. It was the warmest and most sincere human interaction I felt the alien had received thus far on our journey, apart from with its tour guide of course. Never mind the lavish welcoming ceremony awaiting us in Beijing: here, on the humble side road in Ho Chi Minh City, was the emotional and heartfelt welcome to Ocean that the alien deserved. In a sense, it made me feel as if this was where the alien's journey really began: its birthplace on our planet.

The café owner was without judgement of the alien's appearance, without consideration that his new customer might be from another quadrant of the multiverse.

Whatever its origin or its colour of skin, green or otherwise, the alien was here supporting his struggle, supporting his business. Yes, it was ultimately financial, but there was a welcoming of intent as well, a recognition that the alien and I were indirectly assisting him, his family, his wife and his beloved children. And in that moment, it was our simple presence, pregnant with unspoken positive intentions and knock on consequences, which mattered to this decent Vietnamese gentleman.

The subsequent moment, knew both humans, belonged to financial reality. I reminded the alien telepathically that ultimately, the café owner was so welcoming because of our impending purchase. I ordered us two lattés and two dishes of pho, a national staple and popular street food in Vietnam.

As I consumed the pho with a spoon, in a manner that I hoped was culturally acceptable to the locals around us, the alien seemed to take joy once again in our now traditional meal-time game. I called the game bluntly: how the hell does the alien eat? It went a bit like this: I watch the alien intently, but eventually I have to blink; during said blink, the alien's plate or bowl suddenly becomes less full. The desire to learn this mainly inconsequential detail about the alien became increasingly obsessive to me, and increasingly hilarious to the alien. I felt as if I was dining with a one-year-old human baby playing that game of throwing its food on the floor and then cracking up laughing as the parent retrieves it. I could see the alien's shoulders juddering: which in my anthropocentrism, I interpreted as cackling laughter mixed with infantile mischief. My consistent failure to catch the alien in the act of eating continued.

From what seemed to be possibly the funniest game in the multiverse, to an explanation of war. Our world tour had a variety of places within it: places like Cairo and Los Angeles had been selected for multiple reasons, with their ability to teach the alien a wide range of lessons about humanity and our interaction with Ocean. Others, like Ho Chi Minh City and later on, Easter Island, I had selected for more focussed reasons, albeit far from singular. Here, I had to find a conversational segue from our silly eating game to the more serious topic of explaining the societal tendency of humans to engage in nationally sponsored killing. I relieved the pressure on myself by accepting that maybe my desire to make that transition seem smooth was again not only anthropocentric, but also probably culturally specific to my upbringing in the UK.

'So, we have come to Ho Chi Minh City to continue a theme touched on in Los Angeles, that humans have different philosophies around how to organise society,' I blurted. 'For instance, between 1945 and 1986 the communist North Vietnamese, supported by the Soviet Union, China and others, were philosophically in favour of greater state control. This was in contrast to South Vietnam, the USA and other advocates of organising humanity according to capitalist, free market forces and less state control.'

The alien's pho had again diminished. I must have blinked, perhaps mid-way through the word 'philosophically'. I tried to keep focus on the burgeoning teaching.

'Such fundamental differences ultimately led North Vietnam to war in 1955 with the capitalist and anti-communist South Vietnam, supported by the USA, South Korea and other countries philosophically in favour of reduced state control, with more emphasis on individual freedom and liberty.'

Another percentage of the alien's pho had disappeared. I tried not to think about quantifying what fraction of the bowl's contents had vanished.

'The war continued for twenty years, until 30 April 1975 when the city came under control of the North Vietnamese. They re-named the city from Saigon to Ho Chi Minh City, after the communist leader at the time. For some humans the name change was symbolic of the success of the communists, and led to their fleeing the country for places such as the USA. Hence the presence of Little Saigon, rather than Little Ho Chi Minh City, in Los Angeles.'

And with that, the alien's bowl was empty.

It must be a peace without victory. Only a peace between equals can last.
Wilson Woodrow, President of the United States in 1917

To understand humanity, the alien needed to know that both sides in the war thought they were doing the right thing. Both the communist and capitalist ideologies espoused a belief that their way would make life better for citizens. The problem was that even if they ran this subjective debate through the method of thinking advocated in Cairo, it could not produce a meaningful numerical conclusion, because of the entirely different value systems and therefore weightings ascribed to each of the factors. This in turn was a result of the lack of historical precedents: had there been thousands of previous examples of both communist and capitalist societal experiments to draw on, the weightings might have been more objectively assigned to each column. But that wasn't the case. And so this impasse was one of many ways of describing why humans at the time ended up fighting each other.

The communist North Vietnam won the war and then took control of the economy according to their values. However, many would summarise their approach as failing to improve conditions for the Vietnamese people for the first ten years after the end of the war. In 1986 the approach of the Government to its economic organisation made a major shift towards a 'socialist-orientated market economy', with reduced state control and more private enterprise. This development may be seen as a compromise, and explains why the two names of the city are now regarded by locals as interchangeable, rather than political statements.

Casualties of War
(1989)

Having broadly outlined some reasons for the war, it was also important to not underestimate or downplay the horrors of war. I found it hard to communicate this in words whilst on a foldable chair in a side street of Ho Chi Minh City whilst eating pho, and so resorted to film. Back at the hotel I showed the alien the film *Casualties of War* to help it understand in greater depth the personal tragedies and impacts of war.

The film shows how people who look and speak like those in most areas of Los Angeles fought in the Vietnam War against people who look and speak like those in Little Saigon in Los Angeles, as well as Ho Chi Minh City itself. Through the film the alien learned about the concept of war crimes, particularly in relation to gender issues and the treatment of women in war situations. We later expanded on the theme of human rights when we reached Geneva.

Our next stop in Ho Chi Minh City was a textiles factory. I reminded the alien of the fashion show in Los Angeles, where some designers had mentioned their garments were made in less developed countries such as Vietnam. As we arrived at the main office of the factory, I explained to the alien that the textile industry is an important contributor to the Vietnamese economy, as well as an example of inequalities and the current power differential between the USA and Vietnam. I noted telepathically to the alien that the manager who was greeting us at *the office* worked fewer hours for more pay than those on the factory floor in the same building, manually operating various machines.

After a quick tour, understandably so given his limited English, the manager returned to his office. He left the alien and I with some free time to walk around the factory and converse with the workers and machinery operators on the factory floor. The alien was a real hit with the factory workers, who decided to use the alien as a model for their various new child-size t-shirts. They promised that the alien could keep any one of its choice as a souvenir. Apart from its keen interest in the supply chain of its bow tie while we were telepathically chatting during the fashion show, I realised that I still didn't fundamentally understand the alien's attitude towards clothes. The closest analogy I could think of was either naturism – generally unclothed but it knows when to put a dinner jacket on – or perhaps similarly, the *Bugs Bunny* cartoon attitude to the clothing of animated animals; also generally unclothed, except when dressing up for a special occasion, and then clothing is suddenly relevant and helpful.

For the first time I noticed the alien express what appeared to be real hesitation when choosing which of the many colourful t-shirts to receive from its new textile factory friends. Some were shamelessly unsubtle touristy ones with slogans such as 'I Love Vietnam' or more suggestive ones such as 'In Vietnam Everybody Loves Your Dong'. The alien had a choice of other designs that simply said 'Vietnam' or 'Ho Chi Minh City' and a picture of a palm tree or sunset. Fussy alien. I wondered if by chance I had been sent the intergalactic version of Karl Lagerfeld or Louis Vuitton, or perhaps a diva that was hard to please and just could not see itself wearing any of these unfashionable monstrosities. I did not know how to interpret the alien's choice of a completely plain green t-shirt, the shade only slightly off from its own skin tone.

Despite being offered the green t-shirt as a gift, I decided, and the alien seemed to agree, that we should pay in full. We also handed out tips directly to the workers we had been chatting with, ensuring they were paid fairly, at least for this one product. Outside the factory, the alien passed me the t-shirt, and then gestured to a clothing recycling bin on the other side of me. I couldn't read its thoughts, but I projected onto the blank canvas of its void gaze my interpretation that the alien was too much of a fashion victim to be seen wearing such a colour-clashing item. Simultaneously, I could tell the alien was aware of the sensitivities of the situation, and so chose not to reject their gesture in full view of them. Fussy, I thought, but considerate.

We then went on an adventure by bus towards Vung Tau, the closest beach to Ho Chi Minh City. During the two-hour drive the alien was again transfixed, staring out of the bus window as it watched Ocean rushing past. The alien saw children leading buffaloes working the land, and I reminded it of the stark comparison between this, and the sight of children clambering around on climbing frames, swings and slides in a park in Los Angeles.

The bus pulled up in a dusty car and coach park at Vung Tau. From inside the bus we saw the golden sands, palm trees and turquoise waters of the beach. I allowed the alien to step off the bus ahead of me, but in hindsight, perhaps that was a mistake. One foot still in the bus, the alien was met immediately by an enthusiastic coconut seller. I was unable to read the alien's thoughts at this time, but as it rotated its head to look back at me with charming dependence, I detected a sheepishness, an admission that despite some progress at getting the hang of the drill at human airports, it was unclear how that translated to disembarking a bus. And what was a coconut anyway, I projected onto the face of the alien, mainly for my own amusement.

I relieved the alien of its awkward, haven't got a functional mouth to say 'No thanks' issue. I gave the coconut seller a few dongs, and gave the coconut to the alien. The alien held the coconut with peculiar inquisitiveness, inspecting the hairy ball from all sides, rotating it, shaking it, and if I wasn't mistaken, sniffing it. All this was performed in a manner consistent with my assumption that the alien had no idea what it was.

We laid out two large towels on the sand and sat down. The alien seemed unfamiliar with the human practice of sunbathing, and perhaps, I wondered, the very concept of relaxation. Whilst I lay back to enjoy the first few moments of sunbathing on our world tour so far, the alien remained sitting upright, peering awkwardly at the coconut. I saw it begin to formulate a theory as its line of sight switched between the coconut and a family of tourists playing cricket with plastic stumps on the beach.

'No, Alien. Sorry. It's not a cricket ball'.

Feeling a little bit cheated, I sensed the alien telepathically reach inside my brain, and retrieve the answer. It then put the coconut down and copied my sunbathing posture. Why hadn't it just read my mind in the first place to find out what the coconut was? Such were the mysteries of this phase of our relationship, characterised by a one-way rather than two-way telepathic connection.

A few moments later, the alien was snoring on the beach. Loudly. I didn't want to draw undue attention to the alien, and so adjusted its baseball cap and sunglasses, as if to indicate to any human onlookers that all was normal, and I was simply with another sleepy human. The alien snooze was short lived. A local lady woke the alien with the metallic clang of dog tags dangling from her arms.

'From American soldiers. American soldiers. Ten dollar. Ten dollar,' said the entrepreneur.

It transpired that she was trying to sell to the alien the belongings of dead soldiers, such as dog tags and other items, discovered in the nearby woods.

The alien had enough purchases for today, I felt, and so I sent her on her way. I remarked to the alien that this was one of many examples of the long-running aftermath of the Vietnam War. Whether or not the dog tags sold by Vietnamese locals to tourists were real or fake had been the subject of some debate. Either way, their sale highlighted for the alien how desperate some people are for money, and that some humans will go to extraordinary, perhaps gruesome lengths to obtain it. I emphasised that it was another example of poverty and inequality that some humans feel the need to sell the belongings of dead soldiers in this way. I added that there was a sense of irony here as well. North Vietnamese soldiers also died when trying to spread communism in an ideological search for equality, but after their success, many examples of inequality have remained or got worse, to the point where the market for selling dog tags is not to wealthy North Vietnamese tourists, but to tourists they assume to be wealthy Americans, their opponents during the war.

After a few hours on the beach sunbathing, and joining in with the cricket-playing family nearby, we needed to return to our hotel in Ho Chi Minh City. Rather than using the bus again and simply going back the way we came, I decided the alien needed more variety. So in a moment of uncharacteristic bravery, I hired a motorcycle. I plonked a helmet on the alien, then on myself, and rode us towards Ho Chi Minh City. Initially the ride was pleasant, with a feeling of freedom. The alien held on tightly. I sensed it was a little afraid, but not so fearful that it wanted to use another way of getting around.

The level of danger we both felt quickly ramped up as we got back into the city limits. I remembered how this feeling contrasted with the feeling of safety when moving around in LA in our convertible, hybrid car.

With around eight million people living in Ho Chi Minh City, and 8.5 million motorcycles as a result of people travelling into the city for work, the alien was quite right to grip onto me even more tightly, increasingly fearful for its safety on the crowded roads. The flow of traffic was far more chaotic than in Los Angeles. I had been reassured that there was a certain rhythm to the traffic in Ho Chi Minh City, and that when tuned in, one could understand how to motorcycle across junctions without ending up in hospital. But I didn't have the time or disregard for my or my alien's physical integrity to tune in and risk getting it wrong. So we dismounted and walked the rest of the way to the city branch of the same motorcycle hire company, and left the bike with them.

We walked the rest of the way back to the hotel, and chatted with the hotel receptionist about our day. It turned out she was a former doctor. In her previous career she referred to motorcycles in Ho Chi Minh City using the invented term 'Donorcycles', as a result of a disproportionate number of suitable organ donations originating from young and healthy people losing their lives in motorcycle accidents.

The following day we visited the partially forested areas just outside the city, and stood in an area of land cleared in preparation for a palm oil plantation. On the tablet I showed the alien photos of the same land when it was previously covered in ancient tropical rain forest. This showed to the alien first-hand the issue of deforestation, and the concept that some animals and plants have nowhere to live as a result of the loss of forest, hence the protection of endangered species that we later observed in Saigon Zoo and Botanical Gardens.

Having previously introduced the concept of climate change, I referred the alien to another diagram of the global-warming model. It included a picture of a typical motorcycle emitting fumes, and I explained that the loss of the forest is contributing not only to the loss of biodiversity, but also to the warming of the planet, by reducing its ability to absorb carbon dioxide emissions from the atmosphere.

Climate change is real, it is happening right now. It is the most urgent threat facing our entire species.
Leonardo DiCaprio, Actor, in his Oscar acceptance speech in 2016

Further reasons for deforestation became clear to the alien when I reminded it of the Vietnamese mahogany table we were seated at when interviewing a resident of Beverly Hills. I clarified for the alien the connections between countries at different levels: in this example, how forest destruction in some countries is partially driven by demand for products in other countries. Another reason for the loss of the forest is that rapid population growth, as accounted for in Cairo, means that people need to clear land to live and work on, and to produce food for their consumption.

To illustrate another dimension to the reality that wars have effects lasting long after the end of the fighting, I helped the alien to compile a map of the distribution of unusually high rates of cancer and other health problems in this area of rural Vietnam. The cartographically assisted insight became clear only when we overlaid a map of where the Americans dropped 'Agent Orange', or dioxin bombs, during the Vietnam War. The alien discovered the positive correlation. Dioxin can change the DNA of the victims exposed to the chemical weapon, meaning that several generations later, birth defects continue as a terrible legacy of the Vietnam War.

One of the many long-term consequences of the war was a trade embargo between Vietnam and the US, the largest economy on Ocean. I explained to the alien that in 1994 the US President at the time, Bill Clinton, lifted the trade embargo against Vietnam. This demonstrated the symbolic and practical importance of trade in improving relations between countries after conflicts, a theme that continues to be relevant today in other conflicts around the world.

The alien nodded with an air of knowing agreement when I explained that improved international co-operation and relations are often reflected in the physical features and place names within a city. We visited a building in Ho Chi Minh City that in 1975 was somewhat inflammatorily named 'Exhibition House for US and Puppet Crimes'. We learned that it was renamed in 1990 as the 'Exhibition House for Crimes of War and Aggression', and finally in 1995 it was renamed again to the more diplomatic 'War Remnants Museum'. Nomenclature, I concluded for the alien, was always important on Ocean.

Our last excursion in Ho Chi Minh City was to Independence Palace, which displayed on the lawn the tank with which the North Vietnamese had burst through the palace gates, and marked the end of the Vietnam War. I replaced the alien's Egyptian baseball cap with a camouflage styled cap, and allowed it a brief photo opportunity sitting on top of the tank.

I explained that such features preserved in remembrance are important for humans, whose memories are not as functional as that of the alien. Human memory aids in the form of permanent monuments serve not only as a mark of respect for those who lost their lives in a war, but also as a practical solution to the challenge of preventing future wars. Such memorials are a methodical attempt by humans to keep in mind the atrocities of war, in order to help us prevent a recurrence.

The alien nodded. I speculated on its thoughts, and worried that I had underplayed the severity of war, or overplayed the human capacity to prevent further wars. Perhaps this was the reason for the alien's continued telepathic silence. It was certainly something to do with guns, as that had been the final straw in Los Angeles that had prompted the alien to disconnect.

I felt the alien had learned a lot during our time in Ho Chi Minh City and the surrounding areas, and that we were getting on well. I wondered how long it was going to keep giving me the silent treatment, and how the practicalities of its globally televised welcoming ceremony were going to play out in the absence of two-way communication.

PART 2:

welcome and enjoy

CHAPTER 4
Beijing, China

Olympic Song: Beijing Welcomes You
by Albert Leung

This was the official Olympic song released 100 days before the start of the 2008 Beijing Olympics. Its uplifting lyrics and triumphant tone represented the welcoming of other nations to Beijing for the Games. Having taken the alien to places that demonstrate concepts it needed to know about humanity, and doing so incognito, this was the place and the time to announce officially the alien's arrival to the world. I was looking forward to no longer needing to maintain the pretence of the costumed stag do.

One day in the future, perhaps the not so distant future, humanity may wish to put on a welcoming ceremony for an intelligent being from another world. The question of how we design an alien welcoming process can take inspiration not only from political state visits, but also, perhaps even more so, from the welcoming process of host nations before the Olympic Games.

On arrival at Beijing Capital International Airport, the alien was swamped by a mass of people. We got separated and lost each other in the crowd. Luckily, this happened so quickly that we had not even retrieved our bags from the carousel, and therefore both the alien and I thought it sensible to squeeze our way through the crowds and use the carousel as our meeting point. As we reconvened successfully, I was reminded of the concept of convergent evolution, as discussed in Cairo using the alien's snot; this time, there was something more intellectually pleasing about two minds reaching the same solution, independently of each other.

The heaving crowds were, I explained to the alien, partially a representation of us now being not only in the second busiest airport in the world in terms of passenger traffic (the busiest being Hartsfield-Jackson Atlanta International Airport in Georgia, USA), but also the most highly populated country on Ocean. The alien collected its bag from the carousel and paused, waiting to see if a human would approach and offer to carry its bag. Despite being surrounded by so many people, not one offered to do so. The alien looked at me blankly, which I interpreted as being its way of saying it understood that we were again in a somewhat more wealthy and developed country than Vietnam. And then, dumb as you like, I went and lost my alien again.

There were many exits, and we had not discussed which one to use. This time how to find each other again was going to be less obvious. I wondered what the telepathic range was of the alien, but heard no whirring noise, nor felt the proverbial arm of telepathic listening reach into my brain. Perhaps I should have bought the alien a mobile phone so we could get in touch, in case this kind of eventuality arose. Or perhaps I should have fitted the alien with a Global Positioning System tracking device. My mind shifted to my United Nations employers, and the increasing sense I had of them not really thinking through all the challenges and practicalities I would face as the first ever human to work as a tour guide for a life form from another world. It would at the very least be a tad embarrassing if we had lost the alien just hours before the welcoming ceremony here in Beijing. The UN had advised the world's media that they had an announcement to make, but not indicated it was anything more interesting than a tweak to international trade rules, or something equally mundane.

Hunting around the airport like a hungry, panting, painted dog on the African plains, I had many mistaken moments of thinking I had seen my alien. I ran up behind a young man and swivelled him around, only to learn that he was a human, he really was on a stag do, he really was wearing an alien costume, and that his mate, Lee, would physically intervene if I didn't take my hands off his friend. A threatening spit onto the smooth airport floor by Lee followed, as if to underline that he wasn't afraid to escalate the encounter beyond recognition, and that incidentally, that's what he as a real man was willing to do. Everyone watching should know that, and in particular, his potential love interest within the hen party they had met on the plane and who were watching on.

I felt my main task at that point in time was more pressing than helping Lee to impress the ladies by acting as his punch bag, and so I withdrew quickly to continue my one-man alien search party. The ebb and flow of human traffic at the airport allowed my search to speed up. Eventually I stumbled upon the 'Lost and Found' desk at the airport. I found the alien slumped over the desk, convincingly pretending to be an alien costume. It had sort of deflated itself to imitate the human version of an empty alien costume. I didn't know the alien could do that, but thought it was a jolly clever trick.

With the help of the United Nations, the International Olympic Committee, the Beijing Organising Committee for the 2022 Olympic and Paralympic Winter Games, and a chap called Sebastian Coe, I'd been planning the alien welcoming ceremony for months. It took place within the Olympic Stadium used for the 2008 Olympic Games in Beijing. I explained to the alien that Olympic Games' welcoming processes and opening ceremonies could be interpreted as representing the pinnacle of human ability to put on a welcoming show, and perhaps even the pinnacle of human unity itself.

'It's the best welcoming ceremony we can give you as humans, so if it seems pathetic by your standards, please keep schtum,' I concluded for my now re-inflated alien friend.

A limousine was waiting for us at the airport, and took us directly to the Olympic Stadium. We were given black umbrellas to hide our identities as we walked from the limousine, past thousands of reporters from the world's media. Some, I overheard, had got the scoop and were proudly staring into black television camera lenses, telling viewers at home that the most significant moment in human history was about to take place.

Inside the stadium the alien and I were welcomed and greeted by the Secretary-General of the United Nations and other key officials, who referred to me simplistically as the alien's interpreter. Pleasingly, a whirring noise began in my brain, and the two-way telepathic communication between the alien and myself was re-established.

'The alien says "thank you",' I translated.

The Secretary-General walked us, with a gracious sense of occasion, out from a dark tunnel and into the light of the packed stadium. First we heard the roar of the crowds, then we saw the grandstands packed with thousands of evolutionary descendants of a common ape ancestor. On seeing the crowds, my new friend instinctively understood it would be polite to remove its baseball cap and sunglasses.

'Which human should I wave at?' asked the alien telepathically.

'Try to sort of wave at all of them, then just pick one or two at random to make eye contact with, and wave at them personally,' I advised the alien, recalling a book I had read on this subject.

The Secretary-General stopped his important march when the three of us reached the centre of the field within the athletics track.

'In my research I saw that humans throw javelins into this area. Are we expected to measure the distance for the next javelin thrower? Are we at risk of injury standing here?' asked the alien. I thought it was humble of the alien to think it might not be the star of the show right now, but rather had suddenly become a subservient, javelin-measuring official.

'No javelins today. The Secretary-General is just standing us here to make a speech.'

The leader of the United Nations pulled out a microphone and boomed out an important sounding speech that seemed to begin with the evolution of amoeba and to culminate in the alien's arrival. It was nothing new for the alien and me by now, so we switched off from that and, while he talked to the world, we just stood there smiling and exchanging telepathic pleasantries about being back in contact with each other on a two-way basis.

On cue I was prompted to translate a quick word from the alien.

'The alien is delighted to visit Ocean, if only for a short period of time. It comes in peace. It comes to learn. It thanks the people of Ocean for your generosity so far, and it looks forward to completing its world tour before returning home.'

'Add in the bits about guns and climate change,' said the alien to me telepathically.

'What bits? We haven't discussed this. The UN told me to keep it to 50 words or less.'

'To ban guns, and to ban fossil fuel burning for energy generation, obviously,' said the alien, quite rightly sensing we had a unique platform on which to convey two of the most blindingly obvious lessons the alien had learnt about humanity thus far. This gave me a real dilemma: follow the instructions of the UN, or follow the instructions of the alien. I made my choice and began a risky addendum.

'Errrr.... also the alien has asked me to pass on the message that humanity only has a chance of long-term survival if we immediately ban two things. Firstly...'

'Thank you, interpreter!' interrupted the Secretary-General. He had moved the microphone back to his own, operable mouth, and launched into an impenetrable wall of talking about a new era of interplanetary relations. We then walked back into the tunnel, and were ushered to a couple of prominent seats to watch the ensuing fireworks.

The alien made no secret to me that it was frustrated at our lost opportunity to help humanity. Nevertheless, it seemed impressed with the relentless fireworks. Sometimes an explosion made it jump. When they lit a Catherine wheel firework, one of those that spin around, the alien giggled. In contrast, the alien was bored by the lavish speeches by a long list of heads of state throwing in their necessary platitudes about working in harmony across intergalactic borders. But the alien was more entertained when the agenda moved on to an interlude of traditional Chinese music. It seemed both flattered and relieved to see the excessive symbolic imagery of harmony contained within each of the exuberant performances. I wondered if this display of positive human intent was enough for the alien to maintain its switch back to two-way telepathy with me.

'For now,' said the alien, hinting it was conditional on good behaviour.

After the fireworks and with the world watching on, next on the agenda was a ceremonial race over 100 metres between the alien and me. The aim was to symbolise the power of sport and athletics to unite not just humans on Ocean, but intelligent beings across the divides of space.

In the changing rooms under the stadium, we heard the *Chariots of Fire* music playing outside in the stadium. The Chinese ambassador entered with two pairs of high-tech running spikes, plated with gold. One for me, and a smaller pair for the alien. I accepted them with a gracious nod, and the alien copied me.

'Do clothing recycling bins accept running spikes?' asked the alien, the moment the ambassador left the changing room.

'Our recycling units are far behind where they need to be,' I confessed telepathically, before again feeling the urge to add, 'sorry'.

We walked out of the tunnel again and were greeted with a second wave of roars from the crowd. I waved, and the alien copied. We walked to the starting blocks.

'The race result is genuinely unimportant,' I reassured the alien. 'I will be doing my best to win it, mind, and may scream a little at the end if I do win, but that's just how I roll, don't worry about that.'

'I understand,' said the alien.

'I have no idea if you're able to cover the distance far quicker than any human, or far slower. But anyway, let's just enjoy it. It's the taking part that counts.'

5.8 seconds.

'Like I said, unimportant.'

The alien began its victory lap. I tried to keep up.

'What's important here,' I reiterated to the alien, 'is the symbol of unity through a shared, peaceful activity.'

The alien understood this human tradition.

'One of the functions of sport and athletics on my home planet is also to unite individual organisms from different zones of our world, much as you do here on Ocean,' the alien explained. 'And just as it is for you, so it is for us a method of releasing the competitive side of our characters, channelled in a safe and positive way.'

'Competitive?' I asked innocently. 'I don't know what you're talking about.'

I reminded the alien of our discussion in Cairo around the idea that when humans are taking part in a subjective or even objective debate, and use the two-column method, even when scores have been assigned and the result has been numerically concluded, the losing side will often nevertheless reject the result. Metaphorically, it was the equivalent of denying the result of this inter-species race over 100 metres.

'How ridiculous would it be,' I asked the alien, 'if I now said that you didn't really win this race?'

'Very,' answered the alien, simply.

'I'll hold my hands up and confirm that you won fair and square. But watch out. There are humans on Ocean that would run the same race with you, with the same result, but they would succumb to their vested interests and say that in fact you didn't win. They would refer to reasons, such as a faulty start, which didn't happen, but their vested interests prompt them to highlight the possibility, that favourite word of solicitors, that it might have done. It then becomes their opinion that it did happen. And before you know it, a false vagueness is introduced, as it's far more palatable than the cold clarity of defeat. It's one-column thinking. It's abusive, but it happens.'

'I understand,' said the alien telepathically. 'Although we don't have the same problem on my planet.'

As we reached half way around the alien's victory lap, I returned our conversation to the positive potential of sport. I reported recent geopolitical issues in the wider region of China, such as the use of sport in 2018 to bring together the countries of North Korea and South Korea. For China and Beijing itself, in 2008 the Olympic Games re-confirmed China's rise to the top table on the world stage. Olympic Games are also used as symbols of national strength and competence, with particular emphasis on the display of the opening ceremony being a showcase of wider superpower abilities and influence in all areas of humanity. The ability to win the competitive selection process and host an Olympic Games is in itself also seen as a demonstration of national capability.

I wondered if our alien visitor would one day bring other representatives from its own species, and establish a permanent presence and influence on our world stage. If so, we would be wise to accept this with a warmth and a welcoming approach, at least equal to an Olympic Games opening ceremony. I decided to interpret the neutral facial expression and telepathic silence of the alien at this thought as being one of general approval.

The next day we headed out on our first day-trip in Beijing. It was a relief to know that we no longer needed to hide the alien's identity. The welcoming ceremony speeches had made it clear that all questions, coming in from all corners of the world, were to be directed to the specialist team set up within the United Nations, and not to accost the alien and me in the streets whenever we were spotted. The message and plea was, broadly speaking, to leave us alone, to let us get on with exploring the remaining destinations of the world tour. There was a particularly stern warning to the paparazzi to control themselves.

We arrived at the Forbidden City within Beijing. It was so-called because it was originally the imperial palace of the Ming and Qing Dynasties. Ordinary people were not allowed in without permission. This raised for the alien the recurring theme of inequality; an issue that, it noted, had arisen in every place we had visited so far. However, the Forbidden City also symbolised some human progress in terms of inequality: Chinese society has become progressively open over time, and this was symbolised by the Forbidden City, once closed to the public, being now open to visitors not just from any nation on Ocean, but on this day at least, to a visitor from another province of the multiverse.

The Forbidden City is a palace complex in central Beijing, with 980 buildings constructed between 1406 and 1420. It became listed as a UNESCO (United Nations Educational, Scientific and Cultural Organization) World Heritage Site in 1987, as a result of being the largest collection of preserved wooden structures in the world. The alien and I visited a key building within the complex, the Palace Museum, and compared the style of traditional Chinese palatial architecture with the styles we saw at the other places visited on our journey so far. Inside the Palace we saw the extensive collection of artwork and artefacts, and learned about the history of China, including the Ming and

Qing dynasties. The concept of dynasties was perhaps interesting for the alien, showing the idea of power structures within a society on Ocean, and how they are sometimes organised on hereditary rather than meritocratic lines. This concept applies to most societies on Ocean on some level, and may be more or less pronounced in the power structures of the alien's home planet.

'We are exclusively meritocratic,' answered the alien. 'But I am not here to judge your structures, merely to learn.'

The alien was less diplomatic when it came to hunger. As we left the Forbidden City and passed a food stall on the street, I felt a double tug on my left sleeve. The alien watched impatiently as I struggled to communicate with the stall owner. He was as unfamiliar with the English language as I was with Mandarin. I attempted to perform what I thought was a universal hand gesture; I pointed to a collection of small food items on the market stall, then gestured to the stall owner with two, appropriately rotated fingers. The alien joined me in noticing the confusion of the stall owner, not understanding that I wished to have two of those items.

Eventually, after a lot of misunderstandings, I made the transaction. As we walked on, I explained to the sniggering alien that the lesson there was not really my buffoonery, but rather a delicious reminder of the rich cultural differences between people on Ocean, which are certain to be magnified when attempting to communicate with alien cultures. I looked down at the alien for a response, but instead, noticed that the food item had already gone. Again I had been outwitted in our on-going game of 'how the hell does the alien eat?'

Our next stop was the longest man-made structure in the world, the Great Wall of China. Together we recalled that, from our meeting point of the International Space Station, we were unable to see this feature. This was contrary to the popular myth that the Great Wall of China is visible from space. Whilst the feature is approximately 6,000 kilometres long, it is too narrow to be visible from the International Space Station, even from low orbit in most cases, with the exception of the very lowest part of low Earth orbit, combined with extremely favourable conditions.

This raised the concept of popular beliefs and myth busting for the alien. Whilst there are sometimes elements of truth to such myths, in this case the answer was more complex than 'yes' or 'no', but was dependent on a series of definitions and conditions. Humans, rather than relying on factual and objective accuracy, often have strongly asserted beliefs based on cumulative, media or cultural repetition, and the attractiveness of simplifications that are seldom unbiased. This concept is again summarised by the recent term 'fake news', and the struggle of humanity for accuracy, as introduced in Cairo.

'Perhaps,' I speculated with the alien, 'human laziness is so pervasive that we would rather be brief and wrong, than lengthy and right.'

'It takes more words to set out a truthful set of caveats,' summarised the alien for me, as we sauntered along the Great Wall of China.

As we walked we had plenty of time to talk telepathically. I had missed our silent chats. I reflected with the alien on the human practice of building walls between different populations of our species. In the case of the Great Wall of China, it was built mainly by the Ming Dynasty in 1368–1644 to protect the Chinese Empire from the Mongolians. However, this and other such walls around the world have had a tendency to become irrelevant in the long term. This concept remained relevant in 2019 in the USA, where the suggestion of building a new wall along the national border with Mexico was being debated. The alien confided in me that it had been concerned, when telepathically listening in to the minds of Trump voters in Los Angeles, that it had overheard worryingly dismissive phrases about keeping aliens out of the USA.

'I am glad we are now in China,' said the alien. It was sitting perched on an elevated side of the Great Wall itself. Its legs were dangling as it faced inwards to the centre of the Wall where I was standing. I worried it would fall off backwards, but it telepathically reassured me that was not going to happen. I believed in its confidence, but like a parent watching their child happily play near THE EDGE, I continued to worry.

'You have taken me to a place where building new walls is understood to be a thing of your past, not your future. Thank you,' concluded the alien.

Back in Beijing and, as in Cairo, the urban air pollution disturbed the lungs of my sensitive alien. But in Beijing the locals were better prepared. We purchased protective facemasks from a street vendor, and that reminded me that we still needed a decent souvenir from this place on our world tour. The alien was building up quite a collection of memorabilia, with the toy camel from Cairo, the bow tie from Los Angeles, and the coconut from Vietnam.

We continued our walk through the streets of Beijing wearing our protective facemasks. I referred to them in positive terms, as highly sought after fashion items, knowing that the alien had an eye for fashion and might not wear it if it didn't think it was an haute couture facemask – or at least, better than that awful green t-shirt from the factory in Ho Chi-Minh City.

'Beijing is an interesting place. It's in an interesting position on the world stage,' I suggested. 'It leads the world not only on the problem of air pollution, but also on the solutions.'

I took the alien on an excursion to Solar Valley, an hour outside Beijing. Here the alien learned more about renewable energy as a key solution to the challenges of both air pollution and climate change. I explained that China's policy to reduce air pollution in its cities was driven by the social problem of air pollution, rather than the environmental problem of climate change. This raised the concept of how social, environmental and economic issues are intrinsically linked through the widely accepted and astonishingly simple model of sustainability.

Gesturing with the imagined drawing of three circles in the air, I added that the model of sustainability could be visualised as three interlinking 'Olympic' circles of sustainability: Environmental, Economic and Social. The central area where these three circles overlap is where true sustainability occurs. I'm yet to find an example where this model of thinking is not helpful.

So in the example of Beijing's air pollution, although its reduction was driven primarily by the social circle, it overlapped with the environmental circle by simultaneously addressing climate change, and overlapped with the economic circle by moving towards the next economic growth area in the energy sector: renewables. This is typical of the human transition towards sustainability: to find solutions that motivate humans with self-interest and immediate factors such as their personal health or economic needs, at the same time as meeting environmental aims. Interestingly, much has been written on the observation that almost every solution to climate change simultaneously brings social and economic benefits that humans would want anyway, even if they are uninterested in the environmental benefits, or even if they understand that environmental benefits are simply slightly less direct personal benefits.

So the recent history of China is that, in the 2000s it had become the most polluting nation on Ocean in terms of total carbon emissions, as a result of an energy policy favouring fossil fuels. Then, severe air pollution in Beijing and other Chinese cities led the country to reverse this policy, and it became the world's largest producer of renewable energy, with a particular focus on solar power.

Environmental pollution is a blight on people's quality of life, and a trouble that weighs on their hearts.
Li Keqiang, Premier of the State Council of China, in 2016

Our official Solar Valley tour guide was none other than the inventor Huang Ming himself. He explained to the alien that his vision was a human species devoted to renewable energy sources. He described himself as 'the number one crazy solar guy in the world', which made the alien chuckle, albeit silently. I confirmed to Huang that the alien appreciated his humour.

Ming proudly explained that he has created in Solar Valley a 324 hectare site with 3,000 employees, including the world's largest solar-powered building, and a Solar University leading on solar research, development and manufacturing.

As a gift for the alien, Huang proudly presented it with a backpack covered with small solar panels. On the inside, a plethora of adapters splayed out, waiting for connection with every mobile device and gadget on the market. The alien was delighted with this gift. It immediately emptied its current rucksack. A coconut rolled away, to the confusion of Ming, who picked it up and placed it into one of the external zip pockets of the new backpack. The alien seemed neutral about the coconut, but was otherwise overjoyed to fill its new backpack with the rest of its belongings. It handed its old rucksack to Ming's assistant.

'Please find a way of making use of this waste material,' I translated on behalf of the alien.

ALIEN FILM NIGHT

An Inconvenient Truth
(2006)

Whilst I used most of the *Alien Film Nights* to show the alien fictional films that accessed different parts of humanity from the factual nature of our day trips, this was the one documentary film I showed the alien.

An Inconvenient Truth stood out as the key documentary film of its time. An epic tour de force by Al Gore, the film recognises that there are theoretically two columns to the debate around climate change, before systematically showing that each argument in the column 'Against' humans being responsible for climate change is countered. The film shows that, numerically, the conclusion is that there are more points in the 'For' column.

I paused the film when Al Gore got into a crane to reach the top of a graph. The graph shows the cause and effect relationship between carbon dioxide in the atmosphere and atmospheric warming.

The word Inconvenient in the title refers to the vested interests of some humans, who want there to be more points in the 'Against' column. Whilst the 'Against' column is not empty, and humans at their best can recognise and respect that, we conclude there are numerically more points in the 'For' column. How inconvenient. Al Gore similarly recognises that solutions to climate change are sometimes inconvenient to implement, yet by using the word 'truth' in the title, he reminds us of the inescapable reality of this situation.

We returned to central Beijing and found a restaurant. It became increasingly crowded. I ensured our seats were located on the path towards the toilets.

'Am I going to receive a second lavatorial metaphor in as many places?' asked the alien. I noticed an air of sarcasm.

'Not really,' I admitted. 'An explanation, yes. But the point about this one is that the lesson is not metaphorical at all. It is very literal.'

'Is that supposed to be comforting?' asked the alien. 'I enjoy the issue of bodily waste no more than you do. In fact, our aversions to bodily substances intended for disposal are surprisingly similar. Another example of...'

'...convergent evolution,' I completed, enjoying our telepathic tendency to finish each other's sentences.

I placed the tablet on the table between us, and loaded a simple counter app that required a tap of the screen each time we saw a human enter the toilets. Over the course of our hour-long luncheon, wherein I managed again to miss every instance of exactly how this mysterious alien consumed food, the counter reached well into the hundreds. We concluded that nearly every human in the restaurant had visited the toilets at least once.

Why we were doing this, I explained for the alien, related to a debate that rages on Ocean, whereby one column asserts that environmental problems have their root causes in individual consumption levels, and the other column asserts that the sheer number of individuals is the more important challenge.

Both columns contain valid points, each to be recognised and respected. I explained to the alien my view that the more important challenge of the two to overcome was population. This was because even if every individual lived a basic, simple life with no luxuries such as Playstations, smartphones, tablets or dreams of world travel, they would still need to go to the toilet several times per day.

That constant human use of the toilet was not metaphorical. It was literal. The revolving toilet door of humanity is one that consumes resources on a huge scale. Simply the processing of human waste at the scale of over 7.5 billion people is a huge task, requiring unsustainable levels of resources: water, toilet paper from trees, land for sewerage treatment works, chemicals, energy, plastics and metals for the bathroom facilities themselves, and so on. And that's not to even mention the issue of food production, which we were to cover when we reached the Amazon Rainforest. For this explanation, I focussed simply on the delightful issue of wee and poo. I suggested to the alien that with more than 7.5 billion humans, there is simply too much 'wee' to process. As a species, we are too many.

'There's too much wee,' I concluded for the alien.

The alien chuckled, understanding the double meaning. It was, not literally of course, mind blowing to connect with a being from another zone of the multiverse via humour.

'Exactly how we reduce human population is an entirely separate conversation,' I distinguished. 'And in fact, we don't know exactly what the best solution is for this. We do know that it must be and can be done humanely. And we do know that improved levels of education and empowerment for women, particularly in less developed countries, tends to lead to voluntarily reduced family sizes, and more stable populations.'

The alien nodded, then squirmed on its seat, with its legs dangling just slightly off the floor. I wondered if all this talk of going to the toilet was reminding it of its own bodily imperatives.

'Nearly every human is doing what they think is best for themselves and their family. That means you need fewer selves. None of your foreseeable technologies will remove your need to wee and to poo. Even my species still needs to emit bodily waste, and we have been around far longer.'

And with that, the alien slid off its chair and scuttled off into the toilet for disabled people.

The following day we went on an adventure from our base in Beijing. It involved an internal flight to the port city of Yantai. This is where Chinese and European Space Agency (ESA) astronauts conduct joint training exercises at a purpose-built sea survival training centre. The exercises include splashdown training, vital to astronauts returning to Ocean from space.

The alien and I watched on as well educated astronauts splashed around in the water. I commented that astronauts have a surprisingly wide range of training requirements. More importantly, the aim of our visit was for the alien to witness the increasingly important role of China in the human exploration of space. This represented a broader, positive potential for peaceful co-operation, as evidenced not so much by the splashing noises, but by the sounds of Chinese and European languages mixing around in the joint venture of learning how to escape the confines of our planet, look around a bit, and return safely.

'China was the third country to send astronauts into space, after the USA and Russia,' I added. 'China is now an emerging power in the exploration of space.'

'I saw that they landed a probe on the dark side of your Moon,' commented the alien casually. I was pleased at the alien's intermittent revelations that it had been doing some form of homework before arriving here on Ocean.

On the tablet I showed the alien Chinese plans to build a scientific research base on the Moon, and that it would be partly sustained by solar power.

'Huang Ming will be happy with their choice of power supply,' commented the alien.

I believe that the long term future of the human race must be space, and that it represents an important life insurance for our future survival, as it could prevent the disappearance of humanity by colonising other planets.
Stephen Hawking, Theoretical Physicist, in 2015

Back in Beijing the alien and I visited the Grand Canal Forest Park, the final destination of our time in China. The Grand Canal is the longest as well as the oldest canal or artificial river in the world, dating back to the fifth century BC. We hired bicycles and I discovered that pedal bikes were not a familiar form of transport for the alien. However, it was a quick learner, and an excellent balancer. After an hour or so, I had

A L I E N   F I L M   N I G H T

The Martian
(2015)

During our internal flight from Yantai back to Beijing, I showed the alien this film. It summarises the role of China in current human thoughts about the next major step for our species in space: to land a human on Mars. In the film NASA turns to China to help rescue its stranded astronaut. This is a metaphor for the wider reliance on China and the shifting balance of power to Beijing.

The film also shows how challenging it would be to establish a colony on Mars that could provide the basic food and water required for human survival. Watching the film, the alien understood the highly precious ecological balance on Ocean, and the challenges we face in trying to recreate it on another world.

---

taught it to ride a bike, and had returned the stabilisers to the shack from which we had hired the bicycles. We set off along the long, flat banks of the Grand Canal.

'It was no accident that we hired a method of transport involving the concept of balance, was it?' asked the alien.

'No,' I replied, and quickly cracked on with the metaphorical explanation. 'It's a way of explaining what I call my 2p Theory, which concludes our discussion of human exploration of space.'

'The theory centres on the difference between infinity and very large numbers,' I began. 'If you flip a two-pence coin an infinite number of times, then each possible outcome must happen an infinite number of times. Not a very large number, but infinite. And that includes landing on its edge. A bit like we are now, riding these bikes, balancing on the thin edge of the tyres.'

The alien was comfortable with the reality that when flipping a coin there were three, rather than two, possible outcomes: heads, tails, and landing on its rim. I received a telepathic encouragement to continue.

'Landing to balance on its rim is of course less likely to occur within the confines of a finite experiment. When there is a finite number of flips, however large, then certainly the option of the coin landing on its rim will occur less frequently than heads or tails. Perhaps not even once, within that finite number of flips. However, once you move to an infinite experiment, by definition, each option must occur an infinite number of times, as long as landing on its rim remains a theoretically possible option within the laws of physics.'

'I understand,' concurred the alien. 'I am familiar with the analogy, and in fact, have already visited many thousands of planets with intelligent life.'

The alien had jumped ahead, knowing where I was going with this metaphor. Flipping a two-pence coin is perhaps a bit like the question of whether other planets contain intelligent life. Even though the conditions for life are rare, just like the conditions for a coin landing on its rim are rare, if there are an infinite number of planets, then there must be an infinite number of planets with intelligent life.

'Your particular universe is not infinite, and so other intelligent life in your universe is out there, but limited. But that is not the end of the story. On our planet we use the working hypothesis of multiple universes, or the multiverse. I am, for example, not from your universe.'

I was struck by the frankness of the alien. Was this the first major revelation from the alien about our place in the cosmos? I made a mental note to email Professor Brian Cox.

'We operate on a similar hypothesis to your 2p Theory,' continued the alien. 'Part of the reason I am here is to continue our mapping of life forms in the multiverse, which we believe must be, in theory and perhaps in reality, infinitely abundant.'

It was a relief that the alien was willing to share its understanding of the multiverse. I reflected again on who was the real teacher here. Although the trip was ostensibly about teaching the alien, my student was clearly not averse to shoving forward human knowledge by a few centuries. As we headed for the airport to leave Beijing and make our way to Queensland, I became distracted by the sharp contrast between the alien's casual willingness to splurge out profound revelations, and its playful refusal to let me see how it ate.

CHAPTER 5
Queensland, Australia

ALIEN PLAYLIST

Didjital Vibrations
by Jamiroquai

On the plane to Queensland, Australia, I played this track for the alien. The key instrument was a didgeridoo, a traditional instrument of Aboriginal Australians.

As a purely instrumental track, it combined both traditional and modern instruments and technology. This symbolised for the alien the mixture of Indigenous and Western cultures that have combined in Australia.

It was also valuable for my alien chum to hear at least one example of modern human music without lyrics. Doing so helped the alien to understand more fully the role that music plays in human emotion, communication and creating an atmosphere in ways that are impossible through the use of words alone.

The flight from Beijing to Cairns was long. Not as long as from the UK or US, but its duration was sufficient to raise an issue with the alien, one that I was particularly interested why it had not itself brought up already. It was also one that was a little tricky to raise without sounding unappreciative that the alien had travelled many millions of kilometres to get here.

'You know, all this flying about on our world tour. It's not great for the environment. I mean, happy to do it and all, as a one off, since you've come so far to see us. And, well, pretty sure we're learning a lot from you as well. So, worth it. I think. Just worried about climate change.'

The alien rotated its head 90 degrees to look at me.

'Never mind. Not your problem really. Just thought I'd share,' I blabbed unnecessarily.

'You seem to be worried about hypocrisy,' said the alien. 'Intriguing. You are an environmentalist. On our planet we would first criticise the non-environmentalists, if they existed, and then thank the environmentalists. On your planet, I believe there is a concentration of non-environmentalists around Canary Wharf in London. If I wanted to criticise individual humans for their climate impacts, I would start there.'

'Oh, right. Thank you, I think.'

'The flying isn't the problem: it's the method of propelling your planes, combined with your population size. It's in your nature to travel. Change your propulsion method, and change your population size. Fewer of you travelling is more realistic, compared with the option of having more of you, each not travelling,' the alien concluded cogently.

'How do you propel planes on your planet?' I asked, knowing we were about to go far beyond the remit agreed with the United Nations, which was for the alien to learn about us, not vice-versa, unless the alien consented to it. We were forewarned that the alien would be unlikely and unable to share much, due to interplanetary legal and ethical agreements that, despite humans being unaware of, the alien was nevertheless bound by.

'Now, Atul,' said the alien, for the first time addressing me by my name. I felt like a child anticipating an imminent telling off.

'If I reveal to you too much about our technology, your technological advancement will rapidly exceed your societal advancement, and almost certainly lead to the downfall of your civilisation.'

'Happening already,' I retorted flippantly. 'Oh, well. Stakes not the lowest then. I understand. What can you say?'

'We propel planes within our planet using nuclear technology. The opposite to how you use nuclear technology, though. From what I can tell from reading the Internet in the air, you seem to get nuclear energy by splitting atoms. So crass. So destructive. We like to get nuclear energy by fusing two atoms together. It's much less messy with the radioactive waste.'

The alien revealed that interplanetary law enabled it to confirm this, because nuclear fusion was a technology that had been imagined and worked on already by humans. It referred to our Alien Film Night in Los Angeles, and the 'Mr Fusion' device on the DeLorean at the end of the film *Back to the Future*.

'Righto. Thanks. I'll let the United Nations know. Crack on with nuclear fusion then.'

'Just don't ask me about how I reached your planet, that's a different technology. I haven't heard you mention anything close to it yet. I am bound by interplanetary law to not say anything that will vastly change your technological status.'

'Spoilsport,' I huffed.

On arrival at the small airport in Cairns, we retrieved our bags from the carousel. The alien was pleased with its new backpack from Beijing, sporting the shiny solar panels. The alien did not pause before putting its new bag on a trolley: it slung it on confidently in the knowledge that we were in one of the most developed countries in the world. It assumed no humans would emerge, offering to carry its bag.

How interesting it was to watch an alien attempt to pre-empt our human ways. Seconds later, it was contradicted. It was approached by an Aboriginal Australian offering to carry the combined backpack and solar power station.

'Inequality,' I explained telepathically, 'has been evident in all places we have visited so far, but here in Australia, it is perhaps on another level.'

'I understand,' said the alien, which was now eating the intergalactic equivalent of humble pie, and then, to paraphrase the fictional sports commentator Alan Partridge, getting that humble pie all over its green body.

The alien was a quick learner. I felt it would appreciate a statistical accompaniment to my otherwise general chat. I opened up the tablet, not pretending to have memorised the stats.

'Across Australia, and particularly in Queensland, Indigenous Australians are nearly 13 times more likely to be unemployed: 33.3 per cent, compared with the non-Indigenous Australians, at 2.6 per cent.'

'Thank you,' said the alien telepathically, tilting its head subtly in the direction of the local gentleman, reminding me that talking in this way in front of the negative recipient of such inequality might be tactless.

'Saw you on the news, mate' said the Aboriginal, reminding us that our world tour was no longer incognito. 'Short, aren't ya?'

'Is that a compliment?' the alien asked me telepathically.

I didn't know how to answer.

We reached the customs area, and the alien learned from the Customs Officer that Australia, being an island, is particularly concerned about invasive species, which is the world's second biggest cause of biodiversity loss, after habitat loss. He inspected in great detail the paperwork I presented from the United Nations to reassure him that the alien itself did not pose such a risk.

Sceptical but technically satisfied, the Customers Officer transferred his attention to confirming that we didn't have any mud on our shoes, onto which invasive plant seeds might be stuck. He asked probing questions about animals or plants in our bags. The alien declared the coconut, and after a brief inspection of it, the Customs Officer was satisfied we could continue.

'So what are you both doing in Australia?' asked the Customs Officer.

'Well, firstly we're going north to Cape Tribulation, having a look at some of the wildlife up there, then heading back south and...'

'Nah, mate,' said the Customs Officer. 'I mean, why are you here in Australia?

'Cos being on a holiday and looking around is fine, but if you're planning to work, I need to see your Work Visa.'

'Gotcha,' I said, appreciating that for once I was having a conversation out loud, rather than telepathically. 'It comes within the category of holiday. Technically I'm being employed, but by the United Nations, not by anyone here in Australia. Here's the paperwork,' I added, and showed the Customs Officer the various documents provided by my temporary employers to deal with such eventualities.

The Customs Officer, I thought to myself, seemed like a straight up, honest, fair dinkum, typical Aussie bloke.

'Pardon?' asked the alien.

'Oh sorry, I keep forgetting you can hear everything I think.'

The bus from the airport to the town centre in Cairns soon turned into a portable alien appreciation society. It is culturally normal to chat to someone sitting next to you on a bus in Australia, but this time, we were greeted as superstars. Fellow passengers had seen the alien's welcoming ceremony in Beijing on television. The alien was approached repeatedly. During this short journey, I didn't grow tired of explaining that the alien can't talk. As its telepathic interpreter, I noticed that the alien too was unrelenting in its politeness as tourists and locals alike wanted a selfie with what was now the most popular and 'awesome' organism on Ocean.

We reached the bus station in the town centre and took a connecting coach north to Cape Tribulation. This was no ordinary coach: it was a self-described party coach packed with young adult travellers from around the world.

With the outback rushing past the coach window, we had a period without Internet connection. This meant I had to resort to a paper guidebook to look up options for a youth hostel for us to stay in. I decided on a hostel rather than a hotel as I thought it would be good for the alien to experience different types of accommodation at different budgets, and ensure it interacted with a wide range of people. Youth hostels in Australia can be a real melting pot of nationalities, and the alien was likely to meet people from places beyond the ten we were visiting on our world tour. Now that we were no longer incognito, what could possibly go wrong?

On arrival at Cape Tribulation coach station, the alien was first off the coach. It seemed keen to stand opposite the coach driver, second off the coach, as he ticked off each name to account for everyone and, presumably, confirm no one had disappeared between Cairns and here. As each name was systematically ticked off the list, the alien commented to me telepathically:

'Everybody's got a name.'

Occasionally the alien said things whereby I had no idea how to respond. It was perhaps a reference to the fact that it did not have a name beyond 'the alien' or 'Alien'. We had established at the International Space Station that it did have a name on its home planet, but not one that a human could possibly pronounce.

'Do you want me to give you a name? Or perhaps choose a name for yourself?'

I had no telepathic reply. Perhaps this simply reflected some vastly different cultural assumptions on its home planet. But there was a more pressing matter to deal with: to get to our chosen hostel quickly, in order to secure that most coveted of bunk bed locations within multi-bed dormitory style accommodation: the bottom bunks.

The alien and I arrived in our dorm room and there was just one bottom bunk left, so I let the alien have it, and took the top bunk. Probably best, so I could keep an eye on it. We met our Australian room-mate, Greg, who had already been staying there for a few days. On commenting that Greg was one of those names that I had heard of, but not met many, he proudly noted that there are 10,000 people called Greg in Sydney alone, the city he was from. The alien, I mentioned, does not have a name in the human audible range, and so prefers to be referred to simply as the alien, or if you're singing about him and need a name: Alien. They shook hands.

We were getting ready to go to the hostel barbecue when I put on a t-shirt that was relatively tight-fitting, which initiated a conversational cascade ending in the information from Greg that we had accidentally checked into a LGBT hostel. Not a problem, I thought, and hoped the alien remembered the bifurcation fallacy metaphor at the airport in Ho Chi Minh City. It did, although there was a series of follow-up questions from the alien that I dealt with both swiftly and telepathically regarding my booking intentions and propensity for making further mistakes later in our world tour, did it matter anyway, and so on. I felt like a live-television presenter: on the surface having a normal conversation with a guest in the studio, whilst simultaneously hearing in one's head a deluge of other comments and questions. We left the dorm room and walked to the outdoors barbecue area, where we were joined by two older gentlemen from Sweden. One commented that they were on a romantic fortnight away, and the other confirmed their relationship status with: 'He doesn't take me out very often.'

On the other side of us, three African-American ladies had overheard our pleasantries with the Swedish couple. One of them addressed a question to me and the alien: 'Are you guys English?'

'Um, yes. Well, I am. Not the alien. Obviously.'

'Say *Harry Potter*. I just love the English accent. Say *Harry Potter*.'

Happy to oblige, I put on my best Hugh Grant impression: '*Harry Potter*.'

'Oooh! Say it again! Say it again!'

'*Harry Potter*.'

The alien watched on as I parroted various other phrases on command, using my English accent as entertainment for the American ladies. The alien seemed intrigued by the simple joy that humans sometimes take in the different sounds of each other's accents.

After the barbeque we were walking back to our dorm room and saw ahead of us a Finnish lady, frozen not with the low temperatures of her home climate, but with fear. Our hostel was beside a forest, and our dorm rooms were little more than a line of wooden shacks with walkways to link them together. The designs of the roofs meant that wooden beams created triangular shapes for giant huntsman spiders to form webs similar in size, it seemed perhaps to the Finnish lady, to those of a professional soccer net. In the middle of the web was a large spider that was probably better described, from this lady's perspective, as a horse.

The spider had a thick, heavy looking body, not much smaller than a rugby ball. It had eight, hairy grey legs that spanned around 30cm, larger than your average dinner plate. To the Finnish lady, they seemed to span across the Tasman Sea and over to New Zealand.

'Help,' the lady didn't say, too frozen to speak.

'Why is she afraid?' asked the alien.

I launched into a quick telepathic explanation of recent research confirming the evolutionary logic for humans to fear spiders. In a minority of cases they can be lethal, and therefore over thousands of years of living amongst them, humans with a natural fear of spiders and certain other species had a slight evolutionary advantage by avoiding them. Nevertheless, most are not lethal to humans. This also raised the wider issue of human choices around conservation of less charismatic, or downright scary species.

'Her heart rate is dangerously high,' interrupted the alien. 'If the status quo continues for another 55.7 seconds, she will die.'

I was fascinated to learn that the alien had that particular ability. I knew from Los Angeles that it could read my endorphin levels, but this was something else. Although now was not the time to discuss it. The alien offered to intervene. I noticed a benign similarity between the alien's eyes and those of the spider, and wondered if they had some sort of connection. This was confirmed when the alien walked slowly towards the spider, held out a green arm at the lower edge of the web, and the spider calmly scuttled down the web and onto the alien's arm. The alien then walked into the edge of the forest clearing where the hostel was situated, and the spider tapped its feet quietly on the leaves as it disappeared into the undergrowth.

'He's going to find somewhere else to live,' confirmed the alien telepathically. 'His name is Ian, in case she wants to know.'

I chose to pass on this information to the Finnish lady, and she was confused by that decision.

We headed back south on the coach, which involved far more detours than the more direct coaches, which were more A to B focussed. It was a helpful way of teaching the alien a broader range of skills, many of which it would almost certainly never need to use again. Sheep-shearing, for example, was one of the lessons we took part in at a sheep station in the Australian Outback. From our 100 metres race in Beijing, I knew better than to challenge the alien at anything competitive, and so I allowed the owner of the sheep station the honour of not only teaching the alien the standard sheep-shearing technique, but also then immediately racing the alien to see who could shear 10 sheep in the quickest time. It turned out the sheep station owner's prestigious world record was, by definition, unaffected by defeat to a being from a different world.

The sheep station owner then organised, for no obvious reason, a group tug-of-war using a simple and thick, long rope. The tug-of-war involved the alien and me on opposing teams. We were joined by other backpackers staying at the station. I noticed the owner put himself on my team, opposite to the alien. Telepathically I suggested to the alien that intergalactic relations might be improved if it let the station owner win at something.

'I understand,' said the alien. And with that, the fake straining of an organism from one world led to the happiness of a genuinely heaving organism from another.

Satisfied he was back as top dog, the sheep station owner took us out on his Ute in the warm evening. The alien and I stood up at the back of the vehicle, holding onto specially designed bars that allowed guests to do so. The sheep station owner pointed out to us the night-time wildlife on his land. The alien was particularly mesmerised to spot the reflective eyes of a wombat, not realising that it had made this observation several seconds before our insistently non-competitive sheep station guide.

The following morning we had been asked not to set alarm clocks. Tradition was for the sheep station owner's dog to systematically nudge into every room at the station, then bark until it saw human movement, before moving on to the next room. Our first and only activity that day, before continuing our sinuous journey back towards Cairns, was a whip-cracking lesson. It was traditionally an important skill for Australian sheep and cattle owners, and in recent decades had come to be seen as a performing art and competitive sport.

'Australian National Whip Cracking Champion, 2012,' said the sheep station owner. 'Men's category. Freestyle was me best round. Me daughter won her category last year. She's five.'

'Streuth,' I exclaimed, in exactly the impressed manner that he seemed to be requesting.

'Why has he not won again since then?' asked the alien telepathically. 'It's been a while.'

'Best we don't ask that now,' I advised my mentee silently. The alien was still demonstrating that it had yet to grasp the nuances of human competitiveness, and how that can formulate the sentences and behaviour of humans at all levels.

The warm Australian Outback air was filled with the sounds of a professionally cracked whip, combined with the floppy rope noises of a temporary United Nations employee, and the diplomatically awful attempts of an extra-terrestrial under strict instruction to not be good at everything, if it wants to be loved by humans. We were taught a brief history of whip-cracking, and how techniques vary Down Under compared with other parts of the world. We were taught the two-handed whip cracking routine known as the Queensland Crossover, an elaborate routine that reminded me of those ribbon gymnastics routines one sees every four years or so at the Olympics.

We were in the heart of Part Two of Three of the alien's journey: Welcome and Enjoy. This was the middle phase of the world tour, the time when I really wanted the alien to enjoy Ocean. We had indulged in games that were less about learning a specific point, and more about learning general enjoyment and recreation for humans. And there was more of this type of learning to come, particularly here in Queensland.

If one were making a film of the alien's world tour, this might be the time for the musical montage. The jovial coach driver took us inland to the popular O'Reilly's Rainforest Retreat. The alien walked along boardwalks through lush rainforest, across suspension bridges above the rainforest floor framed by orchids and ferns, stood at observation decks to look out over the Green Mountains, and back outside the gift shop area, stood statuesquely for colourful parrots to land on its head, expecting food.

We then arrived at Kuranda, otherwise known as the Village in the Rainforest, and went on a guided rainforest canopy walk to learn about the rainforest ecosystem. From here we boarded the Skyrail Rainforest Cableway, a 7.5 kilometres-long scenic cableway through and over the world's oldest continually surviving rainforest, older than the Amazon that we were heading to later on our tour. In our gondola cabin the alien looked down through the glass floor and into the Barron Gorge National Park. The spectacular cableway has won multiple awards including, in 2012, becoming the first tourist attraction in the world to receive the Platinum EarthCheck Accreditation as a result of reaching the highest sustainable tourism standards: suspended uniquely above the rainforest canopy, there is little disturbance to wildlife. Our gondola on the cableway approached Cairns, and the rainforest canopy below us dropped away gradually, as the land elevation receded, revealing to us the view of the vast expanse of the Coral Sea.

On arrival back in Cairns, snorkels were looming, but before then, there was the opportunity for one more land-based lesson for the alien.

'Why,' asked the alien innocently via its telepathic translator, 'throw something in the expectation that it will simply come back?'

'Boomerangs were invented for hunting,' answered the tutor. 'Win–win, Alien, mate. Throw it at an animal you want to eat. Hit it, and you're all good for lunch. Miss it, and you get your boomerang back.'

'Logical. Impressive,' emitted an alien from a different universe.

I had not seen the alien impressed before. How interesting, I thought, that of all the places we had been so far, and all the technologies we had interacted with, the humble boomerang, invented around 25,000–50,000 years ago, would appear to be the most magnificent from the perspective of an alien.

'It's a shame, though,' started the alien.

'Here we go,' I thought, expecting a tearing down of humanity in some oblique way. The fear was well founded.

'That on Ocean you eat each other. One sentient being eats another. Tragic, we would say on our planet, that beings on this planet ever needed to hunt at all. It's really quite idiosyncratic.'

'Some people here are vegetarian, mate. Not me, mind. What do you eat on your planet then, clever clogs?' asked the boomerang tutor, reducing my role once again to impassive translator of telepathy.

'On our home planet we get the nutrients we need from inert chemicals abundant in the environment.'

'You can keep the boomerang,' said the tutor. And with that, a wooden boomerang knocked against a coconut in a solar-panelled bag that also contained a bow tie and a toy camel.

From Cairns the alien and I went on a guided helicopter tour of the Great Barrier Reef, using the same concept I had explained in Los Angeles, that on arrival at a new place it is sometimes helpful to orientate oneself from a tall building, or from the air. We had technically already done this, having first observed the Great Barrier Reef from the International Space Station. In the helicopter I got the tablet out and telepathically shouted out a few statistics for the alien.

'The Reef is one of Seven Natural Wonders of the World, made of up nearly 3,000 individual reefs and almost 1,000 islands. The Reef is larger than the United Kingdom, the country I come from. It's 344,400 square kilometres, compared with the UK's 243,610 square kilometres.'

'I know the helicopter is loud, but you don't have to shout telepathically,' said the alien.

'Sorry.'

From the air we saw a reef structure that resembled a heart. It prompted us to reflect again briefly on pareidolia, the human search for natural objects that resemble our own cultural iconography. And as it did in Cairo when we were looking up at the clouds, the alien quickly castigated me for being so anthropocentric when peering down at the reef.

Back at sea level the alien and I bought some basic snorkelling equipment, then joined a solar-powered boat tour for an afternoon trip to Green Island. On arrival we walked on to the white coral sand and prepared to go snorkelling. I wondered if the alien really needed to use the snorkel at all. The main emotion the alien expressed when I was putting on my snorkel and goggles was one of feeling left out, rather than its pragmatic need for the apparatus. The alien's indifference at the practical benefit of the snorkel accidentally revealed to me that it was pretty confident in its ability to breathe under water. Interesting. I became distracted by how that might relate to my recurring preoccupation with the alien: how the hell does the alien eat? The sight amused me of this otherworldly being wearing pink goggles and an azure snorkel pushed clumsily against its unopenable mouth.

Snorkelling with the alien was a true joy. The water was warm enough for us not to need wetsuits, and the beaming Sun kept us comfortable as we bobbed on the surface. The sound of breathing through the snorkel was relaxing, although I noticed the alien was not making that particular noise, and seemed to be breathing through its motionless skin, if it was breathing at all.

The sea was full. The glimmering Sun on the surface deceptively suggested it was bouncing off a largely empty body of water, but that was not the case. The water was crammed with clams, coral waving and dancing in the gentle waters, starfish and sea cucumbers. Countless species of fish showed stunning diversity: varying sizes, striking colours and individually distinct facial expressions. For a few minutes we followed a green sea turtle, which let us know if we got too close by a sudden burst of speed, before returning to its usually leisurely pace. Telepathically I mentioned to the alien that our current snorkelling experience was not about learning a specific point, lesson or follow up elucidation, but about enjoying the experience in itself. We were doing this purely to enjoy the moment.

We then had a lesson in the slightly more technically challenging human practice of scuba diving. Again the purely decorative mouth of the alien was a stumbling block for our instructor who, it turned out, had not taught someone with that particular physical feature before. Before we knew it, the alien had signed a disclaimer absolving the scuba diving company of any wrongdoing as a result of the alien's inability to use the equipment in the usual manner.

'It can breathe through water,' I had to explain on the alien's behalf. The statement was met with suspicion, but luckily, the instructor had seen the welcoming ceremony in Beijing on the television news.

'Well, I saw it clock 5.8 seconds in the hundred metres, so I guess I can believe that,' said a man from Down Under.

My subconscious brain had been formulating a theory about how the alien ate. If it could breathe through its skin, perhaps it could also absorb food through its skin?

'You're nearly there,' confirmed the alien. Our attention turned back to our scuba diving lesson.

Having learned the basics, the alien and I put on our oversized flippers. We flopped backwards in unison from the boat into the warm waters of the Coral Sea. The relaxing sounds of breathing through a fully functional scuba diving system were an elaboration of the snorkelling equipment, but were again not shared by the alien with its fancy breathing skin. We were both content, following the instructor into the colourful underwater world.

The instructor used a small underwater whiteboard, similar in size to my tablet, and a non-polluting underwater marker to write down the names of various species that floated past us. I wondered to myself how many times the instructor had misused his underwater whiteboard to flirt with unsuspecting female tourists, writing them platitudinal compliments under water, each time acting as if he had thought of using the device in such a way for the very first time.

'So far this year, 58 times. 71 times in the last complete calendar year. Last year, eight uses of the whiteboard underwater led to copulation with the message recipient within a week,' said a voice in my head. I had forgotten the alien could hear even my most idle of daydreaming thoughts. The alien could read not just my mind, but also the minds and memories of other humans if it chose to do so. And the alien could still not fully understand the paradox of the human rhetorical question. Put those factors together, and I telepathically received the recent romantic history of an underwater player.

'There have been two unplanned pregnancies resulting from the underwater whiteboard,' added the alien. 'Would you like further details on this? A graph perhaps, or a statistical analysis of his copulatory whiteboard results, perhaps correlating by nationality, hair colour or age?'

'That's quite enough, Alien. Thank you,' I replied, making a mental note to remove the whiteboard on my fridge, and find another method of keeping track of my running shopping list.

'Notes facility on your tablet,' suggested the alien, overhearing my new dilemma and immediately resolving it.

'On it. Thank you.'

All evidence was that the scuba diving instructor was straight, rather than gay. This was again confirmed by the instructor stopping our underwater transit and using his whiteboard not to flirt, but to give us some more facts about the Great Barrier Reef.

'Largest structure ever created by living organisms' wrote the instructor.

We read on the whiteboard: '6,000 to 8,000 years old'.

'How does the alien breathe?' was met by the alien with a shrug and general gesture to its overall skin.

Rising sea temperatures over the last 100 years have severely damaged the coral reefs, and during the dive we saw bleached and dying coral alongside healthy and colourful specimens. Reef-building corals grow at their best in temperatures between 23 and 29 degrees Celsius. With climate change accelerating, this optimum range is being exceeded on an increasingly frequent basis.

Nevertheless, we were in the home of thousands of different underwater species, many unique to this particular reef system. Telepathically, the alien showed off that it had counted over 1,500 different species of fish during our brief dive, and its favourite was the clownfish, popularised in the film *Finding Nemo*.

Our exploration of the Great Barrier Reef was not limited to the underwater world itself. The ecosystem overall includes a series of coral islands that pop up above the water. We visited one of these by boat, and learned that the Great Barrier Reef ecosystem overall supports 2,195 species of plants, and 215 species of birds that visit the reef or nest on the islands. There are 30 species of marine mammals including dugongs. There are sharks, rays, six of the world's seven species of marine turtles, at least seven species of frogs, over 5,000 species of molluscs including the giant clam, and thousands more species that live on or around the reef. As one of the planet's most diverse habitats, the Great Barrier Reef has been designated a UNESCO World Heritage Site.

On the boat back to Cairns I introduced to the alien the concept of how humans value biodiversity, wildlife and nature, and that we would return to this concept when we visited the Amazon Rainforest. It is always important to start with the idea that species have an intrinsic value for the species themselves, and that value is independent of human recognition. However, as we have seen throughout our journey, humans struggle with thinking from any perspective other than their own, and therefore intrinsic value is effectively ignored by humans. Biodiversity has been lost in direct correlation with the rise of the human population. This is ironic, and detrimental to humans, given the range of practical benefits of biodiversity to humanity.

Around a billion humans on Ocean have some level of dependence on coral reefs for food and income from fishing. The reef tourism industry, and the livelihoods of people such as the philandering scuba diving instructor, generates revenues in Australia alone of at least US $1 billion per year, as a direct result of hosting the global asset of the Great Barrier Reef.

Coastal protection is another benefit of coral reefs, as they break the power of the waves and prevent coastal erosion and flooding. Coral reef organisms are already being used in treatments for human medical conditions such as cancer and HIV, and we can expect further medical advances to result from coral reefs and overall biodiversity.

Our boat paused on the way back to Cairns, to give us a final dip in the sea. We saw some harmless jellyfish, and I explained to the alien that in 2009 scientists confirmed a discovery of a species that is truly astonishing. An immortal jellyfish, *Turritopsis nutricula*, has been found, and is swarming through the world's oceans. Its numbers are rocketing because it can reproduce, but need not die.

'Eventually something might eat it, but that's not the point,' agreed the alien.

'It may be our world's only immortal creature,' I added. 'It's capable of reverting completely to its younger self. Instead of dying after reproducing, like other jellyfish, it reverts to a juvenile polyp of sexual immaturity and rejuvenates itself. A far better deal.'

'My species operates on a similar system' said the alien, revealing to me that it too, potentially, is immortal. 'We do this through a cell process called transdifferentiation, where cells transform from one type to another. From what I can tell, human cells can also do this, but only in limited cases, such as when parts of an organ regenerate. And even then, it's a bit of a mess.'

'Marine biologists and geneticists on Ocean are trying to learn exactly how this jellyfish manages to reverse its ageing process and achieve eternal youth. Or they might just ask Sir Cliff Richard,' I concluded, wondering if there were any point asking the alien if it could share its secret to eternal youth and immortality.

'Sorry, I am bound by Interplanetary Law and Ethics, and cannot reveal how my species reached this stage. However, I can encourage humans to conserve biodiversity, so you can advance your genetic technology in this area.'

Coral reefs are one of the clearest examples of the cause and effect relationship between climate change and the loss of biodiversity: increase the temperature, decrease the living reef. And within reefs, one of the clearest examples at a species level is the green sea turtle. For this species the gender of any one individual is determined by a simple cause and effect relationship with the temperature at which the egg is incubated. Green sea turtles have evolved to produce normal ratios of males and females according to small fluctuations around the pivotal temperature of 29.3 degrees Celsius. Now that temperatures at the Great Barrier Reef have been higher than that pivotal temperature, only one per cent of sea turtles born in north Queensland in the last 20 years have been male. Green sea turtles in this area are almost entirely female, and scientists are therefore concerned for the future of the species.

The next day the alien and I joined a volunteering group to help the green sea turtle with short-term solutions. We placed shade cloths onto key nesting beaches to reduce the sand temperature, and therefore produce more males in a clutch of eggs. The volunteer group leader explained at the end of the session that the long-term solution is for Australia and the rest of the world to reduce carbon dioxide emissions and bring global warming under control.

I clarified for the alien that its new green sea turtle friends require human action at all three levels to solve the problem of climate change: action at the individual level, action at the business level, and action at the governmental level.

The alien had already implemented action at the individual level through its volunteering. The alien had already supported action at the business level when we organised our coral reef tour with a company that used solar-powered boats. The next, and most impactful step for the alien was to register to vote in Australia. After pulling a few strings with the United Nations, I arranged the paperwork for the alien to become a citizen of Australia, just in time for the national elections. The alien voted for the party with policies that were most closely aligned to the physics of climate change.

'That was not only for the green sea turtle, but also for humans,' stated the alien simply, after voting in a dilapidated village hall turned polling station in Cairns. 'Here, let me show you why.'

My post-voting alien pal ushered me to the nearest beach. Then, in the blazing Australian sunshine, the being drew two concentric rings in the sand. I felt melancholic; I was about to be the only human to experience directly some sort of educational demonstration from a life form that evolved in a different universe. I wished I could be sharing the impending lesson with all of humanity. Instead, I resolved to jot down the impending nugget of wisdom on the tablet, and ping it back by email to the United Nations.

'The central ring represents the self. As we talked about in Beijing, there are rather a lot of human selves on Ocean'.

I often found the alien's wording mesmerisingly clunky. This was such an occasion. It was a result of what it later confirmed to be deliberate prioritisation of precision over a flowing style.

'The outer ring represents society. Notice that the outer ring is larger, and encompasses the self. It is not a separate feature to one side.'

'With you so far,' I reassured.

'On Ocean it seems your political parties on what you call the right are focussed on the inner ring, the self, whereas your political parties on what you call the left are focussed on the outer ring, the society.'

'Huge generalisation, but do continue,' I gestured with an encouraging, anthropocentric arm movement.

'If humans continue to focus on the self, by voting for political parties or candidates that focus on short-term benefits to the self, and not to society, they will become extinct,' the alien said bluntly.

Its total lack of emotion, combined with unbridled confidence in the complete truth of its warning, made my blood run cold in this, the hottest of hot places on our world tour. The alien didn't refer to humans as 'you' this time, as it sometimes did when it was deliberately conflating me, Atul, with my species, humans. It spoke with a detachment this time, even a banality that what it was saying was so obviously correct that it was boring. It was as if the alien were regurgitating a paragraph from a standard educational textbook for teenagers on its home planet about the reasons that civilisations fall. It was as if this were amongst the least contentious reasons, lodged in a platitudinous introductory chapter, before getting to the complex reasons that societies disappear, based on evidence gathered over billions of years of primary research.

'Keep focussing on the self, and societies get dragged down. It's the race to the bottom, as humans say. Societies disappear that way, just like planets and stars disappear into the centres of black holes,' the alien said assuredly.

I wondered how many planets and stars the alien had personally witnessed disappear into black holes, and was met with a brisk telepathic reply of 'several'.

'To avoid the gravitational pull of obscurity, civilisations must do what's in the best interests of society as a whole, not individuals in the narrow sense. Individuals in the wider sense. Voting for a political party that focusses on society is also voting for the self, just in a longer term way. Humans need to change their thinking to longer-term self-interest. It's still self-interest, don't worry.'

'For my fellow humans the problem is that political parties that bring longer term benefits are a bit more complex. Their policies must be more complex, because they benefit not just the self, but also society and the self. That's not one circle, but two. I guess that sand diagram helps a bit, though.'

'Remember Ian, the spider?' asked the alien.

'I do,' I said, not expecting that name to come up again so soon.

'Did you notice his web?'

'Not really, because we were a tad more focussed on helping that terrified Finnish lady,' I said, realising that the alien could probably focus perfectly well on two things at once, even if one of them had mortal implications.

'Its web was complex. It was beautiful. It was beautiful because it was complex. You have real beauty on this planet.'

'Thank you.'

'Just imagine if Ian's web had been simpler. Just a circle, for example.'

'I see where you're going with this. A more basic web by Ian would have been less functional, and less beautiful.'

'Well done. And so it is also with human politics and your civilisation's forward planning. It will be more functional and more beautiful to focus on the outer circle, on society, and on that more complex combination of both the self and society,' concluded the alien.

Feeling indebted to my alien teacher for imparting such clear visuals to articulate my intuitively held understanding, I felt the need to offer something in exchange. And so I taught the alien how to make a basic sand castle. I was quickly outshone in the Australian sunshine, as the alien made the most elaborate sand castle, or should I say fortress, ever seen on Ocean. The alien's more complex sand fortress was, I admitted, more beautiful than my simple sand castle. To passers-by the alien's body, vertically challenged, was sometimes invisible. This enabled me to pretend I was responsible for its astonishing sand sculpture.

Sanity and happiness are an impossible combination.

Mark Twain, American Writer

Having enjoyed the Great Barrier Reef and understood some of the related challenges and solutions, it was time for the alien to have fun participating in some of the other activities available in Queensland, to understand what they said about humanity and our relationship with Ocean. As we travelled south along the Queensland coast to Mooloolaba, I explained to my mate from another quadrant of the multiverse that for many humans, plummeting is fun. Falling from great heights in various ways, as we saw with the BASE jumper in Los Angeles, can be enjoyable. The fact was established, but the reasons were somewhat harder to explain. Each human has its own preference for the balance between risk and enjoyment, and this was exemplified by the human practice of skydiving.

For some humans, a skydive is a one-off experience, an opportunity to try something new, and that novelty in itself is the reason for the enjoyment. Others enjoy the speed and adrenaline. Other humans enjoy rapid descent because the subsequent survival perhaps represents overcoming a personal barrier or challenge. For others it may be a regular hobby, or part of their profession. In 2005 G. William Farthing published a study finding that activities perceived as brave may be a method of humans making themselves interesting to their fellow humans, particularly to the opposite sex, but that this is far more effective when the risk taking has an altruistic purpose. In this case, skydiving for a charity, rather than skydiving purely for the experience, would make human observers more likely to take an interest in the skydiver.

I helped the alien to set up an online donation page to raise funds for a charity as part of announcing its impending skydive. The alien was globally renowned, and raised significant funds. On jump day, the alien was strapped to the front of an experienced instructor. As we ascended in the plane, a colleague of the alien's instructor tried to tease the alien to make it nervous.

'Oh, look, mate, it looks like you've got an old parachute there. Looks a bit frayed. Hope it works.'

'Impact management with the ground is more an issue for humans than for my species,' said the alien telepathically and ominously.

At a moment of the instructor's choosing, the alien tumbled out of the light aircraft and settled into the skydiving position. The green skin of the alien's face flapped only slightly in comparison to the waggling cheeks of the instructor, as they both reached terminal velocity. A minute of freefall passed before the instructor pulled the cord of the parachute. They landed safely on the beach, and when we reconvened, myself having stayed in the perfectly good plane, the alien was somewhat perplexed by this human ritual. It had, at least, experienced first-hand how some humans choose to enjoy themselves.

Perhaps more importantly, we had closed the loop of the parachuting metaphor for human action on climate change that we had begun at the top of the skyscraper in Los Angeles. The alien had now experienced first-hand how useful it was that its instructor had one, large, suddenly deployed parachute, rather than trying to break their fall using multiple cocktail umbrellas.

It was time for the coach to take us inland again. This time to Carnarvon National Park. We went on a guided walking tour to see the Aboriginal cave paintings, some of them believed to be up to 40,000 years old. Our guide was a local Aboriginal Australian leader, who had a different perspective on the presence of the alien to other humans we had interacted with on our world tour so far.

'You seem a peaceful kind of alien,' said the leader.

'Thank you,' I translated from the silent visage of a being so evolved that it no longer used its mouth.

'But think of your visit from our point of view. First we get invaded by white men, saying they are not "invading" but "discovering" us. Then we get a visit from green men. How do we know you don't want our land as well?'

'I come in peace, and do not want your land,' reassured the alien. 'Just on a field trip. What's that?'

A wooden didgeridoo protruded from the guide's backpack. What followed was an hour's didgeridoo lesson for the alien: the conclusion was that a being with a distributed breathing system using its skin was never likely to master this, or any other human wind instrument.

A L I E N   F I L M   N I G H T

Crocodile Dundee
(1986)

That evening in our hotel, the alien and I wore the hotel-provided, matching white bathrobes, and watched *Crocodile Dundee*. It helped the alien to further understand the relationship between Indigenous Australians and non-Indigenous Western cultures.

Early in the film the central character, Mick Dundee, exemplifies a deep and positive relationship of equals with Aboriginal Australians, demonstrating the potential for cultures to be successfully integrated. Mick takes part in a traditional tribal dance, and displays a profound connection with nature. He subdues a water buffalo and, later in the film, vicious guard dogs.

Whilst in New York, Mick is portrayed as being out of his comfort zone. He is initially perplexed and amused by various local behaviours and customs.

The alien confided that it related to Mick, and was seeing human behaviour through similar eyes.

Back on the Queensland Coast, our coach continued south on the Sunshine Coast and stopped at Dreamworld, Australia's largest theme park. Here the alien went on The Giant Drop, a 115-metre vertical drop ride that was the highest in the world from 1998 to 2012. It was not in my plan for the alien to go on this ride, but on seeing it, the alien wanted to try a way of plummeting different from the skydive, to see if it could further understand why humans enjoy falling from great heights. After being hoisted to the top of the tower, held by an electromagnet, hearing a click as the magnet was released, and then avoiding impact with the ground thanks to an excellent braking system, the alien was none the wiser.

There was perhaps more insight to be gained by taking the alien on the BuzzSaw, a steel rollercoaster ride at Dreamworld. I explained that one of the commonplace metaphors we use to describe the human experience is that of a rollercoaster, with the ups and downs of the ride itself representing the highs and lows of life. However, living life on a rollercoaster every day is also not the aim of most humans, many of which prefer a more physically and metaphorically steady existence.

'Do humans go on rollercoasters every day?' asked the alien pertinently.

'No, it's more of an occasional thing, maybe as a treat or bit of fun. Once every few years, maybe,' I guessed, adding that reliable statistics on this are not collected, and that even if they were, there would likely be huge demographic variations.

'So humans enjoy rollercoasters, and other forms of falling, but only if this is occasional?'

'Yes. If even the most ardent fan of rollercoasters or plummeting in other ways were forced to do so all day every day, they would find it very unpleasant.'

'Interesting,' said the alien.

The main reason for coming to Dreamworld was because it hosts the Australian *Big Brother* house. I wanted to show the alien the concept of reality television, and how this particular show has changed over the years from a genuine social experiment, towards a juxtaposition of intentionally conflicting human personalities in close living quarters with each other. The alien was certainly surprised, and somewhat concerned for humanity, that there was an audience for a television show that normalised psychologically unhealthy and destructive behaviour. However, it was not surprised to learn that the *Big Brother* franchise was being discontinued in some countries.

Our coach continued south along the Queensland coast to Surfer's Paradise. The first thing the alien noticed was a tower in the town centre, from which tourists were bungee jumping. The alien had become obsessed with its quest to understand why humans like falling, and insisted it had a go, but learned nothing new. It then dragged me to another tower offering the experience of a reverse bungee jump, whereby the alien sat at ground level in a caged ball attached to two, taut elastic ropes. The cage was then released and hurtled into the air, far above the height of the surrounding hotels, before boinging back to the level of the top of the support struts, and then lowered back to ground level.

'Anything?' I asked.

'Nope,' said the alien.

Surfer's Paradise had in fact been selected on our itinerary not for bungee-related insights or lack thereof, but due to its reputation as a party town for young Australians and international tourists. The alien and I attended a beach party on the sand during the daytime. This involved a beach barbecue with a temporary DJ box playing dance music. We had selected the prime location on the beach, opposite the metal arch with the letters for 'Surfers Paradise' that indicated we were in the heart of the resort. This prime spot enabled hundreds of other tourists to join us. After sunset the alien was keen to continue the partying, so we joined in on the young adult human ritual of the bar and club crawl. This gave the alien a chance to witness first-hand the process by which humans enjoy intoxicating themselves through cocktails with colourful contents and equally colourful names.

 ALIEN PLAYLIST

Cake by the Ocean
by DNCE

At the beach party this was one of the tracks I selected for the alien. It began with the singer attempting to persuade a love interest to talk to him by acknowledging he isn't perfect. This introduced the alien to the idea that humans sometimes struggle to select the right partner for themselves, partly as a result of the challenge of knowing when perfectionism helps, and when it can hinder our lives.

The music video accompanying the track was also set at a beach party, with fun and light-hearted activities such as a cake-throwing competition. This showed the alien another dimension to how humans enjoy themselves, such as with games that on the surface appear to serve no practical purpose. By virtue of its meaninglessness, the activity provided light relief and a sense of enjoyment, perhaps even escapism.

On our final morning in Queensland I discovered, with limited joy over breakfast in our hostel, that the alien did not suffer from hangovers. I then arranged for us to have a surfing lesson, which began on the sand with the instructor getting us to practise standing up quickly on our surfboards. We were able to replicate this on the water, and both the alien and I caught a few waves. In between waves we sat on our boards and had a telepathic chat, where I tried to articulate why humans enjoy surfing and other water sports.

'These activities bring humans happiness for a wide variety of reasons. It's quite hard to put into words why that is. Perhaps enjoying the power of the ocean, the challenge and focus required to catch a wave, the peace of waiting on the water like we are now, or a feeling of being connected to our planet,' I suggested.

'I understand,' said the alien, as a wave approached us. 'Let's catch this one.'

The wave approached and on catching it, the alien stood upright, not on its feet, but on its head. A metaphor, I wondered, for the way the alien was turning various concepts on their head for humanity. Telepathically it indicated for me to never mind that, but to copy its headstand, just for fun. When trying to do so, I felt an invisible force helping me to get into a perfect headstand position on the board. I had no idea the alien had such an otherworldly capability. In perfect synchrony we performed bolt upright headstands as we rode our surfboards majestically to the shore.

CHAPTER 6
Geneva, Switzerland

The Elements
by Tom Lehrer

On our way to Geneva I played this song as a way of introducing to the alien some of the subjects that we would be discussing at our next destination, particularly at CERN, the European Organization for Nuclear Research, derived from the French acronym: Conseil Européen pour la Recherche Nucléaire.

The song listed the names of all the chemical elements of the periodic table known at the time of writing in 1959. Whilst additional elements have since been discovered, the song continues to be featured in modern popular culture, such as the actor Daniel Radcliffe reciting the song on The Graham Norton Show in 2010.

The song's popularity comes from its light-hearted tune and re-arrangement of the order of elements on the periodic table for rhyming purposes. It showed the alien how humans sometimes like to find fun and humour even in the most basic, objective or scientific of scenarios.

On its home planet the alien got the substances it needed from inert chemicals in the environment, rather than eating other living beings. Therefore to the alien, this song sounded like a wonderfully long menu for lunch.

It was the longest flight of our world tour so far – a full 23 hours. I had noticed that my travel partner had not slept much since it arrived on Ocean. There was a snooze at the fashion show in LA, and a snore on the beach in Vietnam, but neither had lasted more than a few minutes. I, on the other hand, appreciated a good eight hours. I explained to the alien two theories about this: firstly, that humans sleep more than other animals on Ocean due to our larger brains needing more processing time when at rest. Secondly, that our ancestors were more likely to survive if their time was focussed on gathering food, reproduction, and sleep. If ancestor A had less sleeping time, they perhaps would have got themselves into trouble messing around restlessly on the African plains, and been consumed by a predator. Ancestor B, on the other hand, kept out of trouble by getting the full eight hours, and so passed on to their offspring, aka yours truly, a genetic preference for solid kip.

Eventually, the alien admitted, it would need to sleep for a full eight minutes. I didn't think much about the potential significance of this, until the alien began sleep-talking. It had left our telepathic connection running, and luckily for me, it was still thinking in English.

'Mind the black hole. Mind the black hole,' said the alien during its nap.

I listened in intently, wondering only briefly if it was unethical to do so.

'Oh, I knew you would get us caught in its gravitational field. You always do that. We were meant to go straight on, not bear left at Quadrant 4,288,944.25.'

It seemed as if the alien was having a dream, arguing perhaps about its partner's driving skills as they went on a routine trip around the multiverse. I felt a sense of comfort once more at the convergent evolution that humans shared with the alien in our tendency to dream. It is thought to be one of the indicators that separates natural intelligence from artificial intelligence. I speculated that this meant the alien was not some sort of advanced cyborg.

'I know a shortcut. Turn on the dark matter energy matrix,' insisted the alien.

This was followed by other sleep-talking moments that I could not decipher, as is also customary when listening to any human sleep-talking. However, I felt what I heard was already useful in understanding how the alien had managed to reach Ocean from its home planet. It had explained to me on the plane to Cairns that it was not allowed to tell me straight, due to being bound by interplanetary law. But it had accidentally told me, here on the plane to Geneva, whilst sleep-talking. Was it really an accident? Perhaps the alien had planned to do this. Was it dropping a snoozy hint to help out its human friend and associated species, nudging us in the direction of focussed research into dark matter as a way to move around the multiverse, whilst not getting itself into trouble with the interplanetary authorities? Quite the triple win, if it was indeed intentional. We were soon to explore CERN, so it would have been quite a coincidence if the alien had just happened to spill the beans immediately before discussing the limits of human understanding of physics. I doubted it was an accident.

On arrival at Geneva Airport the alien noticed that nobody offered to carry its bags. We were in the heart of Europe, a region of the world usually considered relatively wealthy and developed, and few more so than Switzerland. There were not many humans about that needed to earn money by imposing an offer of bag carrying upon other beings perfectly capable of carrying their own. After a short, charmingly uncertain pause, the alien placed its high-tech bag on a trolley, and we walked side by side towards the exit.

The alien overheard an unusually wide range of languages spoken in the airport. Switzerland has four official languages: German, Italian, French and Romansh. English is also widely spoken as a second language, not only in Switzerland, but also in many of the other locations on our world tour. We jumped on a bus to transit from the airport to our first destination in Geneva. On the bus we were again surrounded by people talking in several different languages.

'Why so many languages in this small country?' asked the alien.

I pulled the tablet out of my bag and together we looked up an explanation online that eventually satisfied the alien's curiosity. Historically the multi-lingual aspect of the country was an important element of keeping the peace. The imposition of one group's language on another would not have been seen as diplomatic, and this was particularly relevant in Switzerland, where the central Government had intentionally allowed each of the 26 federal states, known as cantons, to choose their own language. I linked this back to our day trip from Beijing to Yantai, where the concept of hearing a mixture of languages could also be interpreted as a sign of positive co-operation, in that case between Europe and China.

'I understand,' said the alien. 'Although humans will inevitably end up with one common language. I hope you manage to settle on which one peacefully, and without conflict, by using the thinking columns approach we discussed in Cairo.'

'Why do you think that?' I asked, slightly baulked at the alien's confident prediction.

'Have you any idea how many other different languages are spoken out there in the multiverse?'

'A lot, probably.'

'So if you want to interact with them at some point, it would help if your tiny planet selects just one language. Take my word for it, on some planets they were not impressed with having to go through 55 different languages on your Voyager probe. Have some interplanetary respect.'

Before closing the tablet, I added this to my growing list of notes to discuss with the United Nations at the end of our world tour. In fact, I was soon to have a half-way check in with my employers now that the alien and I had arrived in Geneva, but first we visited the centre of global physics research: CERN.

The alien was excited. We were going to discuss some subjects that it knew a lot about. And I was excited about the prospect of the alien dropping further accidental hints, and/or outright instructions, that might vastly benefit humanity and our technological development.

On arrival at CERN, situated in a north-western suburb of Geneva, we joined a walking tour of the site. We learned that CERN was founded in 1954 to unite nations through science, and now operates the largest particle physics laboratory in the world. It was part of a series of international measures after the Second World War, including the creation of the United Nations and what is now the European Union, to unite nations through various measures, including politically, economically, and in this case, scientifically.

Our tour guide at CERN reminded me of the character Amy from the television sitcom *The Big Bang Theory* – professional, knowledgeable and incessantly flirting with the alien. Ethically, I was confused about whether or not to correct her assumption that the alien was male. I decided to apply what I decided, in positive terms, to describe as strategic inaction.

'The creation of CERN was both explicitly and implicitly intended to unite nations together in ways that reduce the likelihood of future world wars. But I guess you don't have to worry about wars on your home planet, do you now, alien,' added our guide goofily, twirling her hair.

'Not any more,' I translated from the alien's telepathic reply to me. I had been reduced to being an organism that was effectively invisible, overshadowed by my celebrity sidekick.

With a cough, perhaps trying to regain her composure, the star-struck guide continued walking.

'CERN's main function is to provide the infrastructure needed for high-energy particle physics research. That infrastructure includes particle accelerators such as the Large Hadron Collider, which we will see shortly. The research creates huge amounts of data for analysis, which is partly why CERN became the birthplace of the World Wide Web, originally set up to facilitate the sharing of information between researchers here at CERN. The first website was activated right here in 1991.'

'Your Internet system has gained some interplanetary interest,' said the alien telepathically. 'But not for entirely positive reasons.'

Places such as CERN become ever more important: places where people from around the world come together to show what can be achieved when people overcome their differences, to work towards common goals that ultimately bring benefit to all of humanity.
Fabiola Gianotti, CERN Director-General since 2016

Hard hats on, the smitten tour guide took the alien and me on another 100-metre journey: this time not horizontally as per our 5.8 seconds race in Beijing, but vertically, underground to the Large Hadron Collider. The LHC is housed in a 27 kilometres circular tunnel, making it the largest single machine in the world. The LHC is a particle accelerator where protons travel at close to the speed of light. It operates most efficiently at extremely low temperatures, and is therefore cooled significantly. This means that, remarkably, it shrinks and expands by 30 metres in length along its 27 kilometres tunnel due to thermal expansion and contraction of the metal.

On first sight the LHC looked a bit like a giant cable sliced in two. Its metallic symmetry had a kind of pleasing aesthetic quality to it. I was momentarily distracted by the question of why humans seem to find symmetry attractive in general, and the biological theory that it indicates health. How interesting, then, to also find beauty in such advanced technology. If the device were to function better with asymmetry, surely it would have been constructed as such, but the symmetrical design was clearly thought to be the most functional.

'We built the LHC to cause tens of millions of particle collisions per second, to gain new insights into how particles behave in these conditions,' continued the infatuated tour guide. It was so obvious she was trying to impress the alien. Get a room.

'This technology is thousands of years behind what we have on my planet,' remarked the alien telepathically. 'Don't tell her that, though, it would be insensitive.'

What was impressive, I thought, was when the alien displayed its concern for the feelings of my fellow humans.

'Huge detectors within the LHC study the particle collisions, which are analysed by a worldwide network of computers. In 2012 the LHC confirmed the existence of a new kind of fundamental particle, the Higgs boson.'

'Now she's being interesting,' said the alien.

'Perhaps better described as a field rather than a particle, this is important because the Higgs boson field gives subatomic particles their mass, and so enables them to join together. Without the Higgs boson, electrons, for example, would continually fly across the universe at the speed of light, without ever being trapped into atoms. And without atoms, there would be no chemistry,' she paused seductively, looking into the blank eyes of the unwooable alien.

'Scientists have described the Higgs boson as being like a famous person arriving at a party, perhaps such as yourself, Alien,' she continued. 'I imagine if you turn up at a party, the other people there would act like electrons and gather around you. But without your being there, other party-goers, or electrons, might just wander around, dispersed. When you show up, as the Higgs boson, people gather around you to form a cluster, or atom.'

'Your analogy is correct,' I translated simply on behalf of the alien, trying not to lead the tour guide on.

The tour guide seemed to change gear in her explanations. I was not sure if this was her giving up on her courtship of the alien, trying another angle, or just getting on with her job.

'Perhaps the alien is more interested to learn of the process by which humanity discovered the Higgs boson. Peter Higgs predicted its existence in a mathematical equation in 1964, which led to physicists working together to design and build the LHC itself, which first operated in 2008. On 4 July 2012, particle collisions at the LHC finally confirmed the theoretical existence of the Higgs boson is now observable and repeatable reality.'

'Very, very slow process,' commented the alien telepathically. I didn't translate that for our guide.

The Higgs boson is believed to have potential to lead on to explanations of other mysteries of the Universe, such as dark matter, whereby again the mathematics is showing that 27 per cent of the Universe seems to be made up of dark matter. But currently we have limited understanding of exactly what this is, or means in terms of potential practical applications. Furthermore, dark energy seems to make up 68 per cent of the Universe, so together they form a whopping 95 per cent of the Universe.'

I recalled the alien's sleep-talking on the plane, and probed the alien to elaborate, wondering if in its waking state it might feel legally able to elaborate.

'Perhaps you have some information you'd like to share with us about dark matter and dark energy, hmm, Alien?' I asked leadingly and telepathically.

'I don't know what you're talking about,' said the alien neutrally.

I had expected this response. So I made up a theory in order to provoke the alien into either correcting or confirming it.

'My theory,' I began out loud, pretending to address the tour-guide, but really aiming at the alien, 'about the nature of dark matter and dark energy is that, like light, they are part of a continuum. Perhaps it's similar to the way that some animals can see ultraviolet light and hear sound that is subsonic to humans. If matter and energy are also part of a continuum, which is inherent in Einstein's famous equation, $E=MC^2$, then perhaps other ranges of matter and energy are present, but simply imperceptible to humans.'

'Interesting,' said the tour guide, looking bored. 'Do you have any equations to back this up?'

'Not at all.'

'Do you have a name for this theory?' she asked, trying to be polite. She seemed uninterested in anything I had to say as an individual, but was very interested whenever I was translating for the alien.

I looked around the LHC chamber for inspiration to name my newly invented theory. Here, in the heart of the most advanced scientific laboratory on the planet, there was bound to be something that sounded clever. Instead, I noticed that the guide was wearing an overcoat with a zip.

'Infinite zip theory,' I said, as if I'd said it a thousand times before. 'Have you noticed that whenever humans find what we think is the smallest subatomic particle possible, we soon find something smaller. Perhaps this phenomenon has no end. Perhaps one of the ways the universe operates is that there is an infinite process of finding smaller and smaller particles. Like a zip on a coat going down, but never reaching the end. Matter and energy are perhaps part of an infinite continuum, an infinite unfurling of smaller and smaller subatomic particles, then going into areas of a spectrum we can't personally perceive, but are very much present.'

The tour guide coughed and smiled, but said nothing.

'Nice try,' said the alien telepathically. 'But you know I'm not allowed to comment. Just tell the United Nations to keep funding research into dark matter and dark energy, that's all I'm allowed to say. Or I'll get into deep trouble with the Interplanetary Ethical Council.'

The flirty guide passed the alien a piece of paper with her phone number on it, and our tour of CERN was over.

 ALIEN FILM NIGHT

The Theory of Everything
(2014)

We checked into a hotel in Geneva, and on the tablet I showed this film for the alien. It helped to elaborate on exactly where humanity currently sits in its journey towards understanding the universe. However, this story is told as a biographical romantic drama, with Professor Stephen Hawking and his wife as the central characters.

Professor Stephen Hawking made a major contribution to the understanding of the universe in terms of black holes. His work made reference to the elusive, unifying theory of physics, hence the title of the film. The film was also interesting for the alien to learn more about people with physical disabilities, and the ways in which humans can overcome obstacles to continue functioning mentally at high levels, despite physical limitations.

The next morning the theme of theories continued over breakfast. I had been formulating a theory about how the alien eats. Whilst snorkelling and scuba diving in Queensland, it had become clear that the alien could breathe through its skin, and so it seemed logical that the alien somehow also absorbed food through its skin. But the skin on which part of its body? And how did it eat so quickly?

I was determined not to blink. The game was on. The alien chuckled telepathically. It waited motionless until I was desperate to blink. I signalled for the waiter, and asked for matchsticks. When they arrived, I placed them dangerously to prevent my eyelids from drooping. A full ten minutes passed. Irresponsibly, I took a Neurofen to take the edge off the pain.

'Fine,' said the alien. And with that, two vegetarian sausages turned into the faintest cloud of dust, and then were sucked directly into the alien's abdomen. The process was faster than the blink of a human eye. I removed the matchsticks.

'I knew it!' I exclaimed loudly in the quiet breakfast area of the hotel. 'You vaporise it and absorb it into your skin, you crafty little alien.'

The alien hiccupped, then giggled.

'That was a little fast, even by my standards. Went in the wrong way. I'll be fine.'

'Why did you evolve like that, instead of keeping use of your mouth and eating that way?' I asked.

'This way is more efficient. The nutrients go directly to all organs that need them. Are you happy now?'

'Well, I do wonder how you vaporise things, and manage to move objects in general, like you did when we were surfing. But I guess you can't tell me that side of things.'

'Bingo,' said the alien.

Having established for the alien that CERN is about more than particle physics, and acts as a symbol of international collaboration and unity, there was no better place on Ocean than Geneva to demonstrate this concept further for an alien. Switzerland is a land-locked country in central Europe, surrounded by countries that have been involved in conflicts and war in recent decades. Yet Switzerland itself has remained neutral and not been involved in armed conflict since 1815. Switzerland's policy of political neutrality means it is not part of the North Atlantic Treaty Organization (NATO), the European Union, and only recently joined the United Nations (UN) in 2002 after it became clear that almost every country in the world would be part of the United Nations. Joining the UN, therefore, was seen as not affecting its neutral stance.

During a walk around Geneva, armed not with weapons, but with the facts on the screen of the tablet, I explained to the alien that Switzerland has the oldest policy of military neutrality in the world. It describes its position as 'armed neutrality', whereby it deters aggression with a sizeable military, whilst barring itself from foreign deployment. Its plan for dealing with a military invasion, known as the National Redoubt, includes mandatory military conscription of males for at least 170 days. Afterwards they keep their rifles at their home, meaning that Switzerland has the ability to mobilise over 200,000 soldiers within 72 hours.

The policy means, therefore, that gun ownership in Switzerland is relatively high, the 16th highest in the world, at 27.6 guns per 100 civilians. This is in comparison with the highest in the world of 120.5 guns per 100 civilians in the United States, and 3.8 in the United Kingdom. I linked this to our discussion and experiment in Los Angeles regarding gun crime, and the alien's successful purchase of a rifle with ammunition. I found on the tablet the statistic that firearm-related murders are a much bigger problem in the US, 4.62 per 100,000, than in Switzerland, at 0.21 per 100,000. To illustrate the point, we ran the same experiment in Geneva. I gave the alien some cash, and once again waited outside a gun store. The alien entered alone and attempted to buy a gun. It emerged from the shop unarmed.

'I didn't have the right paperwork,' said the alien. 'They said something about due diligence checks.'

I was relieved that on this occasion, the alien did not feel the need to break off our two-way telepathic connection, as it had done following our identical experiment in Los Angeles. But I was not out of the proverbial woods. I was yet to raise the stakes from the hand gun, to the nuclear bomb. Risking the alien's intergalactic ire, I took it to one of the many public nuclear fallout shelters in Switzerland, and explained that many people believe Switzerland is the safest place to be in the event of a global nuclear war. Switzerland is the only country in the world to have enough nuclear fallout shelters for its entire population. According to my tablet, the country had enough spaces for 114 per cent of its 8.5 million population, as they have allowed room for population growth and refugee influx from other countries.

We then visited a local Swiss resident's property, to see their private nuclear fallout shelter. All residential buildings built since 1978 are required by law to have their own nuclear fallout shelter, in addition to large public shelters in underground tunnels.

'Ironic, isn't it?' I asked the alien, 'that it is perhaps the least likely country on Ocean to get involved directly in a nuclear war, that is the most prepared for one?'

'Yes,' replied the alien. I noted on the laptop to discuss with my United Nations employers the largely inconsequential trait of the alien to not really understand our cultural quirk of the rhetorical question.

I paraphrased for the alien the significance of nuclear weapons according to the author Michael White in his book, *Super Science*. His theory is that species across the universe might be broadly classified as fitting within one of three categories or stages of development. Stage one species are those from the level of single-celled organisms, up to a level similar to humans with nuclear weapons technology, at which point, most civilisations blow themselves up. Stage two species are those that have nuclear technology and have chosen to use it for reasons other than to blow themselves up, such as developing to the point of harnessing the energy of their home star to move around their galaxy. Stage three species are those that have developed so far that they have been able to harness the energy within their home galaxy, to be able to move between galaxies and interact with a significant proportion of their known universe, all whilst not blowing themselves up. The suggestion was that humanity was currently towards the end of stage one, using this classification, and is currently asking itself the question of whether it wants to blow itself up, or move into stage two of its development.

'There is some truth in that,' commented the alien diplomatically. 'But you know I can't say too much, for your own good. Like I said, just keep researching that whole dark energy, dark matter business. Promise?'

'Promise.' I meant it, at least to do what I could with my humble level of influence as an interplanetary telepathy translator. With no time to lose, I went back into the tablet and added a double asterisk by that particular note about dark matter I had already made for my forthcoming meeting with my temporary employers.

It was a Friday in Geneva, and the year was 2019. I was highly aware that the places I showed the alien, and the activities, processes and concepts discussed in each place, were temporally specific. Had our world tour taken place in the year 1919, or 2119, the places selected and the issues raised would have been undoubtedly different. Nevertheless, there we were, stuck in the year 2019. And in Geneva on a Friday, that meant there was a reasonable possibility that we would witness hundreds of school students skipping, not in their playgrounds, but school itself, to take part in a climate march.

The school strikes for climate began in Stockholm in August 2018 by a determined young pupil, Greta Thunberg, who, instead of attending school on Fridays, staged an action outside the Swedish parliament building, holding a sign that translated as 'School Strike for Climate'. This morphed into a powerful global movement, spreading around the world under varying terminology including 'Fridays for Future', 'Youth For Climate', 'Youth Strike 4 Climate' and similar variations. The strikes raised interesting ethical questions around the value of full attendance at school, in comparison with the urgency of encouraging politicians to take appropriate action to tackle climate change. Articulate fifteen and sixteen-year-olds were flooding the news networks, explaining that if they were marching on weekends, they would not be gaining such high levels of media attention. By 2019, many cities, including Geneva, around the world saw similar protests on Fridays.

As we walked through the streets of Geneva, the alien and I turned a corner and noticed a group of school children holding placards. Three examples included:

Why Learn Without A Future
Change The System, Not The Climate
I've Seen Smarter Cabinets At Ikea

I knew where the alien stood on this issue after it silently helped two young protesters to hold a large banner that read: *We're Missing Our Lessons, So We Can Teach You One.* The alien was aware of its newly found celebrity status on Ocean, and wanted to use it to positive effect. As soon as it began supporting one end of the home-made, wobbly banner, the paparazzi swarmed around, and the image of an alien from another planet supporting the idea of radical action on climate change was soon beamed around the world.

A meeting of the World Economic Forum was coming up on the other side of Switzerland, where we heard that sixteen-year-old Greta Thunberg would be giving a speech. The alien and I jumped on an overnight train to Davos. With a quick call to my United Nations employers, the alien and I had full access to the auditorium.

I don't want you to be hopeful. I want you to panic.
Greta Thunberg, World Economic Forum in Davos, 2019

The alien found the reactions of the relatively elderly politicians in the room fascinating. It looked around at them, and seemed to be reading their thoughts.

'What are they thinking?' I asked my telepathic confidant.

'That she is right,' said the alien. 'Your official leaders are ashamed of themselves. They are terrified about the systemic change she is advocating. You humans really need to get better at change.'

'Quite the dressing down, isn't it?' I asked rhetorically.

'Yes,' said the alien, 'but only metaphorically, not literally.' It still did not fully grasp the human art of the rhetorical question.

'Some are thinking it's really quite easy, they just need to start investing in renewables and nuclear fusion research rather than the dying oil industry,' added the alien. 'Looks like you have a chance, but Greta is right about the need to panic. Why do you think I visited Ocean in 2019 rather than 2020 or 2021?' asked the alien.

I assumed the alien was not asking rhetorically: 'So you can visit us at our turning point, I guess. That would mean you think even 2030 would be too late?'

'Yes,' said the alien. 'The measures need to be already operational, and climate emissions already cut by 45 per cent by 2030, in order for you to stay below 1.5 degrees warmer than your average in your 19th century. That means your turning point needs to be in 2019.'

The real reasons for the alien's visit to Ocean were becoming clear. It was visiting us in 2019 for a reason, and that reason seemed to be related to 2019 being the turning point in our civilisation.

Switzerland's neutrality has led to a number of international and Non-Governmental Organisations situating their offices in Geneva. I took the alien on a tour of central Geneva to give a sense of the variety of organisations. I showed the alien to the Palace of Nations building, which housed the United Nations' Office at Geneva, the second largest of the four major office sites of the United Nations, with the largest being in New York. I had to pop inside for an interim meeting with my temporary pay masters. I left the alien alone to walk around outside the Palace. It seemed suitably mesmerised by the lines of different national flags, and the curious-looking Broken Chair of Geneva, a 12-metre high wooden sculpture of a chair with one of the legs broken, symbolising opposition to the use of land mines and cluster bombs.

I entered an inconspicuous door labelled 'Office for Outer Space Affairs' with the acronym 'UNOOSA' typed neatly below it, and wondered why this important department had such a low public profile. There was a surprise as I entered the room: Barack Obama was there. He was holding a new role within the United Nations known subtly as 'Space Ambassador', specialising in interplanetary diplomacy. The United Nations had, for obvious reasons apparently, decided this role should not be automatically assigned to the sitting US President, but as Obama had now served his full eight years, he was the human for the job. Obama had been taking a keen interest in the alien's visit, what to teach the alien, and what we could learn from it. He had a simple message that he wanted me to pass on to the alien during its time in Geneva.

All people are endowed with inalienable rights, and that principle is embodied in the Geneva Conventions and treaties against torture and genocide, and it unites us with people from every country and culture.

Barack Obama, Former President of the United States

My contribution to the meeting mainly involved telling them what they already knew from the itinerary, shedding a bit of light on how our telepathic connection works, and pressing 'Send' to email them the notes I had already made on the tablet. I re-emerged from the Palace to find the alien smugly sitting high up on the Broken Chair of Geneva.

'Get down from there,' I requested, with the mixed emotions of a parent discovering their child up a tree, and wanting to both assert their authority, and not have the child damaged by an immediately obedient act of descent. 'Carefully,' I added.

It reminded me of the alien's quest to understand why humans like falling, in controlled circumstances, that is. Like a cat jumping confidently from an absurd height, the alien slid off the chair and absorbed its impact with the ground with nothing more than a minor bend of both knees.

I passed on the message from Obama, and the alien understood it. I was under instruction to make doubly sure this was fully understood by the alien, and so we joined a guided walking tour of the United Nations' buildings. Our Swiss tour guide proudly explained to the alien the importance of the Geneva Conventions.

'Four treaties, and three protocols that establish the standards of international law for humanitarian treatment in war. They seek to protect people who are not or no longer taking part in the hostilities, such as the sick, wounded, prisoners of war and civilians.'

'I am guessing that Geneva, rather than another city or territory, was selected to sign these conventions due to its neutrality,' posited the alien to me telepathically, which I converted into an audible statement.

'Correct,' agreed the guide. He seemed a quiet gentleman, focussed on staying professional, and struggled only slightly to not stare into the alien's mesmerising, hypnotic, jet-black eyes.

'The Geneva Conventions represent the unique role that Geneva has in the international community. Switzerland is a neutral, safe and humanitarian haven for the world.'

The guide went on to give examples of how this has played out in different ways and different contexts. The key example that the alien could relate to from its world tour so far was linked to a discussion we had in Beijing, when considering China's influence in the region. Here in Geneva in January 2018, North and South Korea signed to form a joint Winter Olympics team for the first time, a move that had the backing of Beijing. This highlighted the on-going relevance of Geneva as a unique city, with a unique role for diplomacy on the world stage. The city of Geneva is not physically large or imposing, but it plays a critical part in the international community.

A city is not gauged by its length and width, but by the broadness of its vision and the height of its dreams.
Herb Caen, San Francisco Journalist

On our final morning in the city we sat on the shores of Lake Geneva. We saw the 140-metre high water fountain, intended as a symbol of the strength, ambition and vitality of Geneva. I noted for the alien that although 140 metres is reasonably high, the city does not have the grandiosity of the skyscrapers of Los Angeles and Beijing, and perhaps this was a suitable metaphor for the understated nature of how Geneva presents itself to the world. Similarly, the quiet yet extraordinary achievements of Geneva are exemplified by its regular appearances in lists of the top ten cities in the world in terms of Quality of Life; rarely grabbing the headlines with the top spot, yet consistently in the top ten. For example, Mercer's annual survey placed Geneva as eighth in 2018, taking into account factors such as political stability, health care, education, crime, transport and recreational facilities.

Whilst other places on Ocean have much to learn from the approach and values advocated in Geneva, it was time for me to fulfil another promise I had made to Obama during our meeting. Here we were, in the heart of the diplomatic capital of the planet, sometimes referred to as the Capital of Peace, and yet humanity had not succeeded in securing global peace. Obama was particularly interested to hear about the throwaway comment the alien had made at CERN to its amorous admirer, stating they do not need to worry about wars any more on its own planet. It was imperative, therefore, that as its translator I really listened to this extraordinary being, that I learned as much as possible from the alien about how its species had reached that stage of development. I acknowledged the alien's comments in Cairo about using the two-column thinking method to prevent conflicts, but Obama was sure there was more to learn from the alien than that, and I shared the curiosity.

'You know I can't say too much about my species,' reminded the alien when I attempted to probe. 'But there is something I have noticed in how humans talk about diplomacy. As your fellow human Greta has alluded to this, I am able to elaborate.'

'Please do.'

Suddenly I learned that the alien was able to telepathically replay an extract of her speech, not in its own voice, but in the chilling tone of the Swedish teenager.

'You say that nothing in life is black or white. But that is a lie. A very dangerous lie.'

'There is a human tendency towards resolving issues by insisting nothing is black or white. This is part of your problem,' clarified the alien, returning to its own telepathic voice.

'I thought that was wise to say nothing is black or white. I thought, as we talked about in Cairo, that it was good to respect the points in all thinking columns. To recognise and respect the points in the column other than the one you gravitate towards. To conclude on the basis of a numerical assignment of scores, not vested interests, or feelings, which are in reality little more than unarticulated vested interests.'

'That remains true,' said the alien. 'And please keep using that system.'

I indicated for the alien to elaborate.

'Let me demonstrate,' said the alien, fully confirming that our inevitable role reversal was now complete. I was officially no longer the teacher, but the student.

An old lady was walking past us, limping a little as she moved slowly. She was walking on the footpath close to the water, between our seated position on the banks of Lake Geneva, and the lake itself.

'Ethically, I have to ask you to imagine a scenario, as I cannot enact it,' said the alien. 'Imagine that, to make this insight clear to you, I approach the old lady over there, and vaporise her arms.'

'OK,' I said, imagining as instructed.

'Now, would you say that was partially her fault that she lost her arms? 50:50, say? Takes two to tango, does it?' asked the alien sarcastically. It had clearly picked up on the human preference for alliteration of cliché sayings over accuracy. I was reminded of the inaccuracy epidemic we had discussed at the maths class in Cairo.

'Of course not. Fully yours. All on you, that would be, my alien friend.'

'Exactly. It would be 100 per cent my fault that she lost her arms. I could invent justifications, of course. I could say words to the effect that she looked at me in a funny way. Or I could invent that she had been nasty to me the day before. They would be words that do not need to be respected, as they are entirely disconnected from reality. They would misrepresent. They would not represent the external, objective, binary reality that she was entirely innocent, and entirely undeserving of her limb removal. It would be black or white. Greta is right.'

'Agreed.' I understood where the alien was going with this, and it was quite a moment of realisation. Perhaps sometimes, in our human endeavours to be diplomatic and conciliatory, we allow extreme actions to proceed without accurate assignment of extreme levels of responsibility. Even when it is as extreme as 100 per cent versus 0 per cent.

'Too often on your planet, the column that has lost the debate wins in reality. Your climate change deniers have lost the debate, but they have, so far, won the reality to maintain the status quo.'

'Appalling. How can we turn this around?'

'Those who are 100 per cent in the wrong should not be allowed to take only 50 per cent of the responsibility, under the guise of compromise,' said the alien. 'Otherwise, they will always win. Furthermore, it will create resentment within the innocent party, and then they feel justified to retaliate.'

The alien continued with a new, related metaphor, directed at myself this time, rather than the old lady.

'If I steal from you £100, and give you back only £50, I have won £50. Giving back only £50 is not compromise. That is letting destructive forces win £50,' said my hypothetical thief.

'Some humans try to dismiss people like Greta as radical, but the interplanetary community, myself included, would see her as proportionate. Your species needs extreme responses to extreme situations.'

'So we need more people like Greta?' I asked the alien, feeling like I was talking with Yoda from the film franchise *Star Wars*.

'Of course. She is the reflection of an extreme situation. Currently, the extremists are the climate deniers. The extremists are the politicians taking the extremist level of action of zero. Some of those extremists might point to extremely minor actions, which could be rounded to the nearest full number of zero, on a scale of one to 100, whereby 100 is sufficient action as required by physics. Zero is a very extreme number. Yet those extremists are being met by moderate responses,' said the alien.

'I think I understand,' I ventured. 'So using your previous metaphor, extremist thieves might defend themselves by saying they have repaid 25 pence. But actually, that would be rounded to repaying £0, not even £1, whereas they should be repaying £100.'

'Correct,' confirmed the alien.

'There is something I'm worried about,' I confided in the alien. 'Humans encourage extremism, but it seems to be usually in the direction of self-destruction. Not in the direction of self-preservation. Humans are extremely good at causing destruction, but not extremely good at preventing destruction.'

'Your species is suicidal as a whole. Of course there are exceptions, but that is the overall rule. It doesn't have to be that way. Other species out there in the multiverse are not suicidal. You need to find the individuals in your society that are not suicidal, and put them into positions of power. People like Greta.'

'There's hope for us, then?'

'Yes, if new leaders like her are able to ditch the human tendency to focus only on fixing bad things after they have happened, and focus instead, constantly, on preventing bad things, before they happen. Then, and only then, do you have hope,' concluded the alien.

'I understand', I said, echoing the neutral phrase often used by the alien earlier in our world tour, when it was the student in our topsy-turvy, student-turned-teacher relationship.

I wondered whether it was unsurprising, therefore, that the most effective climate campaigners of our time were currently young, often born after the year 2000. They were too young to be in positions of responsibility, and so by definition, could not possibly be held responsible for the climate change inflicted upon them. It is black and white that it is not the fault of such young humans. This is why climate change is sometimes referred to as an intergenerational justice issue.

'Exactly,' said the alien, reading my thoughts. 'That is the next step in human diplomatic development. Some things are not as simple as black or white, and taking the third way is wise, as we saw during our toilet decision at the airport in Ho Chi Minh City. And some things really are black or white. Binary action needs to be taken wherever reality is binary. That is proportionate, and honest. Especially where that binary reality is based on physics, as is your situation with greenhouse emissions.'

On the tablet I found a report from February 2019 that confirmed the alien's assessment of climate change as black or white. Yes, there are two columns, but the column saying that humans have not caused climate change is outnumbered by the column that says humans have caused climate change, by a factor of approximately one million. With mountains of statistics and evidence, such as the last four years being the hottest since records began in the 1800s, scientists have calculated there is only a one in a million chance that global warming is not man made.

'A ratio of 1 to 1,000,000 is reasonable to summarise as black or white. Again, rounding to the nearest percentage figure, that figure is zero,' concurred the alien.

Amazing, I thought, that the alien had in a sense managed to portray our situation around climate change as effectively black or white. It had communicated climate change back to humanity as being more simple than going to the toilet at the airport in Ho Chi Minh City, where there were three valid options.

The alien's tone then turned to become, not identical to, but reminiscent of its reaction to my anthropocentric suggestion that human faces can be seen in clouds, or heart shapes seen in coral reef structures.

'It's not about you humans, by the way,' added the alien, ironically soothing its harsh message with its intergalactic perspective. This stepping back, unexpectedly, brought back a sense of diplomacy. 'The imperative for proportionate response, even when dealing with extremes, is a universal principle. It also applies to all the other millions of species out there.'

And with that, I made a note on the tablet to report this conversation back to Obama. Sitting next to my alien chum, we watched as the now fabled, armless old lady of Geneva continued her hobbling walk along the shores of Lake Geneva. She remained blissfully unaware of her contribution, not only to humanity's future, but also to interplanetary diplomacy.

CHAPTER 7
Amazon Rainforest, Brazil

Bare Necessities (from the film The Jungle Book)
by Terry Gilkyson

During our flight to Manaus, Brazil, I played this song for the alien. The song was about the basic things we need. It can be interpreted as referring to the need for minimal belongings and resources, and it conveyed a message that humans can survive without many of the excesses of modern life.

I suggested to the alien that the song could be re-interpreted as being about consumption of resources on the global scale. This issue had been raised in the previous places during our voyage so far, and was relevant nowhere more so than in Brazil. The lyrics reflected the struggle of humanity to get the balance right in terms of what we need in order to be happy. Whilst Western culture was tending towards greater complexity as technology advanced, the song made the case for a return to the basics and simplicity.

During the flight from Geneva to Manaus, there was something bothering me. I thought I might as well just say it clearly using telepathy, as the alien would soon tune into my subconscious musings anyway, whether I liked it or not.

'I get that you're not allowed to say too much about your species, alien old pal, but really I've learned quite a lot about it now.'

'Purely by accident. I have not intended to reveal such insights,' said the alien telepathically, seemingly covering itself from interplanetary litigation.

'What I don't understand, though, is that if you can vaporise things, why haven't you vaporised each other, and destroyed yourselves in an instant?'

The alien chuckled.

Our food and plastic cutlery arrived courtesy of the air steward. He was bearing the gift of scrambled eggs. Again I noticed that I was unable to read the air steward's thoughts, and was a little frustrated by this.

'We don't share your tendency to attack each other,' said the alien. 'Or if I may speak more glibly: speak for yourselves. The question itself is idiosyncratic, and highly anthropocentric.'

Humbled, I reached for my plastic fork, feeling it was somehow appropriate that the fork was not metal.

It's in your nature to destroy yourselves.
Terminator, in the film: *Terminator 2: Judgement Day*

'Very appropriate,' said the alien. 'Why have you got a plastic fork?' asked the alien, clearly knowing the answer. It seemed to be learning how to use rhetorical questions. I celebrated for a moment in my mind, feeling I could take some credit for this small developmental step in the alien's learned use of this linguistic device. Despite this, I chose to answer its rhetorical question anyway.

'Because humans can't trust each other to not fight each other,' I said with the melancholic air of a human knowing its species cannot be trusted to preserve itself.

'So the answer to your question is: same reason you don't stab yourself with a fork. The only difference is, our species would feel that to vaporise one of our own kind, would be to vaporise a part of one's own body. I have not seen you stab yourself with that fork, so I believe you can at least partially relate to why we do not vaporise each other back home,' said the alien.

My next question was the interstellar equivalent of the chicken and egg question.

'Which came first: the ability to vaporise, or the tendency to not attack each other? Because if the ability to vaporise came first, how did that last without the tendency to not attack each other? And if the tendency to not attack each other came first, why was the ability to vaporise necessary?'

'Atul, you're thinking anthropocentrically again.'

'Yeah, I have a real problem with that,' I confessed.

'Remember our conversation with the boomerang tutor. On my home planet we get our nutrients from the chemical compounds in the environment around us. So the tendency to not attack each other came first. Then the ability to vaporise came later. That ability stayed within us, because we have a tendency to vaporise only things like small plants and bodies of liquid, not the bodies of each other.'

And with that, I continued to use my plastic fork to eat scrambled eggs on the plane. I felt the chicken and egg question was finally answerable. It was the egg. Two birds that weren't technically chickens mated, then there was a mutation, and then the first egg was produced that, by definition, was a chicken.

Our aircraft touched down at Eduardo Gomes International Airport in Manaus, in Northern Brazil. The usual drill followed. We walked to the carousel, waited for our bags, collected them, and the alien tried to guess whether a human was about to emerge to offer to carry its bags in return for a coin, or occasionally, a floppy note of currency. The alien had heard that Brazil's economy was on the up, and so just when it seemed to be confident that no one would emerge, an eager Brazilian gentleman emerged to carry the solar panelled bag on behalf of the alien. The alien deduced that we were again in a less developed region of the world.

Manaus is an isolated city of two million people in the heart of the Amazon Rainforest, with access primarily by air or boat, rather than road. It was once known as the City of the Forest, and I reminded the alien of how this contrasted to an area of Cairo known as the City of the Dead, Los Angeles being dubbed the City of the Car, and Geneva being quietly recognised as the global Capital of Peace.

I had selected Manaus to feature in our global itinerary not so much for the particularities of the place itself, but more because it is the main access point for visiting the Brazilian Amazon Rainforest. From Manaus the alien and I boarded a small, solar-powered boat, and our journey into the largest rainforest on Ocean began.

The Amazon Rainforest is a wet tropical rainforest, which is the most species-rich type of habitat on Ocean. As the Amazon is the largest example of wet tropical rainforest in the world, more than a third of all known species live here, giving the alien the best opportunity to explore Ocean's biodiversity in one place. The Amazon River basin is around 7,000,000 square kilometres, and within this, the rainforest itself covers around 5,500,000 square kilometres, compared with the area of the United States, at 9,834,000 square kilometres. Also known as Amazonia and the Amazon Jungle, it represents more than half of the planet's rainforests. Its sheer and continuous size has meant that an estimated 70 indigenous human cultures have never made contact with the outside world.

We disembarked our solar boat. Our guide was a local gentleman who spoke little English, but understood when I suggested that we make contact with a local, indigenous tribe within the forest. He seemed concerned, but intrigued about how a local tribe would react to the alien. From his experience of the area, the guide had reason to believe there might be a previously uncontacted tribes a few hours' walk into the rainforest, and so our battle through the dense undergrowth commenced.

There was no beaten path, but the guide was able to lead the way, hacking through the rainforest plants with a menacing looking machete. Unknown to the guide, the alien would occasionally help with a targeted vaporisation of a thick branch in the distance ahead of us. Other times, trip hazards such as large, protruding roots on the forest floor would vanish before the guide noticed them. Low hanging branches would move out of the way almost as if by the breeze, in a manner that reminded me of the assistance I had received on my way to a successful headstand on a surfboard in Queensland.

'We make good progress today,' said the guide, pleased with himself. 'Normally not so fast. Your alien is lucky charm.' He had no idea.

'Yes, lucky indeed,' I concurred politely. I was not convinced it would have been helpful to our guide's morale to clarify that he was not responsible for his over-performance that day.

All indigenous traditions, all origin stories provide a large map of where you are.
David Christian, Historian

Through dangling vines we noticed a clearing ahead of us. A circle of rudimentary huts bordered a central area with a fire. Females were nowhere to be seen – presumably inside the huts. I interpreted this as a sign we had not encountered the most egalitarian of indigenous societies, and I worried what this said to the alien about humanity. Standing around the fire, males with elaborate headdresses, painted faces and loincloths talked amongst themselves. Their attention seemed focussed on maintaining the fire, and cooking an animal held above it with the support of a few carefully placed sticks. The men seemed at ease with each other, but the bows slung around their shoulders, and the packs of arrows attached to their backs, suggested a readiness for conflict.

'Alien only,' said our rainforest guide. 'No humans.'

The alien understood, and moved ahead of us. Its green body rustled the bushes, and the tribe reacted instantly with a drawing of bows and arrows. I suspected it looked, from their point of view, like the innocent arrival of more lunch. The alien emerged between two of the huts. It walked through the gap and was greeted with a flurry of arrows; each vaporised long before any impact was possible. The tribesmen were increasingly panicky on realisation that they were not firing at the usual peccary, otherwise known as wild pig, which came oinking into their compound.

The alien came out from between the huts with both of its green arms raised in the air, in what was understood by the tribe as a universal indication of peace. With their arrows ineffective on the alien, they didn't know what else to do, except to stop firing. The more elaborately dressed tribal leader stepped forward, shaking a little. I wondered if he was expecting his own imminent death.

'They do not use telepathy,' said the alien to me telepathically from quite a distance. I realised I had never asked the alien exactly what the geographical limitations of our telepathic connection were. As we had lost each other at the airport in Beijing, I knew there was some sort of geographical limit to our connection.

'Can you teach him?' I asked the alien. The tribal leader was standing close to the alien, face to face, staring into the jet-black eyes of the being from another world.

'Trying. Takes me a minute to tune into their language first. It doesn't exactly resemble English.'

The tribal leader raised a hand to his temple. He seemed to be connecting with the alien, and gestured for his fellow comrades to put down their weapons. After a few more seconds of what I assumed to be alien to chief chat, the leader stood more upright, then bowed to the alien slightly. The alien bowed back in an equally minimal manner, rotated its head back to where I was hiding, then rotated its body to follow, then walked back to me and our rainforest guide.

'He was just hungry,' explained the alien. 'And disappointed I couldn't be eaten. I explained that I'm from another galaxy, but he doesn't know what a galaxy is. Said it would take a while to explain, so will leave them to it.'

I was glad the alien had experienced first-hand some of the instinctive reactions of humans that were uninfluenced by the globally connected culture of the rest of humanity. To the tribesmen, the alien was simply another type of animal that happened to use telepathy instead of audible oinking. And like the wild pig that gets away, so too did the alien, leaving them to find something else for their next meal.

It raised for the alien the issue that, just as humans instinctively think of some other species on Ocean as a potential filler between the mid-afternoon snack and main evening meal, so too might other species visiting Ocean think of humans as potential sustenance. And just imagine if, to other aliens, humans tasted like chocolate, or champagne. How long would we last then? Professor Stephen Hawking referred to similar examples when warning that contact from alien life forms might not end well for humans. Whilst there are theoretical benefits such as sharing scientific and medical advances, looking at the history of the indigenous people of Australia, and Easter Island as we would be learning more about at the next stop on our world tour, contact with the outside world has not always been positive for indigenous cultures.

Our rainforest guide continued ahead of the alien and me, hacking through the dense shrubbery and vegetation. The alien was good at multi-tasking: it silently assisted the progress of the guide, whilst having a telepathic chat with yours truly. I explained to the alien that the Amazon is also known as the Lungs of the World, as it regulates the entire planet's atmosphere. Its mass of approximately 390 billion individual trees are breathing in and storing carbon dioxide from the atmosphere, holding around a third of all carbon stored as land vegetation on the planet, and breathing out oxygen, an essential element for humans to survive more than a few seconds. This demonstrated the value that humans can and should be placing on the Amazon in the fight not just against climate change, but the fight to continue access to the most important atmospheric component for our most basic survival need: the ability to breathe oxygen. Amazonian trees breathe out around 20 per cent of the planet's atmospheric oxygen. Overall, around 50 per cent of oxygen is produced by life on land, with the other 50 per cent being produced by life in the oceans.

The Beach
(2000)

After our indigenous encounter, we paused in the forest to watch this film on the tablet. Humans often have a kneejerk, reactionary, nostalgic or romanticised vision of simpler societies as preferable. It is true that they were more sustainable, but it is also true that the lack of modern medicine meant that life expectancy was much shorter than the 80 or so years that is common in developed societies on Ocean today.

In the film Leonardo DiCaprio's character is a young American in search of an idealised, pristine island in the Gulf of Thailand. The island features a beautiful, hidden beach and lagoon. When he arrives he finds a small, simple community living there in secrecy. However, the apparent paradise soon turns into a more realistic scenario. A shark attack leaves one of the community severely injured, and the leader of the commune refuses to bring in the help of modern medicine, prioritising instead to maintain their secrecy.

This ethical dilemma is the moral centrepiece of the film. Modern medicine is portrayed as a positive, humane and progressive benefit of our world. The alien received a clear message from the film makers that they believed we humans must embrace positive aspects not only of simpler societies, but also of our more complex societies on Ocean.

'Oxygen is not that important on our planet,' conversed my relaxed alien sidekick as it followed our rainforest guide, with me third in line. 'It helps, but we have evolved to draw on a wider range of atmospheric gases and liquids in order to breathe.'

I had noticed when scuba diving with the alien that it was not particularly fussed about using the equipment properly, and that basically it was breathing through its skin.

'For you humans though,' continued the alien, 'cutting down your rainforests is similar to suicide. You wouldn't suffocate yourselves directly, so why suffocate yourselves indirectly?'

> *What we are doing to the forests of the world is but a minor reflection of what we are doing to ourselves and to one another.*
> Mahatma Ghandi, Indian Activist

I was pretty sure the alien was asking the question rhetorically. Last time it asked a rhetorical question I answered anyway. But this time I didn't. The experiment worked, as the alien stayed silent, confirming it had made progress in learning this largely inconsequential skill.

'Legal measures are usually required for environmental solutions,' I said, moving our conversation on to solutions. 'In 2018 Norway became the first country in the world to ban deforestation. I know it sounds very obvious that Brazil must do the same, but it isn't doing it. In fact, the new leaders are encouraging more deforestation.'

'If humanity wants to continue the cause and effect relationship between having trees and breathing, that must change,' said the alien, somewhat stating the obvious, I thought, but it was nice to hear it said from the perspective of a being from another area of the cosmos.

Forests are the world's air conditioning system – the lungs of the planet – and we are on the verge of switching it off.
Prince Charles, Heir to the British Throne

I speculated with the alien that as humans are unable to see oxygen in the air, the invisible contribution by the Amazon and other rainforests is perhaps one of the underlying reasons why rainforests are not valued as highly as they need to be.

'There is an idiosyncrasy to the functioning of the human brain that I have noticed. As you have now alluded to it, I am able to elaborate,' said the alien.

'Please do,' I said, getting the tablet out and expecting to hear something worth making a note of and reporting back to my United Nations employers.

'I would diagnose it as dangerously visual,' said the alien. 'Your brains suffer from a key problem: out of sight, out of mind. This might lead to the end of your civilisation, if you are not careful.'

'Agreed,' I said, entering this observation into the notes function on the tablet. It was true of our current discussion around the invisibility of oxygen, but was also going to be relevant at the final destination of our world tour when we reached the distant, out of sight, melting continent of Antarctica.

'Our brains work in more balanced ways,' confirmed the alien, as if I couldn't tell without the alien rubbing it in – such a show off.

At first, I thought I was fighting to save rubber trees. Then I thought I was fighting to save the Amazon rainforest. Now I realise I am fighting for humanity.
Chico Mendes, Brazilian Environmentalist

The Amazon Rainforest has been in existence for around 100 million years, and combined with the relative stability in its climate as a result of being situated near the Equator, this has enabled a wealth of biodiversity to evolve. I explained to the alien that the age of a habitat on Ocean is important: old-growth forests such as the Amazon usually have higher biodiversity than new forests. The competitive forces of natural selection have had sufficient time to result in more and more specific ecological niches. I summarised the insights of Charles Darwin for the alien, and referred to the supporting evidence of modern genetics, to explain that, given enough time, species will develop specialised adaptations unique to their particular niche.

> *This preservation of favourable variations, and the destruction of injurious variations, I call Natural Selection, or the Survival of the Fittest.*
>
> Charles Darwin, Naturalist in *On the Origin of Species*, 1869

To demonstrate the interplay between ecological niches and the evolution of new species, I asked our rainforest guide to take us to one of the older trees in the rainforest. We found a thick-trunked tree that was around 1,000 years old, and spent a few hours doing a survey of the different species found living in its many nooks and crannies. We identified hundreds of insect species on the tree, including several that were unique to that individual, old-growth tree. We found species new to science, that were not found on any other neighbouring trees, and that were likely to be globally endemic to this single tree.

For the alien this exemplified why the Amazon Rainforest has the highest biodiversity of any region on Ocean. It is the home of 2.5 million insect species, 40,000 plant species, 16,000 tree species, 1,294 bird species, 428 amphibian species, 378 reptile species, and 427 mammal species. The alien and I had a ball of a time finding a variety of colourful, unusual and deadly species that have evolved highly specific adaptations. Our rainforest guide pointed out the wonderfully colourful toucans, macaws, poison dart frogs, snakes, butterflies, jaguars and monkeys.

We returned to our solar boat moored on the Amazon River, and after boarding, the guide excitedly showed the alien an electric eel in the water. They can grow to more than two metres in length and, the guide added, expecting a reaction of surprise from the alien, they can produce jolts of electricity enough to stun and drown a human. Whilst the use of electricity is unusual for species on Ocean, the alien respectfully dampened the guide's anthropocentric enthusiasm: it's a common trick used throughout the multiverse, apparently. It was important to have a sense of cosmological perspective.

'All life is interesting,' began the alien diplomatically. 'Species that use electrical impulses to interact with their environment and find breakfast are present on 14,003,978 planets that I have visited so far.'

This was the first time the alien had quantified how many planets it had visited personally. Up until now it had referred to various large numbers of other planets, but it had not been clear how many of those it had visited itself. I wondered how old that meant the alien was, and indeed, whether it was perhaps in some sense immortal – an issue raised in Queensland when swimming amongst immortal jellyfish. The alien chose not to respond to my thoughts on this, suggesting that, perhaps like on Ocean, it was impolite to ask.

The re-emergence of the theme of biological immortality led us nicely into the next area for discussion with the alien: the question of valuing nature. Diversity of life on Ocean, I explained, brings with it a range of benefits for humans. But biodiversity also has an intrinsic value, regardless of human value, as we had touched on in Queensland. The alien was interested to learn that intrinsic value is the most difficult value for some humans to understand, as there are no direct, personal benefits. It requires a moral or ethical understanding.

'It's unique to Ocean, I'm afraid,' said the alien. 'Some other lead species on other planets struggle to understand the intrinsic value of their fellow species, but as they usually don't eat each other, it's not really a problem out there. Sorry.' The alien's added apology at the end was, I thought, an example of its slight impressionability, picking up my rather British way of talking.

'We do struggle with it here. Some humans do understand the intrinsic value of nature, but even those that do often let that understanding become overridden by short-term, immediate needs, such as providing for themselves or their family, and therefore cutting down a tree in the rainforest, or sanctioning a car park to be built over a nature reserve in order to receive their monthly paycheque.'

'This connects to your population issue,' stated the alien. 'With more people, each fundamentally self-interested, comes more reasons to override the intrinsic value of nature.'

'And that's just when we think about the intrinsic value of nature. What I'm even more concerned about are the direct human benefits of nature, and the fact that we seem to ignore them,' I said, trying to get the alien into a conversation that we could learn something from. I had the tablet at the ready to make notes.

'You are right to be alarmed,' said the alien.

'Short-term human interests override long-term benefits. For example, here in the Amazon the removal of large tracts of the forest benefits a few local families or companies in the short term, but it leads to global climate change, rising sea levels and damage to human coastal communities, not just globally, but also here in Brazil. Yet the people of Brazil recently voted in a government in favour of causing that damage, that self-harm. I know you are limited by Interplanetary Ethics, my alien friend, but on behalf of my species I must at least ask. How can we resolve this? Help. Please.'

'Humans have the solutions already. You simply need to vote in the governments that will implement them,' said the alien concisely.

Medicine Man
(1992)

Back at our hotel in the City of the Forest, I showed this film to the alien as a way to further elaborate on the range of benefits that nature brings to humans. In the film, Sean Connery's character is a researcher in the Amazonian rainforest who has found a cure for cancer. Initially he believes the key compound is a derivative of a flower, and later realises the source of the cure to be a rare ant that is indigenous to the rainforest.

The site where the ants have been found is at risk from a logging company, and the film ends with an ambiguity that represents the real life situation, whereby the story of the Amazon is yet to be concluded. Will humanity destroy the last of the Amazon rainforest and its potential range of medical benefits, or will we find a way to conserve it?

Whilst focussing on undiscovered future benefits, the film perhaps understates the medical advances that had already been achieved from biodiversity, even in 1992 when the film was released. Around 25 per cent of all prescription medicines have originated from rainforest plants, and 1,300 of the 2,000 known cancer-fighting plants have come from rainforests.

Nevertheless, the film is right to focus on the loss of future discoveries: only around 0.5 per cent of the flowering plant species in the Amazon have been studied for medicinal properties, let alone all the other categories of wildlife. The alien understood the clear message of the film: humanity is destroying its pharmacy. It is being lost faster than it can be understood.

The following day we returned to the rainforest. I used the term 'The Seven Es' as a framework to summarise for the alien the overall reasons for valuing nature.

Ethical: the intrinsic value of nature, regardless of human benefit.
Environmental services: such as storing carbon dioxide and reducing flood risk.
Ecological function: such as pollinators.
Enjoyment: the fun of interacting with diverse life forms.
Educational: helping to understand how different species function and interact.
Economic: materials for products that can be sold.
Even if none of the above: health benefits of air to breathe, and DNA study for medical advances.

Our walking, telepathic conversation continued amidst the sounds of the rainforest: the squawks of a toucan in the canopy, the 130 decibels of a howler monkey, the shrill of a yellow-banded poison dart frog, the self-congratulatory mutterings of a rainforest tour guide making unusually excellent progress, the crunching on leaves of an alien explorer, the out-of-breath coughs and splutterings of a human trying to keep up.

'How many species are on your planet, overall?' asked the alien.

'Estimates vary hugely, from the approximate 8.7 million species already identified, up to two billion, or even over a trillion. Some estimates suggest there are more than a trillion microbial species alone on Ocean.'

'So most of your species have not been discovered yet. That means DNA analysis of more species could reveal further medical advances, beyond cures for cancer,' stated the alien. 'Which other conditions have you studied so far with potential solutions from nature?'

'Well, some amphibians and reptiles have the ability to regenerate limbs, but there seems to be a lack of interest and funding to accelerate this research. I do find that a bit odd, to be honest,' I added, once again embarrassed at the attitude of my species towards doing what is vehemently in its own interests.

'You need to study that further,' said the alien. 'I have seen a lot of humans in wheelchairs, and others struggling to walk, as a result of losing limbs. That is really not necessary in the long term. Look into those amphibians and reptiles, replicate aspects of their DNA, and you will be able to share their solutions.'

I opened the tablet and made a note to report that fairly clear instruction back to Obama and the team at the UN. I recalled the armless old lady of Geneva, and how, if the alien had vaporised her arms, it might also have been able to help the innocent victim to grow them back. Or if she was a resident of another planet that had studied limb regeneration with a little more enthusiasm, she might have simply grown back her arms and carried on her walk. I then recalled the section of war veterans in wheelchairs in the stands of the Olympic stadium, during the alien's welcoming ceremony in Beijing.

'Yes, they would benefit from DNA analysis of other species on your planet. It's really not that difficult once you switch around a few genes, you know,' added the alien placidly.

Our rainforest guide stopped the alien and me in our tracks. He made a sort of 'hussshhhh' noise at us, then pointed our attention to a basilisk lizard. The lizard, resting along a tree branch overhanging the Amazon River, initially seemed unaware of our presence, but when it noticed our multicultural trio it panicked as if we were potential predators. Dropping with a light splash into the river, it suddenly exploded into a manic sprint across the very surface of the water surface, its feet tapping rapidly as it propelled forward, not with grace, but with a comical splaying of each leg out to the side.

'Hang on a minute. Does that mean you can regrow your limbs?' I asked the alien, wanting a demonstration, and knowing that the alien could read my thoughts on that.

'Yes. Now is not convenient for your demonstration request, though. Can I show you next time we're on a plane, when I don't need my limbs much?' asked the alien.

It was a surprisingly polite alien at all times really. But especially at this particular juncture of our world tour, given that we were essentially haggling over the exact timing to de-limb itself to satisfy my curiosity. In the circumstances, I felt there was only one appropriate way I could respond.

'Of course.'

We stopped at a natural clearing in the rainforest for a rest. Our guide was looking at his watch and grinning. To my surprise, he then presented the watch to the alien as a souvenir. It was as if the excellent progress we had been achieving had made the guide so happy that he couldn't contain himself. Giving the gift of the watch seemed deeply important to him.

I opened up the tablet and, although I was unable to connect to WIFI in the remoteness of the forest, an anonymous official at the UN had saved onto the tablet a document from a study in 2018. The study had reported that in terms of biomass, humanity is just 0.01 per cent of all life on Earth, compared with 82 per cent plants, mostly in the form of wood, and 13 per cent bacteria. It also revealed that although there was increasing public awareness of the problem of plastic in the oceans, and rising public attention on the oceans in general, this must remain in perspective: just one per cent of total biomass on our planet is found in the oceans, with 86 per cent on land and the remaining 13 per cent as sub-surface bacteria.

The report, by Professor Ron Milo at the Weizmann Institute of Science in Israel, concurred with the alien's implicit perspective of the disproportionately dominant role of humans over other organisms, despite being a tiny fraction of life on the planet in terms of biomass. As with many other reports in recent decades, it listed the top reason as habitat destruction by humans. Habitats are destroyed for a wide variety of reasons, including farming, cattle-rearing and other activities for human food supply, logging, and developments such as palm oil plantations, housing, industry, retail and roads and other transport infrastructure. Combined habitat destruction across the planet has led to the sixth mass extinction of life on Ocean, with an estimated 50 per cent of all animal species having been lost in the last 50 years.

Relating back to the 'Seven Es', one of the impacts of this loss of wildlife that humans need to be careful of is losing the ecological services they provide, such as pollination of our crops for food. Studies have shown dramatic losses of pollinators and insects in general in recent decades, leading to a coining of the phrase *Insectageddon*, a conflation of the words 'insect' and 'armageddon', indicating that human civilisation could collapse as a direct result of the collapse of insect populations.

Our walk ended where the continuous patch of rainforest ended: at a clearing of land populated not with the rich diversity of old-growth forest, but with cattle.

Nothing will benefit health or increase chances of survival of life on Earth as much as the evolution to a vegetarian diet.
Albert Einstein, Theoretical Physicist

Back in Manaus the alien and I went for a meal at a vegan restaurant. I explained that the loss of rainforests such as the Amazon is proportionate to the size of the human population, which by definition is proportionate to the demand for human food supply.

'Farming for cattle and meat production involves the clearing of rainforest land to make space for cattle farming. The clearing of rainforest increases, as the demand for meat increases,' I elucidated for the alien. 'Communities around the world are increasingly aware of this, leading to solutions such as Meat-free Mondays and other efforts to normalise reduced meat diets, vegetarian diets and vegan diets.'

'These are good interim measures,' congratulated the alien. 'But they are not keeping pace with total meat demand, regardless of per capita. You need to control your population.'

I could not disagree with my alien comrade. Rainforest destruction does not physically relate to per capita meat consumption. It physically relates to total meat consumption. That distinction is important. Moving towards vegan diets is positive, but it reminded me of the falling BASE jumper in Los Angeles: individual acts of veganism are like trying to break the fall using a cocktail umbrella. What is needed is the large parachute of reduced human population, achieved humanely through education.

'Taken to extremes,' segued the alien, 'if there were only, say 100 humans on the planet, you could all fly around in planes and eat all the meat you want, and still have little impact on your ecological systems. It is mainly because there are so many of you, in relation to the size of your planet, that you have problems.'

'Agreed. I will again remind my United Nations employers of the need to reduce human population, for this reason, as well as all the other reasons.' Obedient to the logic, rather than the alien itself, I made a note on the tablet.

With an affirmatory nod from the alien, the contents of its bowl of vegan legumes vanished. Then the mysterious, green life form sitting opposite me hiccupped.

PART 3:

going
further

CHAPTER 8
Easter Island, Chile

 ALIEN PLAYLIST

1999
by Prince

On our way to Easter Island I played this song for the alien. Written in 1982, at the height of the Cold War, Prince voiced fears about nuclear Armageddon. The lyrics linked this possibility with the positive message to enjoy our lives as much as we can. Indeed, the prospect of humanity ending as the clock ticked over to the year 2000 was used in the song almost as a justification for hedonism, without the need to consider consequences.

In the years preceding the change in calendar from 1999 to 2000, there were genuine, mortal fears about the 'millennium bug', the concern that computers had been developed cumulatively and entirely during calendar years beginning with the number 19, and it was unclear whether or not they could cope with the switch to years beginning 20. In theory that could have caused the failure of many computers, including those controlling nuclear missiles.

Whilst unfounded in hindsight, the genuine fear represented a recurring 'endism' of humanity: often worrying about its own demise, yet partially accepting of some form of inevitable apocalypse.

The song remained relevant for the alien in the year 2019. It expressed an almost humorous frivolity about the end of humanity. The lyrics call out our species-wide, subconscious mindset of humanity as a project with an inevitable end date, rather than a comprehensive assumption that we will succeed in sustaining ourselves indefinitely.

'What's that?' asked the alien telepathically, looking up. We were in mid-air. Inside a plane, of course. We had already completed our connecting flight from Manaus to Santiago in mainland Chile, and were at this point in time en route from Santiago to Easter Island. Our flight time was just over five hours, and the alien was perhaps getting a little restless, in need of further input. With such an innocent, simple question, it had raised yet another wildly divisive and difficult subject.

'Here we go,' I thought to myself, which the alien overheard.

The alien was looking at the permanently illuminated No Smoking sign above its head. How could I explain the human practice of smoking to an alien, without alienating the significant chunk of humanity that engages in this practice? I tried to stay matter of fact. The alien sensed this.

'Smoking was allowed on flights up until 1988. There was a smoking section and a non-smoking section on each plane. Nowadays, the signs are permanently illuminated, because all sections of all planes have banned smoking.'

'Why have a sign at all, then?' asked the alien, reasonably. 'Isn't it similar to reminding passengers that murder is also not allowed on human planes?'

'Surprisingly similar,' I agreed. 'The difference between smoking and murder is that smoking is allowed in some places, other than planes, on Ocean. Murder isn't.'

The alien had sensed my diplomatic restraint, and was getting impatient. It therefore performed a full, telepathic download of my memory bank of knowledge and thoughts about smoking. To me it felt a little like having a painkiller injection at the dentist, and then, once numbed, a USB stick had been inserted into my temple. The experience was relatively painless, but I was aware there could be complications if I moved in an unexpected way, or did something silly.

'Sorry, your conscious thoughts were too slow, whilst you were dithering over diplomatic wording. Had to go subconscious for a moment there. 93.8GB of data on this subject. Thank you,' said the alien politely. 'So smoking and climate change have conceptual similarities: one is suicide on the individual level, the other is suicide on the species level.'

'Yes,' I thought consciously. It was unnecessary to do so. I wanted to change the subject. 'Hey, so show me that limb regeneration trick we talked about in the rainforest. We have another four hours until we land at Easter Island. You won't be needing your limbs for a while.'

'OK. But I might need a bit longer than four hours to regrow them. Could you arrange for a wheelchair when we arrive at the airport, just in case?'

And a few moments later, an air steward was making a rather unique request into a phone handset connecting to air traffic control. The alien kept its promise and vaporised both its legs and arms in less time than a blink of my laggardly human eyes.

'Did that hurt?'

'Not at all.'

'What about your head? What would happen if you vaporised your own brain?'

'Our brains are distributed differently from yours. It's not all about our heads. But to answer your question, it would be a lot more problematic, yes.'

Within seconds I saw little stumps growing out of the alien's body. It was mesmerising. It was like looking at a plant and being determined to see whether or not one could watch the movement of its growth. I was also reminded of times when I had tried to notice the movement of the full Moon behind a tower at night, the Sun rise at dawn, or the Sun disappear below the horizon at sunset.

On arrival at the small airport on Easter Island, I carried the alien down the steps of the plane and into the main building. Staff were waiting with a wheelchair for their temporarily disabled guest. I plonked the alien into position. Despite being on one of the most remote inhabited islands on Ocean, with a population of just 7,750, the welcoming staff had time to carry the alien's bag for it.

The alien noticed variation in the signs that referred to the name of the place we were in, but from its experience of Ho Chi Minh City, the alien knew not to panic this time. The issue of dual place name identity also arises at Easter Island, as Rapa Nui is the name given to the island by its original, Polynesian inhabitants. It became known to Europeans as Easter Island after a Dutch explorer, Jacob Roggeveen, encountered it on Easter Sunday in 1722.

We had arrived in the early afternoon, and by the time we had wheeled the alien into our basic hotel accommodation and unpacked, the alien had fully regrown its limbs. We were ready to explore. Outside our hotel we met our Easter Island guide for the next two days. She was a highly educated researcher from a university in the United States, residing on Easter Island for several months each year to perform her work in the field. My United Nations employers had selected her on the basis of being widely respected for her insights and research papers about Easter Island. And as we quickly learned, she seemed profoundly positive about everything.

'You have made a great decision to visit this small island,' she began. 'You probably noticed in the plane on your way here, that you had flown over many other islands in the Pacific Ocean. Perhaps you wondered why you have landed on this one?'

The alien started to communicate a response to me telepathically, and then interrupted itself, acknowledging that our guide had asked a rhetorical question. I felt proud of the progress the alien had made in this area.

'Well, over the next couple of days I will delight in explaining what is so different about Easter Island, and its place in the human imagination. So, let's start with the 887 statues.'

The world-famous stone statues are now protected, with the designation of the Rapa Nui National Park as a UNESCO World Heritage Site. Otherwise known as Moai, the statues started to be carved by the Polynesians soon after their arrival on the island, around the year 1200. Many of the statues are placed on platforms known as Ahu.

As the three of us walked towards one of the Ahu with dozens of Moai lined up along it, there was something haunting about the sight of the alien coming face to face with the giant statues. They ranged between two and ten metres high, and weighed up to 70 tonnes. Their faces were distinctively and consistently shaped in a rectangular fashion, with deeply set eyes. As we stood in front of one of them, I could see the reflection of the statue in the jet-black eyes of the alien.

'At first people thought most statues were only heads. Then discoveries in 2012 confirmed that many had full bodies that were simply hidden underground,' said the guide excitedly. I found the recency of this discovery surprising. The alien seemed reflective not just physically, but also in terms of its thoughts.

'Why did their civilisation disappear?' asked the alien pertinently. 'This is relevant to one of my reasons for choosing to visit this planet.' I translated the question out loud for our guide, then my thoughts wandered once more to the real reasons for the alien's visit. It was becoming increasingly clear: it had come here to help us.

'I'm so glad you asked. It gives me a chance to bust out some of the myths about Easter Island,' said the guide with a level of enthusiasm I thought initially was rather inappropriate for an imminent discussion about the collapse of the Rapa Nui people.

'And guess what? Some people thought the Moai were the work of aliens. So maybe you can clear that one up for us, Alien?'

The alien was now unsure if her question was rhetorical or not. It cheated and read her mind, then shook its head. I drew a comparison with a similar theory we had heard in Cairo, that the pyramids might also have been constructed by aliens.

'Knew it!' she exclaimed with only a little restraint, and an entirely unhidden clenched fist. She had clearly been looking forward to this interaction for some time. I wondered if she realised that this alien was just one alien, and did not necessarily speak for all aliens.

'Anyway, we scientists have since found that most of the statues were carved from compressed volcanic ash, or tuff, a rock that was naturally present on the volcanic island. We have also recreated a statue and proven that the islanders could have moved the statue upright in a walking motion with the help of ropes,' she concluded with the air of professional satisfaction.

The guide took us to a site where her colleagues were running daily demonstrations for tourists. A replica statue towered above its human masters, with taut ropes from the top of its head stretching down to groups of scientists on all sides. Each group worked in a rhythm together, making the statue 'walk' along a mud path. The discovery of this technique, using the same technology as the Rapa Nui people would have had at the time, explained the local folklore that the statues 'walked' into their current positions. I extrapolated for the alien that this was another example of humans using science and experimentation to move on from myth and mystery.

After the demonstration the guide produced three packed lunch boxes, and found us a picnic bench close to a line of statues. Having explained the basics of the statues, she was keen to move the conversation on to the symbolic importance of Easter Island.

'It plays an important role in the human imagination, with its isolation amidst a vast and inhospitable ocean acting as a microcosm for humanity on our planet, surrounded by vast and inhospitable space.'

'I understand,' replied the alien via its translator.

After a brief explanation for the tour guide about why the alien's sandwiches vanished so suddenly, I added for the alien that humanity has long been preoccupied with 'endism', the idea that something significant, particularly our own civilisation, is coming to an end. In the 1500s Nostradamus made multiple, less-than-cheery, although cheerfully inaccurate, predictions about the end of the world. Shakespeare was also partial to the occasional reminder for his audiences that civilisations do rather tend to rise and fall.

I related this back to places we had already visited on our world tour, with many believing that the global superpowers of the USA, as well as the UK in the context of the former empire and Brexit, were already in decline. Conversely, most would agree that China was on the rise, to say the least.

'Back in Shakespeare's day, which marginally overlapped with that of Nostradamus, the rise and fall of civilisations was depicted as somewhat more dramatic, sudden and often coinciding with celestial events, such as solar eclipses. There is a solar eclipse here on Easter Island, starting in 10 minutes. Did you know that?' the guide asked.

'Of course,' I replied. 'All part of the itinerary.'

The guide handed out special eclipse-viewing glasses, and we looked at the sky to see that the partial phase of the solar eclipse had already begun. The disc of the Sun was already partially covered by the Moon. I realised the light around us had already started to dim.

I had got to know the alien quite well by now, and was not surprised to detect the recurring theme of its unreserved anger at any hint of anthropocentrism. It had an entirely apposite question.

'Why associate the ecliptic with the apocalyptic?' it asked concisely. 'Are humans aware that the arbitrary link between the alignment of objects in a solar system, and cultural events relevant to one of millions of species on a planetary ball is, of course, yet again, explained by your extreme anthropocentrism?'

'Yes,' replied our guide happily. 'As you are here to learn about humanity, that includes the illogical and the superstitious. We can now explain eclipses with science, but before this was possible, they held great cultural significance. Listen, I have a special recording for you.'

The guide brought out her smartphone and, using the voice facility, played back the booming, deep voice of a man who sounded like Brian Blessed. I could think of no more spectacular location on Ocean than Easter Island to hear a passage from Shakespeare recorded specially for the alien. Our guide had prepared well for her time with the alien. As we looked skyward, we watched the incremental coverage of the Sun by the Moon. Darkness progressively cloaked the three of us at the picnic bench. The epic, melodramatic, spooky passage was from *Hamlet*:

> *In the most high and palmy state of Rome,*
> *A little ere the mightiest Julius fell,*
> *The graves stood tenantless and the sheeted dead*
> *Did squeak and gibber in the Roman streets...*
> *And prologue to the omen coming on,*
> *Have heaven and earth together demonstrated*
> *Unto our climatures and countrymen...*
> *As stars with trains of fire and dews of blood,*
> *Disasters in the sun, and the moist star*
> *Upon whose influence Neptune's empire stands*
> *Was sick almost to doomsday with eclipse.*
>
> Horatio in *Hamlet* by William Shakespeare: Act 1, Scene 1

The 'Diamond Ring' effect appeared as we looked to the dark sky. It was the moment when the last sign of light from the Sun shone through a valley on the Moon just before totality, producing a single jewel of light set in a narrow ring of sunlight. When we watched that last glow of light fade, it was because we were watching the movement of Ocean.

Totality was the moment when the partial eclipse turned total, as the Moon completely blocked out the Sun. The difference between the partial phase of the eclipse and the total eclipse shocked the alien. It has been described as like the difference between a friendly kiss, and a night of passion. It was as if a dimmer switch had jumped from being 'ON' and simply a little darker than normal, to being completely 'OFF'. It was so completely pitch black that we even had to stop eating our sandwiches.

> *It gets darker, very gradually darker for an hour or so. And then*
> *right at totality it gets, all of a sudden, ten thousand times or*
> *more darker.*
>
> Professor Jay Pasachoff, International Eclipse Committee, in 1999

I explained that there was also a total solar eclipse back in 1999 that was visible from much of Europe. In the run up to that eclipse it was feared to coincide with the end of the world, as predicted by Nostradamus (who was, I clarified for the alien, not the most reliable of forecasters). On that occasion, however, many of the world's eclipse scientists were able to express its beauty without reference to the supernatural.

> **By sheer luck, nothing more, they appear the same size in
> the sky.**
> Sir Patrick Moore, Astronomer, in 1999

Our guide was in her element. Sitting across the wooden picnic bench from us, she was watching a solar eclipse with a being from another world. It seemed to be the highlight of her life.

'The global has met the global, but is producing a distinctly local zone of totality. If you look out to sea, you can see a line of shadow, where the eclipse goes back to being partial,' explained the guide importantly.

> **An eclipse gives you a smaller kind of you… and it gives you a
> unique feeling that you are part of this incredible expanse
> of nature.**
> Fred Espenak, Head of Eclipses at NASA, in 1999

Nature around us seemed confused. Birds were tweeting more than a millennial smartphone addict. It was as if all wildlife on the island was trying to articulate that dusk seemed much earlier than expected. A sheep, for example, bleated. The humble noises contrasted with the inter-global sense of occasion. It was giving all three of us a different perspective, a reminder that ultimately we are all beings that have evolved on variously sized balls that float about in the cosmos. Occasionally, one rocky ball gets in the way of light beams emitted by another ball, which happens to be a burning gaseous ball, on their way to another rocky ball.

After two minutes of totality, light returned to the island, and the alien vaporised another sandwich, then absorbed it through its skin. I could tell the alien was not particularly impressed with the eclipse that had seemed so significant to its human companions. Referring to the quote from *Hamlet*, the alien mentioned placidly to the anthropocentrists at the picnic bench that no civilisation had collapsed during this eclipse, as far as it was aware.

In our post-eclipse deconstruction at the bench, I introduced a more metaphorical and philosophical dimension to our discussion. In contrast to the sparsely populated Easter Island, I referred to the total eclipse of the Sun on 11 August 1999 that was visible in far more populated areas across Europe. Back then, as the Moon was drawn ever nearer in the sky to the Sun, so the cultural interest was drawn out of its latency and brought into focus. The cultural interest could be said to have accelerated almost to the point of 'totality' in the sense of complete cross-cultural interest. Even individuals who showed no interest in going outside or looking outside to observe the partial phases, perhaps because they were unable to take two full hours off work, still came out of their workplaces for totality. People were particularly struck by the very rare feeling that everyone who was outside was interested in the same thing, with no exceptions. There was a feeling that the eclipse was bringing people together in the context of realising that humans all share one planet that moves through the cosmos. The eclipse had become an occasion for environmentalism.

Can we therefore speak of a moment of 'cultural totality'? Part of Cornwall in south-west England was in the zone of totality of the eclipse in 1999. A local radio station, Pirate FM, reflected a 'totalitarian' sentiment by trying to find a person in Cornwall who claimed to be not particularly interested in the eclipse. It was as if the radio station had observed the accelerating cultural interest, and extrapolated to believe that cultural totality would be reached, whereby nobody would be completely uninterested in the eclipse. Having found Zoe, a young woman who claimed to be particularly uninterested in the eclipse, Pirate FM challenged her to remain shut in the specially created Pirate FM shed during the eclipse, with the incentive of a two-week holiday to Mombasa, Kenya. She was informed prior to accepting the challenge that the shed had no windows, and that during the entire two and a half-hour process of partial and total eclipse she would be forced to listen to Des O'Connor songs, and watch old episodes of the comprehensively mocked television soap opera *Eldorado*.

> **We've all heard people moaning about the eclipse. They're bored with it. But would you honestly miss the eclipse for a holiday to Mombasa?**
> Phil Angel on *Pirate FM*, 6 August 1999

For the two or three days prior to the eclipse in 1999, this challenge was highly publicised on local radio and was a key component in the landscape of anticipation. It generated many discussions among Cornish residents as to whether they themselves thought they would leave the shed. The shed became a metaphor for enthusiasm for the eclipse. On eclipse day Zoe resisted the temptation to leave the shed, demonstrating that even when considering an extremely rare total solar eclipse, an event that will not occur in the UK again until the year 2090, any idea of 'cultural totality', a grand theory of cross-cultural interest in an event, is likely to fail.

In 2019, as in 1999, we were within what has been described as the post-modern era: an era that recognises that events such as an eclipse mean different things to different people. As the authors Cook and Crang put it in their book, *Doing Ethnographies*, societies are always messier than our theories of them. In the erroneous presumption that nobody could bear to remain inside during the eclipse, Pirate FM's shed represents a failed, forever doomed attempt at cultural meta-narrative. The post-modern notion of 'deconstruction' is a warning against human presumption. There will always be someone in the shed. For deconstructionists such as Algerian-French philosopher Jacques Derrida, meaning can never be present in its totality at any one point.

'So I believe that we should both intellectually and physically deconstruct the shed in order to expose the person inside,' I concluded.

The alien had been telepathically quiet whilst I had been explaining the metaphorical shed deconstruction. It seemed thoughtful. More interested in the shed than the eclipse itself, I would say. For the alien it was perhaps a variation on its running theme of anti-anthropocentrism. Basically, it's usually difficult, unwise or impossible for humans to generalise in totality: there will always be exceptions to our rules.

It was important for the alien to note that the necessity to make generalisations and summaries in order to progress communication, does undermine the numerous and significant exceptions to the rules. The shed, forever occupied with at least one individual, represents exceptions. So the alien chose to agree with what the shed represents; but in its own, inimitable style.

'If we ever lose each other again during this world tour, like we did at Beijing airport, you will always find me in your metaphorical, exceptional shed,' said the alien. Smarty pants.

It was mid-afternoon, but as the light had returned, it felt like morning again. We walked and talked, coming across different stone faces embedded into the landscape in various ways. Some were sticking out of the mud, half exposed as part of an on-going archaeological dig. Others stood proudly in lines on their Ahu. The guide returned to the alien's key question about why the civilisation on Easter Island had disappeared. She was aware she had not yet answered it.

'Researchers initially believed the population of Easter Island was once much higher than the 3,000 recorded by Roggeveen in 1722. This prompted questions about why the population collapsed. At first, the leading theory was an ecocide prior to the arrival of Roggeveen,' she explained.

I telepathically filled in the alien on the definition of her word 'ecocide'. It was, like *Insectageddon*, a linguistically pleasing conflation, this time of the words 'ecological' and 'suicide'. Their child, *Ecocide*, refers to the self-harm of humanity via the environment.

> ***What I'm seeking for is to have ecocide recognised as an international law. And that's to criminalise mass damage and destruction.***
>
> Polly Higgins, Ecocide Law Advocate

'The theory was that the statues were partially responsible for the downfall of the society, as natives had cut down the palm forests in order to move the statues into position, as well as make space for agriculture,' added our guide.

We had been walking uphill for some time, and had finally reached the highest point on the island, known as Maunga Terevake. We stood at the top and enjoyed the 360-degree view of the entirety of Easter Island, surrounded by the Pacific Ocean stretching to the horizon in all directions. The island itself was only 24 kilometres long and 12 kilometres wide, and so from this highest point, it was possible to see the whole island.

'This means the person who cut down the last tree is likely to have been aware they were cutting down the very last tree on the island, and did so anyway. This is why there was the theory of the Rapa Nui committing an act of conscious ecocide,' explained our guide.

'Her positive tone indicates there is a 'but' coming,' said the alien to me privately. It was an increasingly perceptive alien.

'Whilst a valuable concept and cautionary tale for humanity to keep in mind, the evidence for ecocide on Easter Island has since been falsified,' said our guide with a hint of smugness that suggested to me that she had written the paper that falsified it.

Feeling a little bit like tangent expert comedian Ronnie Corbett, I clarified for the alien that one of the criteria for a human to consider a theory scientific is that it is falsifiable, rather than impossible to demonstrate it is incorrect. This position was first advocated by the 20th-century philosopher of science Sir Karl Popper.

'New evidence,' continued our guide, prompting me to suspect immediately that she was referring to her own, 'shows that Easter Island inhabitants were skilled agricultural engineers, fertilising their fields with volcanic rock. Objects that were initially assumed to be arrow heads used in the battles over declining resources have been re-analysed, and concluded to be tools for cultivating the land.'

From her bag emerged a small agricultural implement. She gave it to the alien and indicated it was a souvenir for the alien to keep. A symbolic reminder, she added, of the misinterpretation of Easter Island. The alien placed the tool carefully in its solar-powered backpack, next to a toy camel, a bow tie, a coconut, a boomerang, a phone number and a watch.

'Furthermore, whilst the population had fluctuated over the years, it started to decline terminally only after contact with Europeans in the 18th century that brought new diseases, and then finally the Peruvian slave raids of the 1860s.'

Our guide brought out her smartphone again, this time to show us graphs demonstrating that, after European contact, the progressive decline in the human population of Easter Island was mirrored by the progressive collapse of the statues. The cause, she speculated, was perhaps a deliberate toppling of the statues as they were perceived to become ineffective in looking after the islanders.

'Or perhaps it was the other way around,' suggested the alien. 'Perhaps the statues represented particular, important individuals in the community, and when they died, the community toppled the statue to indicate they had died.'

The guide was thoughtful at the alien's suggestion. She made a note on her smartphone, and thanked the alien for this potentially important contribution.

'A new perspective. I will investigate. Thank you.'

As we walked from one end of an Ahu of statues to the other, she explained that in 1722 Jacob Roggeveen recorded around 3,000 Rapa Nui people, and that all the Moai were standing upright. Jacob's arrival is recorded to have involved a fight, the death of around 12 native people, and the wounding of many others. His records described the Rapa Nui people as healthy and robust. Then 48 years later, in 1770, another explorer, Gonzalez de Ahedo, recorded that the population had declined to around 2,000 Rapa Nui people, although no Moai were had fallen at this stage.

As we reached the end of the line of statues, her voice and her enthusiasm dropped. She seemed personally affected by the story she was telling. It was her life's work, after all, I assumed.

'Just four years later, in 1774, James Cook recorded a population of merely 1,000 Rapa Nui people. He recorded that some of the statues had been toppled, and human skeletons littered the landscape. Then over the years other records showed fewer and fewer standing statues, in direct correlation with the decreasing population. By 1877 the human population was just 111 on Easter Island. The people were described as riddled with disease, and none of the statues remained upright.'

The alien telepathically coughed. We were standing next to a line of standing statues. I put this to our guide, confident in her ability to answer any question about what was possibly an unhealthy academic obsession.

'All Moai monoliths that you see standing here on the island today were stood back up by archaeologists since 1950. And all Rapa Nui people on the island today are the descendants of those 111 people. Which leads us to the next thing to understand. The latest archaeological evidence shows the human population here was never much higher than the 3,000 recorded by Roggeveen, and that the soils were never particularly fertile.'

Extinction is the rule. Survival is the exception.

Carl Sagan, Astrobiologist and Science Communicator

'This means, to answer the alien's question, that we have started to accept that we need to rewrite the story of Easter Island. We need to change it, from one of a rich environment that was destroyed by ecocide, to a success story of islanders thriving here for 500 years, and then destroyed not by ecocide, but by contact with Europeans and Peruvians.'

'I recognise this concept,' said the alien in my skull. 'Relative civilisation duration. She is saying the Rapa Nui actually survived a very long time, not a short time. Interesting.' I translated this for our telepathically challenged guide.

147

'Spot on, Alien. The skilled Rapa Nui people persisted for 500 years on an isolated island with limited resources. Everything is relative, as Einstein would have said. So, comparing like for like, we looked at the evidence and records from other, nearby islands: none of their civilisations survived anything like as long as 500 years.'

Mind blown, it was time to return to our small hotel for the evening, and mop up my proverbially blown mind with a massive sleep.

A L I E N   F I L M   N I G H T

E.T. The Extra-Terrestrial
(1982)

E.T. is widely considered one of the greatest films ever made by humans, and this cultural significance was encouraging for the alien. It portrayed humanity as a species that is capable of being positive about the concept of a benign alien visitor, albeit a fictional one

The plot elaborates on the idea that, even if unintentionally, any interaction between life forms can lead to problems such as disease, illness, misunderstanding, violence and fear, and that such interactions need to be managed carefully.

E.T. also invites us to humanise and respect the 'other', and to recognise they have feelings and concerns of their own. The positive portrayals of E.T.'s abilities, such as building a psychic connection with the character Elliott, telekinesis and the revival of the chrysanthemum, reminded the alien that humans are capable of positive interaction with other intelligent species. However, the film also highlights that this may not come naturally to all humans.

The following morning the alien and I had just finished breakfast, and emerged from the hotel to find our impressively keen guide waiting outside. She had a rental car ready for us, and we jumped in. We were travelling to a remote corner of the island where archaeologists were exploring exactly how the statues were carved, before they were moved.

'The story of Easter Island is one to replicate, not avoid,' she said whilst driving accurately. Her face was beaming with professional pride. I had been mulling on this overnight, and the alien seemed keen to hear more as well. She referred to the research of her colleague, archaeologist Dr Carl Lipo from California State University.

'The first thing to replicate is their co-operation. On an isolated island, such as our planet as a whole, it is important that we co-operate with each other in the way that the Rapa Nui people did. The shared goal of building and moving the statues was probably a factor in uniting and stabilising the community. Perhaps humanity needs to find a shared goal again, such as clearly uniting around solutions to climate change and the loss of our biodiversity.'

We arrived at the site, got out of the rental car, and walked to an archaeologically intended hole in the ground. A giant head was sticking out. It had an elongated nose, a defined chin, rectangular ears, deepened eye sockets, and heavy brows. It had been carved from compressed volcanic ash called tuff.

'The second lesson to learn from the Rapa Nui,' our guide continued, 'is that we should maintain diversity. This means not only our biodiversity, but also a diversity of approaches. We can apply this to mean focussing not only on one environmental challenge and solution, but also on many at the same time. Other colonised islands also had statue construction, but on Rapa Nui it became very important to the society. They were unlikely to know in advance that this particular aspect of their culture would be the factor that helped their stability and success, relative to other islanders. Similarly, it is currently unclear to modern society which of our many environmental solutions may become the one to scale up in future: is it solar, or is it nuclear fusion, for example? So it is important to encourage diversity of many solutions simultaneously, until we really know for sure which solution to throw all our effort into. For the Rapa Nui, it was statues. And maybe they were not even consciously aware of that.'

I felt there was some sort of metaphor for humanity in front of us: the statue was incomplete. It had been abandoned during the process of carving.

'A metaphor,' suggested the alien, 'for the incomplete human history. You are still carving your story.'

'Exactly,' said our guide, after I had translated the telepathic exchange. 'And thirdly, it's important to allow the environment to regenerate. The Rapa Nui succeeded for 500 years in managing their soils so that they were able to cultivate enough food, whilst not over fishing their surrounding seas. They were excellent at preventing ecocide, not causing it. Perhaps spreading diseases and slave raids, although tragic and barbaric, are easier to prevent than ecocide in future. Or it is perhaps direct human conflict, not ecocide, that is humanity's biggest danger.'

'Thank you, that has answered my question,' said the alien.

And with that, it was clear to the alien that the isolation of Easter Island in the Pacific Ocean was a microcosm of the isolation of our planet in our particular corner of the multiverse. Until the alien's arrival, humanity was isolated from other life forms on other planets.

The microcosm function of Easter Island also worked on more specific examples, such as the loss of biodiversity on Ocean. After habitat destruction and fragmentation, invasive species is the second highest reason for biodiversity loss around the world. Similarly, Easter Island has taught us that the unintentional introduction of diseases from Europe to the Rapa Nui was an even more significant cause for their decline than their own mismanagement of their environment.

'So why am I so happy to learn through my research that the Rapa Nui died out not because of ecocide? Well, it's because the message is positive. It means that Easter Island teaches us that success in preventing ecocide is possible. So there is real reason to hope that our species can do the same,' concluded our guide uninterrupted, now that the alien had finally got the hang of when humans ask rhetorical questions.

CHAPTER 9
Challenger Deep, Pacific Ocean

 ALIEN PLAYLIST

Something in the Way
by Nirvana

I played this song for the alien during our voyage in a solar-powered boat across the Pacific Ocean. The lyrics challenged the way in which humans treat animals on Ocean.

The writer of the song, Kurt Cobain, ended his own life in 1994. I used his life story for the alien, like Easter Island, as a microcosm for humanity. Kurt was on a path to suicide when writing this song. Something is in the way of rapid and comprehensive implementation of the environmental solutions that humans already have available.

A shiver went down my spine. It was not due to the air of the Pacific Ocean surrounding our solar-powered boat. We were voyaging from Easter Island towards the Mariana Trench, from which we were to descend into the Challenger Deep. The air was still and warm, as we were close to the equator. The shiver was from the sight of the alien looking at the construction of a new oil-rig in the ocean. The rig protruded from the water like a cigarette from the mouth of a smoker, as if the personified planet itself had been forced by humans to take up smoking. I thought back to our conversation on the plane to Easter Island about the conceptual, suicidal similarities between smoking and climate change.

The alien did not need to say anything telepathically for me to understand what it was thinking. In fact, I noticed the alien had been silent for a relatively long time. For some reason, it had decided to disconnect telepathically. Perhaps that was the alien's version of chill-out mode, a bit like when one is on a long car journey, and all is fine with your travel companion; you simply want to be with your own thoughts for a while. Or perhaps listen to embarrassing music through headphones, without letting anyone know.

The alien's telepathic silence had not been accompanied by the silly plopping noise I heard when it disconnected at the end of our time in Los Angeles. I was intrigued to see the alien's blank expression again, without the chitter chatter of words. It was like holding up a mirror to humanity – not only metaphorically, but literally: the alien's jet-black eyes occasionally had a slight shine to them, and in that shine I could see the reflection of the towering oil-rig stretching to the stratosphere. What does this say about humanity? After all the alien has learned, after all it has seen and heard about climate change and its threat to the survival of our species, it was looking at an oil-rig in the ocean. This was not one that had been around a few decades, perhaps put up in the height of the 1980s when the television show *Dallas* was in its prime, and the characters JR Ewing, and even 'good boy' character Bobby Ewing's portrayal of the oil industry at the time making little if any reference to climate change. This was 2019. Millions of children had been marching through the streets of the world demanding instant action on climate change, as we saw in Geneva. The group Extinction Rebellion had been protesting across the globe. And yet here was a new oil-rig being constructed. A new one. And a few hours later our solar-powered boat passed another new oil-rig. And then another new one.

From a side angle I looked at the alien's impassive countenance. We had not communicated for hours. It was freaking me out. I missed our usual intergalactic chin-wagging. Something was wrong. Something was in the way of the usual, often comical jibber-jabber between me and the alien. The last time it was this silent was immediately after the gun store experiment in Los Angeles. Perhaps a pattern was emerging: when the alien was severely concerned about humanity, it disconnected. Only last time, it had forewarned me it was going to do so, and even clarified it was in my, perhaps meaning humanity's, best interests to not know what it was thinking. Its lack of precursory remark this time was altogether more sinister. And it was something to do with the new oil-rigs. Previously I had assumed the disconnection meant the alien thought there was at least some hope for humanity. That the alien wanted to disengage subtly this time was unnerving. It implied only one thing.

'Humans are a temporary species,' I said, intentionally unclear if that was a statement or a question for the alien. Either way, I hoped for a response, but was disappointed.

The alien and I were standing at the front of the solar boat, with the elderly, bearded, boss-eyed captain in the cabin behind us, cosily at the wheel. The captain had been brought in especially from Cornwall in south-west England, renowned for its fishing industry. He was the only one available who knew how this latest solar boat worked. His thick, gruff, Cornish accent gave you the sense that he had seen it all before, and if he hadn't, well then it couldn't be that important. He showed no sign of being star struck by the alien, but had, apparently, "eard of 'im'. My correction, that the alien was in fact gender neutral, was met with a noise of confusion that seemed splendidly consistent with the captain's permanently crossed eyes.

With a clunk, the captain turned the quiet whirr of the electric engine into the silence of unpowered drifting. The alien maintained its gaze up at the lofty cranes and busy construction workers. Our boat was floating quietly past an oil-rig, this time particularly closely. The alien seemed transfixed by the human activity. The workers bustled about their business, unconcerned by their contribution to climate change, it seemed. Each individual worker, of course, was doing what they thought in the short term was in their personal, best interests. Perhaps they had a family to feed. But I wondered if in the medium term, they connected their short-term actions with the increasing likelihood that their own children might eventually drown as a result of the rise in sea levels caused in part by the very object of their own professions.

A couple of construction workers cheerfully waved at the alien, which did not respond. It was the first time, perhaps with the exception of stealing the sunglasses in Los Angeles, that I had seen the alien not conduct itself towards humans with respect and consideration, with politeness and courtesy. I waved back on the alien's behalf. Then, feeling it was impolite to stare at them, I stood on the other side of the front of the boat, and looked out at the horizon.

I had been silently hoping for a response from the alien for some time. Eventually I accepted it was not going to happen, and looked back around at the alien. It was looking directly at me, holding a gun to its own head.

My first thought, perhaps insensitively, was to wonder how the alien had got the gun past the multiple customs and security checks we had gone through since Los Angeles. I guessed the alien had some sort of cloaking skill, similar to that invisible cape in *Harry Potter*. In the alien's case, it had already shown an ability for telekinesis, so it seemed reasonable to believe it could also sneak stuff past low-tech human metal detectors.

Instinctively I leaped at the alien to grab the gun, but it shifted out of the way. The alien maintained the gun's place at the position that, on a human, would be the temple. We stood in silence looking at each other. From our 100-metre race in Beijing, and the alien's multiple, otherworldly, acrobatic abilities demonstrated in Queensland, such as its victory in the sheep-shearing contest and our surfing headstands, I knew that there was no point in my entering into a competition – I had to talk it down.

The alien offered me the opportunity to do so. A childish whizzing noise entered my head, and our telepathic connection was restored.

'Is this because nobody is going to carry your bags for you, when we get to the Challenger Deep?' I asked, trying to keep it light.

'When is the agreed end date of humanity?' asked the alien.

I didn't know how to answer. Worryingly, I understood exactly why the alien had assumed we humans might have agreed on a date to end our species: we are acting as if we have set an end date, and don't need to think beyond it. And that end date is in the very near future.

'I am trying to fit in with humans.'

'Come again?'

'A significant proportion of humans are suicidal. We have talked about Kurt Cobain as a named example. We have talked about smokers as a larger section of the human population. And here, as we pass the construction of new oil-rigs, I see the institutional and governmentally sponsored support of collective, mass human suicide. I understand that not every human is suicidal, of course, such as Arnie, Obama and Greta. There are always exceptions to the rules.'

On the plane to Easter Island I had worried about communicating with the alien about smoking for this very reason. The alien occasionally showed signs of being impressionable, or at least remaining teachable. So the last thing I wanted to do was let the alien understand that conscious beings, aware of the dangers, still make the repeated decision to smoke cigarettes. That concern was not even about the impact of smoking on climate change and plastic pollution. It was even more immediate than that. The concern was the immediate self-harm of the carcinogenic habit. Maybe in the 1920s when the cause and effect relationship link between smoking and cancer was not understood, one would interpret their actions very differently. But this was 2019.

Smoking and oil-rigs combined had, for the alien, painted a picture of humanity at war with itself. Not just collectively in terms of climate change, but at the level of individual self-harm as well. And it is supposed to be at the level of individual action that one would expect self-interested humans to do what's in their own interests, at least in the short term. In the medium term smoking is one of the most effective ways known to humanity to bring cancer upon themselves.

'On our planet we understand the concept of self-interest. But we exercise it in a way that helps ourselves and others at the same time.'

'So like when we gave money to the homeless person in Cairo. It was not just to help them, but to also feel good about ourselves. Smug, even,' I recalled.

'Yes,' agreed the alien. 'That is where smoking and climate change are going so wrong for you. One human smoking does not help another human. One human voting for a climate inactive government does not help any other human. These actions do not even help the individuals committing them. Sometimes, it doesn't even make them feel good in the short term, because subconsciously they are aware it is attempted suicide.'

'I agree, old chum. Smoking is not like attempted suicide. It is attempted suicide. Just slower. Medium term. It's a bit slower than a bullet to the head, but to someone like yourself with perhaps another perspective of time, I can see there is not much difference. The end result is likely to be identical to shooting oneself in the head. So how can we change? We are so bad at change.'

'Pride is a big problem in human psychology. Try saying something like: it's such a good idea to change, I'm embarrassed I didn't think of it myself, or sooner.'

It was an interesting suggestion from the alien: a phrase we could use as humans, perhaps, to help unlock our currently blocked potential for change. The phrase acknowledges both our pride and our humility. It transitions us from unhelpful pride to helpful integrity. It helps to overcome our embarrassment at our previous thinking, and yet at the same time, it bridges the gap to new thinking. It wasn't immediately obvious that this was a phrase from another world, but it was, in a very literal sense. It wasn't a phrase that I'd heard any politician on Ocean say in the past, but I hoped I would in the future. What did it mean for humanity that this potentially useful nugget of wisdom came from the alien only when it had been driven to the point of putting a gun to its head? Sometimes the greatest clarity comes when we are at rock bottom. In this case, it came when the alien was at rock bottom psychologically. Physically, we were both floating above rock bottom: the deepest part of the oceans on Ocean.

'Thank you. Mind if I quickly make a note of that phrase on the tablet?'

'Please do,' said the alien, gun still at its temple.

After an awkward few moments of note making, I nodded to the alien that we could resume.

'Where were we? Oh yes. Suicide,' I segued like a ninja.

'Our species does not share this suicidal drive. I am interested to learn what that feels like,' said the alien, maintaining a steady aim at what, on a human, would be its cerebrum.

I had been concerned about, but not fully prepared for, our conversation taking this turn. I understood its point. After everything it had seen of humanity thus far, self-harm was a reasonable conclusion, a recurring, common theme to draw from the data. There were of course, like the shed, exceptions. But exceptions do not mean there are no general rules from which to deviate.

'Part of your learning about our species, then?'

'Yes.'

'Gotcha.' I turned away calmly. I did my best to clear my head, so the alien would not hear my tactical thoughts about engaging it in conversation as a way to talk it down. I wanted to prevent the alien from covering the bow of the captain's solar-powered boat with a delicate furnishing of cranial fluid.

The captain was never the most jovial at the best of times, but at this point, through the glass of the cabin, his concerned gaze caught my eye through his bearded face and straggly white hair. He had seen a lot in his time, I thought, but probably not an alien suicide on the bow of his boat. I could tell that even he was alarmed. I gave him a reassuring nod and casual gesture to engage the electric engine again and drive the boat as normal, in a manner that reminded me of David Brent in the TV programme *The Office*. The calm gesture belied my inner panic.

'You do realise,' I continued, not looking at the alien, 'that for humans, suicide is irreversible, by definition. We do ethnographic studies of other cultures here on Ocean as well, but joining in on a spot of suicide would be taking it a little far. I know you can grow limbs back, but if I remember correctly from our chat at 35,000 feet above sea level on the way to Easter Island, shooting yourself in the head would be a tad more inconvenient. Can you grow that back as well?'

'I don't know. None of my species has ever tried. Not really our thing.'

The guilt I felt was enormous. Here was a being from another world, evolved presumably over billions of years, and it had never come across the terrible act of suicide, nor even heard any information about the consequences of a violent trauma to the head. And yet, give it a few weeks here on our planet, and this pliable, presumably young, alien had been dragged down to our level so horrendously that it was now thinking that suicide was normal and interesting. What low standards we have.

'How old are you, by the way? I keep meaning to ask.'

'Thank you for asking. I can reveal that I am, in the years understood on your planet, 999,999,999 years old. Tomorrow is my birthday.'

'Blimey! So your one billionth birthday is tomorrow?'

'Yes.'

'Happy birthday.'

'Thank you,' said the alien. There was something disturbing about it being so polite, whilst holding a gun to its own head.

'Well, look, stick around for that, old chap. We can celebrate your birthday tomorrow, at the bottom of the sea. Wait a minute, so you knew you'd be on Ocean for your birthday?'

'Yes. This journey to Ocean is a present for my one billionth birthday from my parents. One of the reasons we selected your planet instead of others is the nice round number. On other planets, for example, I'm already over a billion, and on some others, I'm under a million years old, in their years.'

'How old are your parents?'

'I could answer that, but it would take about eight full Ocean minutes to say the number.'

'So the reason you're visiting us is a birthday present. But I've been getting the feeling you want to help us, as well. Can't really do that if you pull that trigger now, can you?'

'Hmm,' said the alien. It was one of the few times during our world tour that I felt I had really got through to the alien – and one of the few times that I had sensed it was indecisive, and unsure of itself.

Feeling that was as far as I could go with that line of persuasion, I was both encouraged by a sense of progress, yet disappointed that ultimately the gun had not been lowered. I changed tack, and paced around the bow of the boat for a few moments, hands behind back, trying to devise a plan, whilst trying to prevent the alien from understanding my thoughts. I realised the latter was pointless, but also, perhaps it was very anthropocentric of me to assume it would be a bad thing for the alien to understand that I really, really didn't want it to kill itself. Perhaps the genuineness of my aim to keep it alive, and my cranial hunt for a method to do so, was exactly what the alien needed to hear.

Perhaps I could lighten the tone again, as a method to remind the alien of the joys of staying alive. I thought of the television series *Blackadder Goes Forth*, and the importance of the character George, played by Hugh Laurie. I tried to emulate his approach to bringing some morale to the trenches. Blind optimism, some would say.

'Understood. Well, look, Alien, my old mucker, my old chum, my old bosom buddy, bestie, my BFF you. It's been jolly fun travelling around with you so far. Would be an awful shame to stop it here with your neurons hanging off the boat. And think of that poor old captain. It'd break his back clearing up the bow of this boat here, what with all your cerebral matter splattered everywhere.'

The alien and I both turned our heads to look at the boss-eyed captain, who couldn't hear a word of our telepathic conversation. He gave us an angry shrug as if to say: 'What are you looking at?' The alien turned back to face me, gun steady as a rock, pressed firmly into its green head skin – its magnificent green skin, capable of breathing under water, capable of absorbing sandwiches. It would have been such a waste to lose this amazing life form.

'I mean, think of all the weird and wonderful species you'll be missing out on if you blow your brains out now, before you get a chance to see the Challenger Deep. A lot of us silly humans might be suicidal, but those underwater species aren't. Get to know them a bit. We'll give you an hour to swim around by yourself, get away from humanity for a while. It'll be good for your mental health. Literally. In fact, my old alien comrade, m'colleague, if you will, if you don't mind me saying, I'd be awfully sad to see your head scattered across the bow of this boat. I'm enjoying our time together. Don't leave me now! At least get to the end of our world tour!' I meant it. The alien knew it.

The alien's shoulders were juddering. It was crying. It lowered the gun. Then the alien placed the gun back into its solar-panel-covered rucksack of souvenirs, amongst the toy camel, the bow tie, the coconut, the boomerang, the phone number, the watch and the agricultural tool.

'We still cry despite having lost our lungs over millions of years of evolution. And despite having a more distributed breathing system,' explained the alien matter-of-factly. 'No tear ducts, anymore, but emotions remain useful on occasions such as this,' it concluded with a precision I was not particularly expecting.

'You kept the gun from Los Angeles?' I asked, giving the alien a quick hug, in full knowledge that such a gesture may be utterly meaningless from its point of view.

'Important souvenir to show my species,' the alien nodded, reciprocating the hug.

We released our hug in the same way that two rugby player bloke friends might do awkwardly after a heart to heart chat. Not that this alien was male.

The immediate danger of the alien suicide was temporarily over, but it was not resolved. I didn't want to change subject prematurely without closure, only to find later a green ooze covering the bow of the boat the minute my back was turned again. Or possibly the contents of its head would be another colour, or translucent, perhaps. I didn't think it would be polite to ask.

'More positive messages are still to come at the last two places of our world tour. Chin up, alien. If we're going to die eventually anyway, we might as well enjoy a bit more exploration first. A bit more adventure. And besides, the point of going to the Challenger Deep is that there are no other humans around to distort your overview of life on Ocean.'

'It would be a pleasure to escape anthropocentrism for a while,' agreed the alien.

'We've been swimming through a metaphorical sea of human self-importance. It's time to hang around with a few non-human species that are not suicidal,' I concluded.

Perking up only slightly at the idea of avoiding death, the alien turned to its bag, withdrew a sandwich it had kept from our picnic bench at Easter Island, and nonchalantly absorbed it. I wondered if it was really aware of the gravity of what had just happened. Telepathically, I was swiftly reassured that it was.

'All right, my handsomes! We're here now we are. Here we be,' said our Cornish captain in an almost deliberately incoherent arrival message. It contrasted with the clear, crisp announcements that the alien had become accustomed to from the tannoyed flight attendants immediately before the touchdowns at most of the other places in our world tour so far.

There was no land in sight, but a bleeping radar in the captain's cabin asserted that we were directly above the Mariana Trench, within which was the Challenger Deep – at 10,994 metres it is the deepest part of all oceans on Ocean. We were floating south of Japan and east of the Philippines, within the ocean territory of the Federated States of Micronesia. The closest land was Fais Island, part of Micronesia, 287 kilometres to the south-west. The next closest was the US territory of Guam, 304 kilometres to the north-east.

Waiting for us at the back of the boat was our submersible vessel. It was drenched, not yet in water, but in the latest, state-of-the-art technology. The captain's ragged clothing, straggly hair and unkempt beard reminded me not to judge someone's technical knowledge on the basis of their appearance. He was in charge of operating the vessel from the surface, and we had to trust him. The alien reminded me that the submersible was more for my benefit than its own.

The captain clumsily operated a series of levers. Eventually, through law of averages I worried, he moved a lever that lifted the submersible vessel. After the conclusion to what I believed was his internal game of 'eeny, meeny, miny, mo', the captain prodded a button that moved the vessel to the edge of the boat and held it above the lapping Pacific Ocean. He nodded with poorly hidden uncertainty, as if to pretend that everything thus far was intentional.

Before we entered the submersible vessel, a breeze snatched from the alien's four-fingered hand the plastic bag it had been using to carry its sandwich. If the plastic bag was empty, it might have simply floated on the surface. But within the alien's rucksack it seemed to have been mixed up with various other items, and now contained the agricultural tool from Easter Island. The bag began to sink. It was descending through the largest water column on Ocean. The alien's sense of fun then returned.

'Let's race it,' suggested the alien.

The alien had enjoyed our 100-metre race in Beijing, and decided this was another opportunity to compete. It was a simple reminder of how the alien was helping me to think differently. Of course, why should races usually take place on some sort of horizontal plane? Why not vertical? Alien vs plastic bag. Small joys. Good job the alien didn't kill itself a few minutes ago; we were having fun again already.

Our submersible vessel was a slightly updated version of the one that film director James Cameron had used to reach the Challenger Deep in March 2012. I noticed that its shape was not too dissimilar to the cigar-shaped Oumuamua that whizzed through the solar system in 2017, and was thought possibly to be an alien spacecraft.

And so we jumped inside the vessel, closed the various, wheeled doors, and our descent to the Challenger Deep commenced. The craft bobbed on the surface for a while, as the captain established radio contact with us from his boat, which was due to stay, sensibly, on the surface.

'Proper job, my 'ansomes. All them dials working all right then? Are they be?'

'I believe so,' I communicated nervously.

'Goin' down dreckly then.'

After a few minutes of reassuring bleeping noises to indicate we were maintaining contact with the surface, I explained to the alien the metaphorical nature of our current descent, connecting with our earlier conversation about suicide.

'The feelings you had with that gun to your head were perhaps an example of depression, my alien friend. Perhaps this journey to the depths of the ocean is a metaphor for the depression that humans feel when contemplating our inbuilt tendency towards self-harm.'

'I understand,' said the alien, now clearly more interested in our progress relative to the plastic bag.

The alien was rather cavalier about the need for the vessel. To me, the word waterproof was a bit of an understatement about the benefits of using it. But it seemed that to the alien, agreeing to use it at all was more out of politeness and to keep me company. I needed protection from the crushing pressure, a thousand times more than the atmospheric pressure at sea level. To the alien, such changes in pressure required little more than a nose-holding, blowy equalisation.

The Challenger Deep is an underwater valley, around 11 kilometres long and 1.6 kilometres wide. It is the deepest section within the much larger Mariana Trench, which is around 2,550 kilometres long and 69 kilometres wide. We were without WIFI connection, but I had pre-loaded onto the tablet the Challenger Deep portrayed diagrammatically with Mount Everest, Ocean's highest mountain above sea level at 8,848 metres, placed inside it. Everest was still about two kilometres under water.

I had pre-loaded another diagram, showing that the Challenger Deep is not the part of the sea floor that is closest to the centre of the planet. Ocean is not a perfect sphere, but an oblate spheroid. Isaac Newton was the first to realise this, and the alien recalled the same observation soon before its arrival at the International Space Station.

'Squashed at the poles. It made me laugh when I first saw it,' said the alien, remembering the shape of our silly planet with a charming fondness. I had seen the alien enjoying itself many times during our world tour, but there was something nice about knowing our oblate spheroid planet had made it chuckle even before we met. Ocean is slightly swollen at its equator, and as a result, parts of the Arctic Ocean sea floor are at least 13 kilometres closer to the centre of the planet than the Challenger Deep sea floor.

The alien was surprised to find out how little humans know about the Challenger Deep and Mariana Trench. Indeed, some would say it is the most unexplored region of Ocean, and that humans know more about the surface of Mars. Conversely, the creatures and microorganisms that live in the Mariana Trench have very little or no knowledge that life exists above water, or indeed, that there is an 'above water', as some species live out their life cycles entirely without reaching the surface of the ocean.

A recurring theme of our world tour had been the need for humans to escape their anthropocentrism. It was not surprising that this self-importance would annoy, wind up and taunt no one more than an alien. I drew the alien's attention to the fact that enormous effort was required to design and build a suitable submersible vessel. That engineering effort itself was yet another metaphor for the titanic psychological effort required by humanity to escape its deeply embedded anthropocentrism. Not easy.

Looking out of the window of our vessel, the alien and I observed the progressively different life forms as we descended, further and further away from the anthropocentric surface, and our bearded, radio life-line. Initially we saw whales and dolphins, and I explained that despite outward appearances, these species have surprising similarities to humans. For example, the presence of spindle neurons in the brains of whales is thought to be involved in feeling emotion. The concentration of spindle cells has been measured to be three times higher in cetaceans than in humans, perhaps suggesting that humans are not the most emotional beings on the planet.

As we descended further, the species the alien and I saw became progressively less familiar. They were getting strange, at least compared with the species we had seen on land so far on the world tour. Looking out of the window, the alien struggled to see a telescope octopus, a species of octopus that is almost entirely transparent.

Songs of the Humpback Whale
by Roger Payne

This is the only song that I included in the *Alien Playlist* that was repeated from the Golden Record of the Voyager 1 space probe.

In 1970 a bio-acoustician, Roger Payne, released an album of recordings of songs sung by humpback whales. The sounds on the album are the animals singing. As we descended to the Challenger Deep, in our valiant effort to escape anthropocentrism, what better song to play for the alien than one not written by humans?

The album was in the charts alongside the likes of Led Zeppelin, on its way to becoming the bestselling environmental album in history, at over 100,000 copies. It raised awareness of the intelligence and culture of whales, and is credited with contributing to the 'Save the Whales' movement, which in 1972 led to the United Nations Conference on the Human Environment adopting a 10-year global moratorium on commercial whaling.

Our bullet-shaped vessel plunged further into the darkness, and at 7,000 metres below the surface, the alien saw a dumbo octopus. Despite their evolutionary history having little in common with that of humans, it was still difficult for us to escape human influence, although in this case, simply because of nomenclature. At least its name was amusing, prompted by the title character of Disney's 1941 cartoon film, *Dumbo*.

We arrived in the Mariana Trench, and were in complete darkness. We kept the lights of the vessel turned off, so that the alien could see bioluminescent creatures emitting their own light. A deep sea dragonfish glowed: its prey swam mindlessly towards the light, and therefore, to its doom.

Life at these depths can grow to extraordinary sizes, due to a process known as deep-sea gigantism, also known as abyssal gigantism. This is thought to be a result of the decreasing temperatures, reaching as low as one degree Celsius. I activated the lights on our vessel, and from our window the alien saw a giant amphipod, around 20 times larger than amphipods we had seen earlier, closer to the surface. A giant squid seemed of more interest to the alien, as the largest eye in the world floated past, inspecting us as much as we were inspecting it.

As we quietly propelled ourselves through the Mariana Trench with our headlights beaming out like a surprised tourist crossing Dartmoor in heavy fog, we saw Japanese spider crabs clambering on the sides of the trench, using the largest leg span of any known arthropod. We then saw odd, giant, single-celled organisms called xenophyophores, which demonstrated for the alien just how different life can be at these depths.

'Oh, they look familiar,' said the alien casually.

'Really? They looked like kitchen sponges.'

'If they work like similar creatures on my planet, they extract minerals from their surroundings to form their exoskeletons. None of that horrific killing for protein you get on the land surface of this planet.'

Before our descent the captain had given me what he had unsettlingly described as a crash-course in how to steer the submersible. He was assisting remotely from the surface, acting as an extra pair of eyes as a result of the many cameras covering the vessel. I was generally concentrating on steering us away from impacts with rocks, and more importantly, the walls of the trench itself.

'Look. Look over there,' advised the captain, unclearly. There were many directions in which we could have looked.

'Vents. Vents. Proper hot they are. 'ot, I tell you. 'ot they are. 'ot they be,' he cautioned.

We had arrived at a series of hydrothermal vents. Whilst the surrounding water was nearly freezing, the hydrothermal vents bubbled up water around 370 degrees Celsius as a result of the plate tectonics and subduction of the Pacific Plate. Due to the water pressure at that depth, however, the water wasn't boiling. Minerals were spewing out of the vents, providing food for the deep-sea life to feed and thrive on, despite being in complete darkness. Some believe vents such as these were the places where simple life first evolved on Ocean.

The distraction meant we had lost track of the plastic bag for a worrisome few minutes. Incoherent objections from the surface indicated that it was a pointless task, but I insisted it was important to give our alien visitor the sense of enjoyment it craved from the race, especially given its recent brush with suicide. Our lights spun around searchingly in the darkness. Eventually, we found it again, several metres below us, and therefore winning the race.

As we followed the plastic bag and steadily caught up with it, I explained to the alien the plastics crisis that has been building on Ocean, following the invention of plastic around a hundred years ago.

'So humans invented a material, used it comprehensively, and then had a think about what to do with that material after it had been used?' asked the alien.

The alien had really got the hang of rhetorical questions by this point; a relatively late stage of our world tour. It had now used another one with ease. We both knew it needed no direct response from me. I shifted to an explanation that many forms of plastic do not biodegrade, and if they do break apart, they are often simply reduced to smaller pieces. On the tablet I showed the alien a report by the Ellen MacArthur Foundation and

World Economic Forum in 2016, which estimated that by 2050, in terms of weight, there would be more plastic than fish in the oceans.

The issue of plastic in the oceans is not just an environmental, conservation or animal welfare issue. Whilst fish and seabirds are suffering from mistaking plastic for food, humans are also ingesting plastic by eating fish that accidentally ingest plastic. That means the concentrations of plastic can become even higher for species further up the food chain. This process is known as bioaccumulation, and in 2018 humanity had the first confirmation that micro plastics have entered human bodies, by discovering micro plastics in human stool samples. Poo, once again, as in Beijing, had become relevant.

'Unfortunately this realisation has all happened rather recently, and we don't yet know the health impacts of micro plastics in the human body,' I concluded, once again humiliated at being a member of the human race. The alien looked back at me emptily, unable to provide comfort, but instead, to draw a connection with previous themes.

'So in a sense, the situation is similar to smoking?'

'Oh, in what way?'

'Humans created something that became widespread. And then learned of the health impacts. And then kept using it anyway.'

I found no solace in the alien's ability to draw that connection. But it was not trying to comfort or alleviate. It was simply trying to understand, and to help.

'Floor of the deep. Floor I tell you. There that it be. Right there it are. There. Right there it be. Can you see it, my 'andsomes?'

We were, of course, approaching the floor of the Challenger Deep. I took control of the headlights and shone them directly down.

'Don't disturb that floor, you won't see nothing if you do, I tell you. Dusty it is. Dusty it be. Land on it gently, my 'andsomes. Gently. Right you are. Right you be.'

'Yes, captain,' I interrupted, as was necessary to end the Cornish accent filling the vessel from nearly 11 kilometres above us.

'Sorry, Alien, old chap, but looks like it might be best if we let the plastic bag win. We need to slow down to land.'

The alien folded its arms in what I assumed to be a sulk. I wondered where it had learned such a mannerism, or whether it was also natural to the alien's own species, especially in individuals as young as to be approaching only its billionth birthday. With our lights shining downwards, we watched as the plastic bag fell and settled on the floor of the Challenger Deep, accompanied by a small puff of displaced dust.

I explained that the geological process of sedimentation is on-going, with new layers of rock being formed from whichever material settles on the sea floor. If we left the plastic bag where it settled, it too would eventually become part of the geological layers of the planet's future history.

'Plastic is now becoming a major component in the mixture of sedimentary material. Some have speculated that millions of years from now, plastic may show up in the future geological record as a visible, thin layer of a slightly different colour to the surrounding geological layers. This layer would consist of the different, man-made materials such as plastics falling to the seabed at this period in our planet's history. The current period is being referred to by some humans as the Anthropocene, with the future fossil record expected to show "techno-fossils" such as plastic.'

'I understand,' said the alien grumpily. It was still brooding that the race with the plastic bag had been called off.

As our vessel approached the floor of the Challenger Deep, I ensured we slowed down our descent even more, in order to prevent stirring up the dust from the sea floor and obscuring our vision out of the windows. This mistake was made during the first manned mission to the Challenger Deep in 1960, and was successfully avoided in 2012 when film director James Cameron became the second manned mission to land here. A retired naval officer had plunged to the Challenger Deep earlier in 2019, and found plastic when he got there. The alien and I were therefore the fourth successful landing at the Challenger Deep.

With the lights of our vessel still activated and beaming out into the darkness, the alien and I reflected on our sense of isolation. With no other humans, we were in an environment that was as alien as it gets on Ocean. The alien commented that there were more similarities to its home planet here than on the surface, but refused to elaborate.

The silence, darkness and isolation of the Challenger Deep was an important reminder not really to the alien, but more to us humans, that our planet is not all about us. Most of Ocean, the solar system, the galaxy and the universe is uninhabitable for humans.

'It's now my birthday, to the exact second,' said the alien, breaking our silence.

I was largely unprepared for this scenario, but after learning that the alien's birthday was imminent at the surface, I had asked the captain if he had anything to hand that could work as a gift. He found a party horn from a previous group that had been celebrating a birthday party.

'Happy birthday, my deep-sea alien friend. I know you don't have an operable mouth and all that, so I'll blow this for you.'

The vessel filled with the noise of a party blower that extended, then retracted in a sort of futile yet joyous act that brought considerable mirth to the alien. We agreed it was almost certainly the first time in the planet's history that such a noise had been heard at nearly 11 kilometres below sea level. I presented the party horn to the alien as its birthday present, and we telepathically toasted to the next billion years of its life.

On the floor of the deepest part of the world's oceans, we were not entirely alone. The alien had exceptional vision, far in advance of humans, and reported that it was able to see protists, single-celled organisms that are thought to be the very first life forms on

Finding Nemo
(2003)

With our vessel resting on the sea floor at the Challenger Deep, I showed the alien this film. It built on the theme discussed earlier in our descent, that humans are not the only species on Ocean with feelings.

The format of the film was necessarily animation, as it personified the underwater characters, giving them human traits and emotions. The central characters are two clownfish: Nemo, and his father, Marlin. In the story, humans inadvertently capture Nemo, who ends up in a fish tank in a dentist's office. The plot is about Marlin's journey to rescue Nemo.

Complex human journeys are added to Marlin and Nemo's character arcs, such as Marlin overcoming his tendency to be an overprotective parent, and finding the right balance between being careful and care free. The film portrays the main characters as equally, if not more, human than the humans in the film.

The alien applauded the anti-anthropocentric sentiment of its special, underwater birthday film.

---

the planet. Other life forms, such as those we saw on our way here through the Mariana Trench, occasionally passed our motionless vessel sat on the floor of the Challenger Deep. With so few expeditions having reached this depth before ours, we used the video cameras of the vessel to film and log passing deep-sea life, which, according to the radio shrieking of the captain, appeared to be previously unrecorded species.

The alien was pretty relaxed about the idea of leaving the vessel for a bit of a swim around. On the surface I had agreed to give the alien some alone time down here, so felt I had to honour this promise, and allow the monumentally risky event to take place. The vessel had an airlock device that was designed for this kind of scenario, but had never been tested at this most extreme depth before. The alien left the vessel. Less than a minute later it was back.

'Not staying long, just wanted to retrieve my souvenir from Easter Island. It was in the plastic bag. Oh, and here's the plastic bag. I understand deep-sea littering is a bad idea. Back soon,' said the alien, before disappearing again.

'You've got one hour,' I called after it.

As it swam away into the darkness, I noticed the alien was glowing intermittently. It seemed to be having a bioluminescent chat with the other incandescent species in the darkness. Bioluminescence is used as a form of communication by species here on Ocean. Indeed, some researchers say it could be regarded as the most common form of communication on our planet, as it is ubiquitous throughout the oceans. Scientists have also found that the human body glows tiny quantities of light. So why not on the alien's planet as well, I thought, rhetorically, to myself.

I knew I was going to miss my glowy chum for that hour. After a few minutes, I made use of the time to make radio contact with the captain, and reassure him the airlock was functioning fine at this depth.

'Well, good to hear. Good to 'ear. Made that airlock myself you know. With me bare hands. Me bare hands I tell you.'

'You did a jolly good job, captain.'

The fact that the alien was able to pop in and out of the vessel without being affected by the pressures, and without any protective suit, reminded me of the exceptionally specific requirements that we humans must meet at all times, in order to stay alive. We have evolved in such precise pressures, oxygen levels, temperatures, light levels, and thousands of other factors, all of which must stay within extremely narrow parameters. The alien had clearly evolved to live within a far broader set of parameters, including the extreme water pressures that would crush an unprotected human swimming in the Challenger Deep.

As I sat alone at the bottom of the sea, while the alien was out enjoying itself, I made a note on the tablet to feed back to my United Nations employers this moment and this insight: humans have evolved in such specific circumstances that it makes those parts of Ocean that are hospitable to humans so much more precious to protect. In the intergalactic scheme of things, humans are not particularly adaptable, in comparison with species such as this alien. This makes it essential that humans manage the areas that we can tolerate much more effectively, so that they remain within the same, tiny parameters that we evolved within.

CHAPTER 10
Antarctica

 ALIEN PLAYLIST

Imagine
by John Lennon and Yoko Ono

On our journey to the final place of our world tour, I played this song for the alien. It helped to convey the transformative scale of fundamental, radical changes that many believe humanity needs in order to survive in the long term.

Antarctica is perhaps the best example of a place on Ocean that meets the criteria in the song. No country owns Antarctica, and there is no official religion. There is no permanent population, meaning that scientists who work there keep most of their possessions back in their home nations. It is a peaceful place, and although there is occasionally some form of crime, it is rare and usually minor.

When we caught first sight of Antarctica from our light aircraft, I asked the alien to think of the continent metaphorically. The blank canvas of the ice sheet can represent the future of humanity as a blank sheet of paper, yet to be written on. Antarctica is sometimes referred to as the final frontier on our planet, and therefore a place where humanity perhaps has an opportunity to start again. I suggested to the alien that an alternative future for humanity can be imagined and implemented in the unique circumstances of Antarctica, and that future can be a positive one.

After our return ascent from the Challenger Deep, we travelled by boat to the nearest airport, and then onwards to Antarctica. Within the icy continent our first destination was the Amundsen-Scott South Pole Station. Heading straight to the centre of the land mass meant that the alien had a few hours to look out of the plane window at the white continent beneath us, as blank as the alien's expression itself.

As our plane began its descent, I prepared by padding myself up with multiple layers of clothing. The alien was fine with its multi-purpose skin that had evolved, as it had so clearly reminded me at the Challenger Deep, to be comfortable in a much wider range of environments than my fussy human epidermis.

The pilot was relieved to skid only a little as she brought the aircraft to a halt on the runway at the Amundsen-Scott South Pole Station. Howling winds greeted us as the plane's door opened. We walked down the steps of the plane, and the alien paused at the bottom, wondering if anyone would emerge to carry its bags. It read the situation well, and realised that this place was not heavily populated, and that nobody was going to make that particular offer. This was partly a reflection of the extremely limited population at the research base, with around 150 scientists in summer, and around 45 in winter. We were on the only continent with no indigenous humans, and each human that was there had a very specific job. Given the harsh conditions, it was not worthwhile for anybody to travel there speculatively, hoping to find basic work such as receiving tips in return for carrying bags.

There was something else the alien noticed shortly after descending from the small plane. Its engine was left running. The temperature was so low that there is a constant risk of plane engines ceasing up, if they are left without running for long periods of time.

'Ironic,' I narrated for the alien telepathically, 'that the continent most sensitive to climate change, and most dangerous to humans if it melts, is the very one that requires humans to leave engines running and emit carbon emissions in such a wasteful way.'

'Human lungs are not designed to be filled with floodwaters of melting continents,' said the alien chillingly, in more ways than one.

The pilot gestured for us to walk directly into the research station. Just inside the door, I showed the alien a screen with a temperature reading for the outside: −30 degrees Celsius. This is the mean temperature for the Antarctic summer. If we had been visiting in winter, the screen might have read around −60 degrees Celsius. The lowest temperature ever recorded at the surface of our planet was in Antarctica in 1983, at −89.2 degrees Celsius.

We were greeted by our guide for the next few days. She was from the British Antarctic Survey, and played a key role on the Scientific Committee on Antarctic Research, or SCAR. The alien giggled at the acronym. We set our bags down in our small cabin, then began a tour of the research station. It is mainly run by the United States, one of 40 nations that runs research stations in Antarctica. The Amundsen-Scott Station is the most southern and the largest research base on the continent, and the only base at the Geographical South Pole. Its co-ordinates are exactly 90 degrees South latitude, and zero degrees longitude.

Preserved for posterity on a wall in a corridor was a battered old sign that previously marked the Geographic South Pole. It acknowledged the Norwegian explorer Roald Amundsen, and the British explorer Robert F. Scott, the first two expedition leaders to reach the South Pole in 1911 and 1912, and after which the research station is named.

'So it is important for humans to be first in things. Interesting,' said the alien, teasingly.

'Rich coming from you, who thrashed me in the 100 metres,' I retorted telepathically.

Our guide wondered what she was missing.

'Sorry, we communicate by telepathy. It comes from a competitive species as well.'

'No, I don't. Tell her I don't.'

I said nothing.

'Tell her!' urged the alien.

The alien reminded me for a moment of the angry emotion character from the film *Inside Out*.

'I guess being the first to achieve something brings a kind of immortality,' I said to the guide, veering away from the alien's preferred clarification.

'Indayd,' said our guide. Her accent was cockney. I wondered where she had grown up, and concluded it was probably on the set of the television soap *EastEnders*.

''Eee looks foine. Nuffink wrong with 'im. Bit green 'vo.'

'Begging your pardon?' I queried.

It was the alien's turn to play translator. It explained that she had assumed the alien was male, and that she had reason to believe the alien was, for some reason, not fine. Finally, she seemed to think the alien's green complexion was not a major issue.

'I see. Yes, the alien is all good, thanks. I mean, bit depressed earlier in our world tour, nearly shot its own brains out and all that. But that's all in the past now.'

'I woz told you woz comin' 'ere wiv an ailing visita.'

'Hmm,' I pondered. The alien translated.

'Oh, ailing! No, no, alien. Alien visitor. Its health is fine. Great, actually. Not ailing. Alien. Thanks for checking, though.'

After a few minutes of explaining what the guide had missed on the world news, having been quite literally in the dark for the last six months during the Antarctic winter, our tour of the research base commenced. The guide showed us the greenhouse within the station. We saw the various laboratories and communications rooms, as well as the gym, music room, library and TV room. Our guide confessed to not having spent much time in the latter, but in hindsight, perhaps she should have done, as such rooms are important for the physical and psychological health of humans in remote and confined spaces. They are also considerations for humans if we were, one day, to travel to and colonise other planets. Indeed, scientists from NASA and the European Space Agency are using research stations in Antarctica to examine the potential effects of long space missions, such as the challenges of crew living in complete isolation, in order to assist with planning manned missions to Mars.

As we unpacked in the evening, the alien was not as surprised as I was about the Sun not going down. Seen it all before, on many planets, apparently. The research station was located at the South Pole, and we were at the only inhabited place on the surface of Ocean from which the Sun is continuously visible for six months, with the angle of elevation of the Sun remaining above the horizon. Conversely, in the winter, when Ocean is tilted on its axis away from the Sun, Antarctica remains in darkness for six months.

The following day the alien and I covered 100 metres once again, but this time it was not a race. Our first excursion was a short one: the 100-metre walk from the research base to the Geographic South Pole. As the research station is located on a moving glacier, the walk is getting 10 metres shorter each year. The Geographic South Pole is one of the two points where Ocean's axis of rotation intersects its surface. It is on the opposite side of Ocean from the Geographic North Pole. The point of the South Pole is marked by three objects: a simple metal pole, a flagpole suitable for interchanging the displayed national flag, and a notice board.

Our guide then took the alien and me just a few metres to the Ceremonial South Pole, consisting of a metallic sphere on a short bamboo pole, surrounded by the flags of the original 12 Antarctic Treaty signatory states. I explained to the alien this example of cool co-operation.

'This is why I included Antarctica at the end of our world tour. The Antarctic Treaty System is nothing less than a potential template for further human co-operation. It is symbolised by the interchangeable flags here at the South Pole. It is a unique international agreement, specifying that nobody owns Antarctica. The Antarctic Treaty does not recognise, dispute, nor establish territorial sovereignty claims. It clarifies that no new claims shall be asserted while the Treaty is in force.'

'I like it,' said the alien simply.

Our guide went on to explain, through her cockney accent that required occasional translation by the alien, that the Antarctic Treaty reserves the continent for peaceful purposes, with military activities banned. It sets aside Antarctica as a scientific preserve, and establishes freedom of scientific investigation. It came into force in 1961, and now has 53 signatory states.

We looked at the various flags surrounding the Ceremonial South Pole.

'Thank you for bringing me here,' said the alien. 'You are showing me that humans can combine science and diplomacy. You can move on from inaccuracy and vested interests. This means you have potential for further co-operation and peace. First impressions weren't great on that front, if I'm honest.'

Our next chilly jaunt involved crossing the blizzardy continent in the light aircraft westwards, towards the Amundsen Sea. Even from the plane's height it was impossible for the alien to see that Antarctica can be divided into three major regions: West Antarctica, East Antarctica, and the Antarctic Peninsula. West Antarctica and East Antarctica are separated by the Transantarctic Mountains. The alien had noticed that division from the International Space Station, the observant little monkey.

We boarded a research ship and joined a team of scientists studying seawater temperatures in the Amundsen Sea. Six glaciers drain into the Amundsen Sea, and the scientists explained to the alien that three glaciers in particular, the Pine Island, Thwaites and Smith Glaciers, were losing more ice than is being replaced by snowfall. The melting of these three glaciers alone is contributing an estimated 0.24 millimetres per year to observed rises in worldwide sea level.

Antarctica has land beneath it, whereas the Arctic doesn't. Glaciers emptying into the Amundsen Sea are the fastest melting in Antarctica. As they leave the land and meet the sea they form floating ice shelves. However, as a result of climate change the sea temperatures have warmed, meaning that those ice shelves melt as they come into contact with warmer water. If the Amundsen Sea hadn't warmed, they might have remained as ice.

'So the glaciers become smaller,' explained one of the scientists. She was Norwegian, and generally more understandable than our guide at the research base. 'They release their water that otherwise would probably have remained locked up as ice.'

The alien watched as a floating ice shelf broke apart, and crashed into the warmed Amundsen Sea.

'These West Antarctic glaciers are vulnerable because they sit on bedrock that is below sea level. So the land is below sea level. The land slopes down, not up. Very unusual, obviously,' continued the scientist. 'In most parts of Antarctica, and the world, that's obviously not the case. Land usually slopes up from the sea. But here is a really bad place to have land that slopes downward. It means the warmed Amundsen Sea pushes the glaciers back inland, causing them to melt from below. Unless the temperature of the Amundsen Sea water drops immediately, there is no known mechanism that humans can use to stop this melting. As an immediate decrease in sea water temperature is unrealistic, even if global carbon emissions stop today, this glacial retreat in this region is almost certainly unstoppable.'

The alien tugged at my sleeve, and indicated it didn't understand. The scientist walked us inside the ship, where she had a diagram on the wall that showed the ground sloping inland, and how this meant that water was constantly pushing against the glaciers. She then placed an ice cube into each of two test tubes. In test tube A she added warm water, and in test tube B she added cold water, close to freezing. The alien saw that the ice cube in test tube A melted far more quickly than in test tube B.

'Glaciologists believe we are past the point of no return, and that the glaciers surrounding the Amundsen Sea will inevitably complete their current melting process, raising global sea levels by 1.2 metres within around 200 years,' concluded the Norwegian.

We probably can adapt to a certain extent. The problem is that we're not planning for it.
Don Chambers, Sea Level Researcher, University of Texas

'If all the ice in Antarctica, the Arctic and mountains around the world melted, global sea levels would rise by around 70 metres. This would submerge around half the world's major cities, including London and New York, as well as entire regions, such as Florida and Bangladesh. That is not inevitable. It's just the 1.2 metre rise that is too late to stop,' said the scientist, trying to be positive.

'Come back in 200 years, see how we're getting on?' I asked the alien.

'Your continental land masses are likely to look very different, much smaller,' said the alien. 'I will have to be careful that I don't think I've taken a wrong turn and reached a different planet.'

'If your alien friend wants to come back in 200 years, it might need scuba diving equipment to see landmarks such as Big Ben and the Statue of Liberty,' concluded the scientist, unaware that the alien doesn't need scuba diving equipment.

'I would like to see them without swimming,' said the alien telepathically. 'For your sake, not mine.'

A L I E N   F I L M   N I G H T

Waterworld
(1995)

We returned to the Amundsen-Scott South Pole Station, and I encouraged our cockney research station guide to join the alien and me in the TV lounge for our Alien Film Night. *Waterworld* helped the alien to visualise the comprehensive impact that climate change and sea-level rise may have on a planet that is already mostly ocean.

The film was released in 1995, but it is set around the year 2500, when the aforementioned melting process has, in the story, completed. The polar ice caps have melted entirely, and water covers nearly all of the land on the planet. Human civilisation has been reduced almost to extinction, with a few remnants living on floating communities. Land-based civilisation in their past is not regarded as a historical fact, but is a contested issue, with some people believing in and searching for the mythical 'Dryland', whilst others are erroneously sceptical it ever existed.

The film was critically acclaimed for the strength of this premise, portraying a potential future where humans are reduced to the goal of simply finding dry land. It demonstrated to the alien the fragility of human civilisation, and how human progress may not continue indefinitely if we do not take the decisive action required to sustain one of the most basic requirements of our species: land.

I reassured the alien that while a sea-level rise of around 1.2 metres is probably inevitable, it can be capped at around that level if solutions are implemented. Just as the cause and effect relationship between carbon dioxide and warming can work against humanity, so it can also be used to cap the initially unstoppable sea-level rise at around 1.2 metres.

Antarctica, whilst being the main place on Ocean that may provide the floodwaters, is also a place that can remind humans of the solutions to the challenge of climate change. In addition to the success of co-operation that the alien saw at the Ceremonial South Pole, with the 53 flags representing the success of the Antarctic Treaty in securing the continent as a place of peace, Antarctica is also the venue where two further environmental success stories have played out through the use of legal measures: limits to whaling, and the rejuvenation of the ozone layer.

The following day the alien and I went on a day trip south to the Ross Sea. Like the Amundsen Sea, the Ross Sea is also part of the Southern Ocean, which surrounds the Antarctic continent and includes the planet's largest marine mammal feeding ground. In the Ross Sea we caught glimpses of dolphins, minke whales, blue whales and killer whales, otherwise known as orcas.

The alien was particularly interested to see a blue whale. Our Ross Sea guide confirmed that the blue whale is the largest species to have ever lived on Ocean, including all known dinosaurs. The heart of a fully grown blue whale is typically around 1.5 metres long, 1.2 metres wide, and 1.4 metres tall. Some of its blood vessels are so large that a human could swim through them, explained the guide, doing a sort of front-crawl gesture towards the nonplussed alien.

'During the early 20th century many species of marine mammals were hunted to the brink of extinction by humans for meat and other commercial products,' said the guide, adjusting himself back upright into a sensible position. 'In 1982 the International Whaling Commission, or IWC, prohibited the commercial killing of all large whales, minke whales and orca. In 1994 the IWC established the Southern Ocean Whale Sanctuary, to ensure the long-term recovery of the whale populations.'

The alien chortled telepathically. I realised the pattern: it was finding human use of acronyms increasingly amusing. Even here at the last place on our world tour, I realised there was still so much more to learn about my alien playmate.

A humpback whale leapt out of the water, twisted in the air and slapped down on the surface. The splash drenched us at the side of the boat. The fact that the alien was able to be soaked in this way was testament to the success of international co-operation, with some populations of whales now recovering to the estimated sizes of populations before commercial whaling began in Antarctica on a large scale in 1904.

We can turn things around.
Sir David Attenborough, Broadcaster in *Blue Planet II* in 2017

The guide was rightly cautious, however, as there remains issues of lethal whaling for questionable 'scientific' purposes, and many organisations believe additional Marine Protected Areas, or MPAs if one wanted to amuse the alien further, are needed.

A few minutes later a Japanese fishing vessel emerged from behind an iceberg, apparently pursuing a minke whale. Our guide blew its horn, and the Japanese vessel disappeared. The horn was markedly louder than the party horn I had blown for the alien on its birthday in the Challenger Deep.

'That's told them,' said the guide. 'They know they'll get reported if they're spotted.'

I explained to the alien that international co-operation at its best can be effective, but rarely perfect, with individual nations looking for ways to advance what they perceive to be in their own, short-term interests. Japan is taking a 'one-column' approach to the issue of whaling, justifying the practice in terms of short-term, vested interests, rather than calculating the points in the column against their practice, and concluding on the basis of the balance of points in each column.

Back at the Amundsen-Scott South Pole Station our cockney guide invited the alien to assist the team with their weekly balloon launch. The balloons are fitted with small devices that record ozone levels in the stratosphere, approximately 20–30 kilometres above the surface of Ocean. The practice dates back to 1986 in its current form. She explained to the alien that the ozone layer absorbs most of the Sun's ultraviolet radiation, which otherwise would damage life at the surface, such as increased risk of skin cancer in humans. I checked in with the alien regarding its need for sunscreen in Antarctica as a result of the thin ozone layer, in combination with reflection of sunlight from the ice. I was not surprised to learn that its green pigmentation was more than sufficient.

The alien was granted the honour of releasing a balloon. With a cheer from the team, the alien let the balloon go and watched as it rose to the stratosphere. Our guide explained that in 1976 their atmospheric recordings revealed that the ozone layer was being depleted. This was being caused by chemicals released by industry, mainly chlorofluorocarbons, or CFCs. I asked the guide to pause for a moment while the alien stopping sniggering.

'Dem CFC's woz used in millions of 'ass'old products. Fridges, aerosol sprays...'

It was my turn to chuckle, more at the unintentional implications of her accent. She continued, with the help of the alien translating for me where her pronunciation posed challenges, that in 1985 the annual depletion of ozone above Antarctica was announced, and subsequent international co-operation and legal regulation was successful. The success of the legal measures was attributed to the ozone case being communicated more effectively than current attempts to communicate climate change. For example, sequential linguistic methods and metaphors such as 'ozone hole' and then 'ozone shield' proved useful in communicating an imminent risk followed by tangible solution. The public were able to relate a hole in the ozone layer directly to their personal health risk of skin cancer.

Global decline in ozone depleting substances shows that we can make positive change when we act decisively.
William Ripple and 15,364 Scientist Signatories from 184 Countries in 2017

In 1987 an international treaty known as the Montreal Protocol was agreed that banned the use of CFCs. The treaty was legally binding. A reason this was possible was because of efforts to ensure substitutes were available. This meant the public had a smooth transition, and did not experience a disruption when moving from CFC to non-CFC products. All 197 nations on Ocean have signed the treaty, and by 2003 scientists announced that the global depletion of the ozone layer was slowing down, with a gradual trend towards recovery announced in 2016.

Perhaps the single most successful international agreement to date has been the Montreal Protocol.
Kofi Annan, Secretary-General of the United Nations, 1997-2006

The ozone success story depended on international co-operation and, specifically, legal measures that simply prohibited CFCs. I asked the alien if it was concerned for humanity given the fact that although legal templates exist, there seem to be more pervasive vested interests that act as barriers to implementing similar, international, legal approaches to banning carbon dioxide emissions, or even moderate approaches such as the Paris Agreement, as discussed in Cairo. It assumed my question was rhetorical.

The final concept I introduced to the alien before it left Ocean was intentionally and necessarily the last. Leaving it until the end was important: its positioning was a metaphor. It was the concept of death itself, which is, by definition, the last experience of all humans. The alien had been around for a billion years, and judging by the way it responded to the question about the age of its parents when we were on the bow of the boat above the Challenger Deep, it had quite a few years left on the clock. Did the alien die at all? Was the alien immortal?

'I cannot reveal that information, yet. Sorry,' shrugged the alien, seemingly also frustrated by those pesky Interplanetary Ethical Rules.

'Humans are in a technological battle, fighting with ageing, and fighting with death itself. We talked about limb regeneration and other medical lessons we can absorb from nature, but here in Antarctica, the coldest continent, the temperatures are a metaphor for another technique we can learn. Cryonics.'

'Ah, now you're being interesting,' said the alien.

> *Being cryopreserved after death is the second worst thing*
> *that could happen. The worst thing is dying without being*
> *cryopreserved.*
>
> Ben Best, Screenwriter and Actor

From the Amundsen-Scott South Pole Station the alien and I went out for our final adventure together on Ocean. We were in a search of a particular insect, the Antarctic midge. The cockney guide ahead of us insisted she knew where she could find us one. The Antarctic midge is able to survive losing up to 70 per cent of its body water, and therefore is able to survive temperatures as low as –20 degrees Celsius without ice crystal formation that can damage cells and tissues in the body.

What started as a discreet sprinkling of soft snow from the sky turned into a maliciously billowing blizzard. But it was not a blizzard of snow from the sky: Antarctica receives very little snowfall, to the extent that it is considered a desert. Indeed, in some areas of Antarctica it has not had snowfall for about two million years. The snow that was surrounding us had been whipped up from the ground by the strong winds. It was gathering on our heads, shoulders and progressively less visible feet. Our guide pressed on ahead.

'Come on! Bit of the white stuff never killed anyone,' encouraged a cockney accent fallaciously.

The alien had skills in this area, and knew what to do. Just as it had assisted our Amazon guide to make excellent time as he hacked his way through the thick undergrowth, so now, in order to prevent an impromptu burial of two humans under a snowstorm, the alien used its mysterious, invisible force to help a cockney lady and a temporary United Nations contractor carve their way through the snow. Our guide retained her belief that she was doing it all herself.

We approached a rocky area. The guide stopped, said nothing, then faceplanted herself deliberately into the snow. She emerged upright again, proudly holding up what looked like a snowball, insisting it contained a frozen Antarctic midge, and that we should get back to the research station sharpish, not to avoid our own burials, but so she could show us the unfreezing process.

Back at the Amundsen-Scott South Pole Station we rushed to the laboratory. From our jackets fell trails of snow behind us through the corridors. The guide placed the snowball in a tray, then carefully poured a jug of water all around it. A black line soon revealed itself to be a frozen midge. After a few minutes, the apparently lifeless insect began to twitch, then fully reanimate. She placed it in a small, Perspex box, and presented it to the alien.

'Ere you go. Souvenir.'

I explained to the alien that this was another example of the value of biodiversity, as discussed in the Amazon, and the vast range of lessons that humans might be able to learn from nature. There are other examples around the world of wildlife being able to survive freezing, such as Arctic ground squirrels and wood frogs, which have evolved diverse solutions to the challenge of surviving freezing.

'Humans can learn a lot from the animals around you,' said the alien. 'This is a good example. Thank you. But the learning is not for me. It is for you. If you can study these creatures more, learn from their DNA exactly how they are able to survive freezing, then you can apply such lessons to human cryopreservation. Biodiversity holds nothing less than the potential for significantly extending human life. You don't live very long, compared to the rest of the species in the multiverse,' clarified the alien.

'Is that how your species learned to live to be billions of years old? Learning from the other species you evolved with?'

'Since you raised the question in those terms yourself, I can answer whilst staying within the limits of Interplanetary Ethics. Yes.'

Cryonics has been referred to as 'an ambulance to the future' whereby humans opt for 'time travel' rather than 'space travel'. Instead of travel to a hospital to try to prevent death, cryopreservation involves being frozen shortly after death, in the hope that the technology to unfreeze and reanimate will be developed.

'Trouble is, my old alien pal, we humans don't yet have the technology to reanimate a cryopreserved human,' I ventured, seeing just how much we could learn from the alien on this most fundamental of subjects: preventing death, or rather, preventing a permanent death.

'There are of course no guarantees that you humans will ever develop this technology, but remember, it's not all about you.'

'I don't understand. But if I'm being anthropocentric again, I do apologise. I know it makes you narky.'

'Freeze more humans. As we learned at Easter Island, diversity of approaches is the key to species survival. If the bodies stay frozen long enough, maybe humans will develop the technology to unfreeze them and give them a new life. If humans don't, maybe another species will visit this planet, like my own species, and share with you the unfreezing technology. Death is a choice, as we say at home.'

'You mean you'll come back and unfreeze some of us?'

'Of course. And show you how to regenerate your bodies. You're already surprisingly close, actually, just need a bit of help with your DNA tricks. Keep studying species like that immortal jellyfish we saw in Queensland. In the meantime, I need to get around a bit of Interplanetary Ethics Council paperwork, then I'll be back to share the technology. Bureaucracy is the real bore here, not the techie bit.'

And so the alien ended our world tour with the promise to share the most precious gift imaginable with humanity: the ability to beat death itself. To fulfil the desire to keep living for ever. The elixir of life itself. Immortality. Eternal life. It was subject to a bit of interplanetary red tape, of course. This was my final note on the tablet, and I emailed the full set of notes to Obama and the United Nations team back in Geneva. The genie was out of the bottle, and could never go back in. It was now clear that our low human standards, our acceptance that a mere 80 or 90 years of life should remain our expectation, was now confined to the history books.

ALIEN PLACES
Departure

Nessun Dorma (No one shall sleep)
by Giacomo Puccini

I hadn't selected a song for this part of our journey, but the alien had been keen to borrow my tablet and go through songs on the Internet to make its own selection. It chose Nessun Dorma.

Strapped into our secure seats and facing vertically within the rocket, the alien finally confirmed to me the real reason it had decided to visit Ocean. It had come here to help us. To nudge us in the right directions. I had suspected this was the case, particularly since it was sleep talking on the plane to Geneva, and the alien confessed that it had been very much a case of pretend sleep talking.

The alien's visit had indeed been its birthday present, but one with a purpose: to save our ailing species. My new friend considered itself to be a conservation volunteer, and humans were the subject of that conservation. Perhaps the situation was similar to an intergalactic version of one of those conservation volunteering holidays where you have to pay a contribution to the organisation that runs it.

The altruistic aim was to motivate us, the people of Ocean, to win the fights for a sustainable population, for a stable climate, for the conservation of biodiversity, and for longer and healthier lives. To stay awake as a civilisation, rather than to sleep walk into our eternal sleep.

My United Nations employers had arranged a private space shuttle for the alien and me to return to the International Space Station, from which the alien was due to continue its return journey to its home planet. The world was tuning in to bid the alien farewell, with a live Internet feed inside our shuttle. Space suits on, our shuttle docked with the International Space Station. We floated through the airlocks and met the crew members, who indicated where to put our bags down. As a final gesture for the alien, I made sure I carried its bag.

The solar-panelled bag was full of souvenirs the alien had collected during our world tour. We had time to empty out the alien's bag, and have a quick review of the objects it had acquired.

From Cairo there was the small toy camel, bought from the lady wearing a shop. It reminded us of when the alien was tricked into riding a camel for free, but being charged to dismount. This said a lot about trusting humans, and the pervasive importance of money.

From Los Angeles there was the bow tie, a reminder of the inequalities between humans. There was also the gun. I removed the bullets, and let the alien keep the gun as a symbol of the inability of some nations to do what is very clearly and obviously the right thing to do in terms of changing laws, but vested interests are preventing them from doing so. The gun represented the inherent ecocidal and suicidal nature of humanity, justified often by short-term rather than medium-term interests, and that this is perhaps the underlying psychological battle we need to win.

From Vietnam there was the confusing coconut. We had never resolved why it was selected as a souvenir, and the alien now expected an answer. I explained that it simply represented a natural object found on the planet. I felt it was important for the alien to have at least one object that would have looked exactly the same in appearance as if humans had never existed on Ocean.

From Beijing there was the solar-panel-covered bag itself. It represented the transition of humanity towards sustainability, albeit slowly, and that this type of technology, as well as many other aspects of humanity, was increasingly being led by China.

From Queensland there was the wooden boomerang. This represented an ancient tool used by humans for thousands of years, in the era when humans behaved in a truly sustainable way. Rather than designing a tool that would be lost, or become waste, the boomerang always returned. It represented nothing less than the circular or 'spaceship' economy that humanity needs to return to, one way or another.

From Geneva there was simply a piece of paper, on which was written the phone number of the amorous tour guide at CERN that had been flirting with the alien. On closer inspection, I saw that the accomplished scientist had used rather endearing bubble writing, and expressed her zeros as love hearts. The alien had an admirer. I suggested it represents the drive of humanity for love and reproduction of our species. I was not convinced that this, or any one object could do justice to the sagacious lessons and themes we had discussed in Geneva. Nevertheless, I suggested the alien should take it as a compliment.

From the Amazon there was the gift of the watch worn by our guide. We remembered the simple joy and satisfaction the guide had felt for making progress through the rainforest faster than usual. This represented the need for humanity to return to taking delight in basic achievements in life. The symbolism of a watch is multi-faceted, however. Humans are not yet immortal: we all have a watch on our wrists, counting the days we have to live. But it doesn't have to be that way, and if we learn from biodiversity, we can learn how to regenerate our bodies and continue to make medical advances.

From Easter Island there was the agricultural tool. The alien and I recalled how this symbolised a civilisation that had been successful, rather than ecocidal, and that it was ultimately disease and human conflict, rather than environmental mismanagement in this instance, that they had needed to watch out for. It was an important lesson in perspective, and choosing to interpret things positively, which many humans struggle with.

From the Challenger Deep there was the party horn. Blown at the bottom of the world's oceans on the alien's billionth birthday, it was a reminder of the sheer age of the alien, and that humanity needs to think much bigger than we do at the moment. We need to raise our standards, not let them drop to the lowest of depths. We can evolve as a civilisation to the stage where we too might one day celebrate our billionth birthdays, if we behave as if we want to stick around.

From Antarctica there was the Antarctic midge. It was the only living souvenir that the alien was taking with it back to its home planet. A pet midge, we decided. As it could survive freezing, the alien said, it would place it in a state of cryopreservation, and unfreeze it years later when the alien finally arrived. It was a reminder that humans too may one day need this technology, not just to extend our own lives, but also to travel between the stars, and to explore the multiverse.

If I had to distil our world tour into one key message that I would like the alien to leave Ocean with, it would have been that the broad identification of how to implement a truly sustainable and moral human society is still absent. Or to put it another way: we don't know. We don't know what we need to know, and we don't know what we don't know. For example, we know we need to fight our own instincts towards short-term rather than long-term thinking, but we don't know how to do this consistently, in all circumstances, for ever.

Before the alien could depart our colleagues at the International Space Station needed to deploy some ingenious netting devices to clear space debris. Decades of human pollution of orbit had meant that thousands of tiny particles of human litter now raced around in orbit. A collision with any one of them could have been disastrous for the alien's departure vessel. I suspected the alien's technology could handle it, but as it served as one, final lesson for the alien, I allowed their orbital game of catch to continue. It showed the alien how humanity has trashed the planet at all levels, from the depths of the Challenger Deep, to the heights of orbit itself, and beyond if you include those Voyager probes.

Inside Out
(2015)

Whilst waiting for the space debris to be cleared, we had time for a final film. After scanning through thousands of film reviews on the tablet at light speed, the alien selected this Oscar-winning animated film. It is set within the mind of an eleven-year-old girl called Riley. Five personified emotions in the film are: Joy, Sadness, Anger, Fear and Disgust.

There were parallels between the developmental journey of Riley and the alien. Both were initially filled with Joy: in Riley's case, at the idea of moving house, and in the alien's case, at the idea of arriving on Ocean. However, whilst some aspects of Joy remained, Joy quickly became mixed with Sadness, as both Riley and the alien realised the realities of their new situations.

Rather than deny their negative emotions and accept only the positive, both Riley and the alien resolved their journeys by accepting that multiple emotions can and perhaps should be accepted simultaneously. And so this was the way that the alien chose to conclude both its emotional and its practical assessment of humanity and our conservation status following the alien intervention. Mixed.

After the alien departed, I woke up. The imagined world tour was over. I had been dreaming on the sunny beach of Surfer's Paradise in Queensland. There was no alien coming to help us. No alien to save us. It is up to us, humanity, to nudge and to propel ourselves in the right directions. To save ourselves. There never was an alien. It was an imagined journey, but the lessons, the practical solutions and the calls to action are real.

Further Reading, Listening and Viewing

Books

AESOP. *Aesop's Fables in Aesop's Illustrated Fables* (2013). Barnes and Noble, New York.

DE BOTTON, ALAIN (2009). *A Week at the Airport: A Heathrow Diary.* Profile Books, London.

GAARDER, JOSTEIN (1995). *Sophie's World.* Phoenix House, London.

PACKHAM, CHRIS et al. (2018). A *People's Manifesto for Wildlife.* Chris Packham, Southampton.

VOLTAIRE (1752). *Micromégas* in *Micromégas and other Short Fiction* (2002). Penguin Classics, London.

WHITE, MICHAEL (1999). *Super Science.* Pocket Books, New York.

Songs

Ellie Goulding, 'Anything Could Happen' in the album *Halcyon*. UK: Polydor Records, 2012.

Christine and the Queens, 'Tilted' in the album *Chaleur Humaine*. France: Because Music, 2014.

Rootjoose, 'Can't Keep Living This Way' in the album *Rhubarb*. UK: Rage Records, 1997.

Michael Jackson, 'Speed Demon' in the album *Bad*. USA: Epic Records, 1989.

Edwin Starr, 'War' in the album *War & Peace*. USA: Motown Records, 1970.

Songs (cont.)

Albert Leung, 'Beijing Welcomes You', performed by various artists, in the album *The Official Album for the 2008 Beijing Olympic Games*. China, 2008.

Jamiroquai, 'Didjital Vibrations' in the album *Travelling Without Moving*. UK: Sony Soho Square, 1996.

DNCE, 'Cake by the Ocean' in the extended play album *Swaay*. USA: Republic Records, 2015.

Tom Lehrer, 'The Elements' in the album *Tom Lehrer in Concert*. USA: Lehrer Records, 1959.

Terry Gilkyson, 'The Bare Necessities', performed by Phil Harris and Bruce Reitherman, in the film *The Jungle Book*. USA: Walt Disney Records, 1967.

Prince, '1999' in the album *1999*. USA: Warner Bros., 1982.

Nirvana, 'Something in the Way' in the album *Nevermind*. USA: DGC Records, 1991.

Roger Payne, all tracks in the album *Songs of the Humpback Whale*. USA: Capitol Records, 1970.

John Lennon and Yoko Ono, 'Imagine' in the album *Imagine*. UK: Apple Records, 1971.

Giacomo Puccini, 'Nessun Dorma' ('No One Shall Sleep') in the opera *Turandot*. Italy: 1926.

Films

Arrival, directed by Denis Villeneuve. USA: FilmNation Entertainment, 2016.

Quantum of Solace, directed by Marc Forster. UK: Eon Productions, 2008.

Back to the Future, directed by Robert Zemeckis. USA: Amblin Entertainment, 1985.

Casualties of War, directed by Brian De Palma. USA: Columbia Pictures, 1989.

An Inconvenient Truth, directed by Davis Guggenheim. USA: Lawrence Bender Productions, 2006.

The Martian, directed by Ridley Scott. USA: Scott Free Productions, 2015.

Crocodile Dundee, directed by Peter Faiman. Australia: Rimfire Films, 1986.

The Theory of Everything, directed by James Marsh. UK: Working Title, 2014.

The Beach, directed by Danny Boyle. UK: 20th Century Fox, 2000.

Medicine Man, directed by John McTiernan. USA: Hollywood Pictures, 1992.

E.T. the Extra Terrestrial, directed by Steven Spielberg. USA: Universal Pictures, 1982.

Finding Nemo, directed by Andrew Stanton. USA: Walt Disney Pictures, 2003.

Waterworld, directed by Kevin Reynolds. USA: Davis Entertainment, 1995.

Inside Out, directed by Pete Docter. USA: Walt Disney Pictures, 2015.

Acknowledgements

Many people have supported the publication of this book, either directly or indirectly through enthusiasm and positivity about the concept.

Thank you to Creative Byte for the cover design, interior design and the *Alien Places* logo. Thanks also to Pete Nicholson for designing the logo for Atul's Earth.

Thanks to Luke Wooltorton for reading drafts and giving feedback, for co-developing the '2p Theory', and for our surfing headstands.

Special thanks to the editor, Sylvia Sullivan, for her detailed input and engagement with the book.

Thank you to all participants of the *Alien Places* podcast so far: Nick Crane, Dan Sansom, Patrick Kendrew, Lucy Tadman-Troup, Sammy Brisden, Jason Birt, Abigail Maiden, Nicola Morris, Lizzie Daly, Adam Clark, Abi Thommes, James Fair, Amy Williams.

Finally, I thank Professor David Matless at the University of Nottingham, for setting an essay question involving an alien in 1998, during my BA Geography undergraduate course.

Printed in Great Britain
by Amazon